Praise for Mark de Castrique

Murder in Rat Alley

"Nicely plotted...intelligent, kind protagonists and an eye-opening historical background help make this one winner."

—*Publishers Weekly*

"Mark de Castrique fabricates an elaborate, multi-layered mystery that employs espionage elements to deepen the intrigue. The author's skill creating divergent clues that he deftly connects makes for a fascinating read at a compelling pace."

—*Reviewing the Evidence*

"*Murder in Rat Alley* is definitely a very compelling mystery with some surprising twists and unexpected connections!"

—*Fresh Fiction*

"Someone trying to bury the past kills again and threatens Blackman and Robertson before the full, convoluted scheme, involving more decades-old murder and espionage, is revealed."

—*Booklist*

Hidden Scars

2018 Thomas Wolfe Memorial Literary Award nominee
"With its strong sense of place, depiction of racial tension that still lingers in the new South, and appealing sleuths, de Castrique's well-plotted mystery is a winner."

—*Library Journal*

"De Castrique combines an examination of the South's troubled racial history with a smart probe of current political-financial shenanigans."

—*Publishers Weekly*

"De Castrique's sixth delivers a vivid gallery of suspects, lively dialogue, and an attractive pair of sleuths."

—*Kirkus Reviews*

A Specter of Justice

"A good choice for anyone who enjoys small-town mysteries and ghost stories."

—*Booklist*

"An entertaining whodunit with colorful characters, swift-footed plotting, and a confident narrative voice."

—*Kirkus Reviews*

A Murder in Passing

"This solid whodunit offers readers a glimpse into a curious chapter of cultural history."

—*Publishers Weekly*

"This fascinating mystery, merging past and present, brings some little-known history to light and shows that laws change much faster than attitudes, as Sam and Nakayla, an interracial couple themselves, discover."

—*Booklist*

The Sandburg Connection

★ "Stellar... A missing folk song, a buried treasure from Civil War days, and a pregnant goat all play a part in this marvelous blend of history and mystery seasoned with information about Carl Sandburg's life."

—*Publishers Weekly*, Starred Review

"A suspicious death on top of Glassy Mountain turns two laid-back private sleuths into prime suspects."

—*Kirkus Reviews*

"Folk songs, Sandburg, and Civil War history—what a winning combination!"

—*Library Journal*

The Fitzgerald Ruse

"An excellent regional mystery, full of local color and historical detail."

—*Library Journal*

"The warmth of Sam and Nakayla's relationship and Sam's challenged but determined heart make for a great read…"

—*Kirkus Reviews*

"Readers will hope to see a lot more of the books' amiable characters."

—*Publishers Weekly*

Blackman's Coffin

★ "A wealth of historical detail, an exciting treasure hunt and credible characters distinguish this fresh, adventurous read."

—*Publishers Weekly*, Starred Review

"Known for his effortless storytelling, de Castrique once again delivers a compelling tale blending fact and fiction…"

—*Library Journal*

"In the struggling Sam Blackman, de Castrique has created a compelling hero whose flinty first-person narrative nicely complements Henderson's earnest, measured, and equally involving account."

—*Kirkus Reviews*

Also by Mark de Castrique

The Blackman Agency
Investigations
Blackman's Coffin
The Fitzgerald Ruse
The Sandburg Connection
A Murder in Passing
A Specter of Justice
Hidden Scars
Murder in Rat Alley
Fatal Scores

Mysteries for Young Adults
A Conspiracy of Genes
Death on a Southern Breeze

The Buryin' Barry Mysteries
Dangerous Undertaking
Grave Undertaking
Foolish Undertaking
Final Undertaking
Fatal Undertaking
Risky Undertaking
Secret Undertaking

Standalone Thrillers
The Singularity Race
The 13th Target
Double Cross of Time

SECRET LIVES

SECRET LIVES

MARK DE CASTRIQUE

Poisoned Pen
PRESS

Published by Poisoned Pen Press, an imprint of Sourcebooks
P.O. Box 4410, Naperville, Illinois 60567-4410
(630) 961-3900
sourcebooks.com

Library of Congress Cataloging-in-Publication Data

Names: De Castrique, Mark, author.
Title: Secret lives / Mark de Castrique.
Description: Naperville, Illinois : Poisoned Pen Press, [2022]
Identifiers: LCCN 2022006642 (print) | LCCN 2022006643
(ebook) | (trade paperback) | (epub)
Subjects: LCGFT: Detective and mystery fiction.
Classification: LCC PS3604.E124 S42 2022 (print) | LCC PS3604.E124
   (ebook) | DDC 813/.6--dc23/eng/20220225
LC record available at https://lccn.loc.gov/2022006642
LC ebook record available at https://lccn.loc.gov/2022006643

Printed and bound in the United States of America.
POD

For new granddaughter Lucy
Welcome. A world of books awaits you…

"There is something addictive about a secret."

— J. EDGAR HOOVER

Chapter 1

Jonathan Finch saw the dark sedan parked where he'd been told it would be—on the top level of the parking deck near Whole Foods in the Clarendon neighborhood of Arlington, Virginia. At four in the morning, the county across the Potomac River from Washington, DC, came as close to shutdown as anytime, except for the occasional snowstorm. Finch's Ford Escape SUV and the sedan were the only vehicles in sight, and with headlights off and windows tinted, they appeared as shadowy shapes illuminated by a half-moon and the ambient light from the streetlamps below.

Finch would have preferred a more crowded, public rendezvous site, but he also understood anonymity figured predominantly in any transaction. Security meant precautions, and those precautions varied from person to person, or p2p, as expressed in this world. Peer-to-peer.

As had been prearranged, Finch opened the laptop on the passenger seat, connected it to the hot spot of his cell phone, and logged in. He used the special password-protected software program to call up the private key to his anonymous account. The next steps were simple. He typed a message to the nameless address that was the destination of the transfer:

I'M READY. BRING FIRST HALF MIDWAY.

The driver's door of the sedan opened, but the interior lights stayed off. Finch cursed that his counterpart displayed more caution than he'd anticipated. It was too late for him to disable his own courtesy lights. Instead, he reached inside his nylon windbreaker and unsnapped the flap of his shoulder holster. The Beretta would slide free in a matter of seconds.

Holding a gym bag with both hands, a figure in a hoodie rounded the back of the sedan. The stranger appeared to be no more than five-foot-six in height, and the slender build suggested a lithe, muscular body. The movements were catlike, sure-footed, and agile.

The hooded figure dropped the gym bag on the concrete. The smacking sound told Finch the bag was full. Without giving him a second look, the carrier turned around and returned to the car. Finch eased out of the driver's seat, facing away as the SUV's dome light came on. He strode toward the bag, keeping his eyes focused on the back of the dark figure until it disappeared into the sedan. He knelt, still watching the car and listening for any footsteps. He grabbed the bag's straps with his left hand, stood, and slowly walked backward until he sensed his Escape was within reach. He lifted the bag to cover his face as he sat back in the driver's seat and closed the door.

Finch picked up a small flashlight lying beside his laptop and flicked it on. The narrow beam glinted off the shiny zipper. He opened it, spread the sides of the bag apart, and sucked in a deep breath as he looked at the rolls of hundred-dollar bills inside. He slid the rubber band from one roll and counted twenty-five Benjamin Franklins. He made a quick calculation that the bag was large enough to hold one hundred rolls. Two hundred fifty thousand dollars.

He re-zipped the bag and tossed it into the back seat. Then he picked up the laptop. He'd already entered the appropriate amount of cryptocurrency, clicked the transfer icon, and watched as his account balance reduced accordingly. Then he set the laptop on the passenger seat and turned back to the sedan. The faceless person was already walking toward him, carrying a second bag. Everything had worked perfectly for stage one.

Stage two carried the greater risk. The other driver, or an accomplice, had proposed Finch go first in this second exchange—transfer his remaining funds and then receive an identical gym bag holding more U.S. dollars. But Finch wouldn't agree. There was no reclamation if the recipient simply sped away, stiffing Finch out of the final two hundred fifty thousand. His coins would be irretrievably lost, whereas the gym bag of cash physically existed and could be physically recaptured if Finch tried to make a break for it. And he wasn't entirely confident they couldn't track him down.

The second bag smacked against the concrete, and the figure retreated faster this time. Finch stayed as cautious as before, this time sweeping his eyes in a wider arc across the deck as he approached the final payment. This time he kept his right hand on the butt of the holstered Beretta as he carried the bag to the car.

Again, he pulled out a roll of currency at random. Twenty-five one-hundred-dollar bills with enough other rolls to increase the total cash value of the haul to a half million. He tossed the zipped bag into the back seat with the first, and then turned his attention to the laptop. With a few keystrokes, he set up the second transfer, moved the cursor to the icon, and paused. If he'd been heading up a sting operation, he would have called in his backup. He now had a record of the transfer and the cash as evidence. On his signal, all exits to the parking garage would have been sealed, and a computer forensics team would have descended upon the car, primed to confiscate all electronic equipment before it could be wiped clean.

If he were heading up a sting operation.

He started the engine. Then he clicked the icon to initiate the second transfer, deleted his private key, and slammed the transmission into reverse. The vehicle rocketed backward so fast, the tires laid rubber. The laptop tumbled onto the floorboard, shutting the screen against the keys. But Finch wasn't taking the time to watch the balance of his account decline. He was hell-bent on getting the half-million dollars to safety. The tires continued to screech in protest as he raced down the ramps to the exit.

The crossing bar was down. If he'd been set up by the mysterious other party, the exit lane could be the ambush point. He'd checked that there were no surveillance cameras on the entrance or exit. So, without stopping, he crashed through the bar, sending it splintering onto the pavement. What was a dent or busted headlight in exchange for the untraceable windfall that rode with him?

He breathed easier as he disappeared into the backstreets of one of Arlington's residential neighborhoods. He slowed enough to turn off his phone and eliminate the hot spot used by his computer. Though the odds were slim his signal was being tracked, why take a chance? The next step would be to ditch the gym bags and then begin banking the cash in amounts less than ten thousand dollars. Multiple accounts until he could consolidate them into a trust fund. The plan would take time, something of which he had precious little.

Three blocks from the parking garage, two men sat in a black SUV. In DC and the surrounding area, the vehicles were as common as politicians. The two men inside watched a computer monitor wedged on the console. A red blip moved through a grid of streets.

"He's slowing down already," the driver said.

A voice crackled from the speaker of a cell phone. "I've lost his signal."

"Copy that," the driver said. "We've got the GPS tracer."

"Do you need me to head him off?"

"No. We'll retrieve. Good job. Check your wallet in the morning."

"You know I will. I'll wipe down the car and leave it where we agreed. Good hunting."

"Let's move," the second man said. "We don't want him to get out of range."

"I think he's going to nest close by," the driver said. "But better to intercept before he stashes the money somewhere. Let's go introduce ourselves to our new best friend, whoever he might be." He eased the SUV away from the curb and headed for the blinking red light.

Jonathan Finch found a parking place on North Highland Street in front of the house. Fortunately, his landlady and her other boarders should be asleep, but if anyone happened to see him, he would say he'd just driven in from Richmond. That was true. They were used to the odd hours of his work. He could explain the bags as heavier clothing now that autumn was right around the corner.

Carrying one of the gym bags, he walked to the rear door, where a back stairway took him closest to his room. He used his key to unlock the bolt and tiptoed up the steps. Still, the old, dry floorboards creaked beneath his feet. He opened the door to his small room. There was a dresser, an armoire, a desk, and a single bed with a nightstand. He knelt and pushed the gym bag as far under the bed as he could.

He returned to the car and opened the rear door. He reached across for the bag that had fallen behind the driver's seat.

"Back out slowly." The hoarse whisper was more growl than voice.

Finch froze.

"Do as I say. Leave the bag, and we'll go get the other one together."

"It's a boardinghouse," Finch said without turning around. "People are stirring."

"Then we'll just have to hope you're quiet. Now get out."

As Finch slowly withdrew from the car, the rear door opposite opened and a second man grabbed the bag. He looked up at Finch. The blood drained from his face. "Jesus."

Finch lunged backward, spinning rapidly and throwing his left elbow at the height where the voice had sounded. The blow caught the man in the throat. Finch kept spinning, yanking the Beretta free and aiming through the open doors. The second man had dropped the bag and replaced it with a Glock.

The two gunshots exploded as one.

Chapter 2

Jesse Cooper stopped in mid-sentence. The bang sounded like a bomb had detonated beneath his window. Gas explosion, he thought.

The young woman on his computer screen jumped. "What was that?"

Without answering, Jesse ran to his window and parted the curtains. At four thirty in the morning, houses were dark, with only streetlights casting an illuminating glow. Jesse saw an SUV parked at the curb, saw a man sprawled by the rear passenger door, and, more ominously, saw two men running away, one carrying a square object under his right arm, the other clutching a gym bag in his right hand while his left arm dangled by his side.

"Something's happened, Tracy. I've got to go." He hurried from the room, leaving the woman on the screen frantically calling his name. Clad only in a T-shirt and boxer shorts, he bounded down the stairs two at a time. As he reached the bottom, an elderly woman cinching a powder-blue robe stepped into the hall.

"Ethel, stay inside." Jesse was out the front door before she could reply.

He ran barefoot across the yard to the vehicle. An engine roared to life half a block away. For a few seconds, he heard the squeal of tires and saw a dark SUV accelerate down the street, its headlights off.

The pool of light from a streetlamp just reached the figure lying faceup on the sidewalk. Jesse recognized one of his fellow roomers. Jonathan Finch, a Secret Service agent. Blood stained his chest and flowed onto the pavement. A pistol lay at his feet.

Jesse knelt beside him and heard rapid, raspy breathing. "Jonathan, hang with me. I'll call for an ambulance."

But he had no phone and hesitated to leave the man. He turned and saw Ethel hurrying across the yard. He opened his mouth to yell for her to go back inside and phone for help, but she spoke first.

"I've called for an ambulance and police. Put pressure on his wound."

Jesse placed his palms on the spot that seemed to be the center of the injury. Blood flowed between his fingers. The man's short breaths struggled to become words. Jesse bent closer till his ear nearly touched the man's lips.

"Tell Ethel… Tell Ethel…the secret…" The last syllable was no more than a faint puff of air.

"Move." Ethel Fiona Crestwater barked the order as she slipped out of her terrycloth robe and wadded it into a ball. Wearing only a gray flannel nightgown, she nudged Jesse aside and pressed the makeshift bandage against the wounded man's chest with one hand, while feeling his neck for a pulse in the carotid artery.

Ten seconds later she whispered, "May your soul fly with angels." Then she pulled her blood-soaked robe from the dead man's chest and unraveled it until she reached her cell phone jammed in a pocket.

Lights began coming on in neighboring houses. A distant siren wailed.

"Jesse, we don't have much time." Ethel used a dry corner of her robe to wipe the blood off her phone. "I want you to observe everything you can." She activated the phone's light and video app and then ran it up and down Jonathan Finch's body.

Jesse stared wide-eyed, having trouble pulling his gaze from the elderly woman to the target of her recording.

"Come on. I want an extra set of eyes. I don't depend upon technology." She bent down and studied the pistol for a few seconds. "A Beretta. Interesting." She looked through the open rear passenger door of the SUV. The one opposite was also open. She hurried around the front of the vehicle, pausing to film damage to the grille.

Jesse followed. In the crease of the dent, he noticed white paint streaked onto the SUV's green. The driver's door stood ajar, and he looked over Ethel's shoulder to see a cable dangling from a twelve-volt socket. "Looks like a power adapter for an electronic device."

"Phone?"

"No," Jesse said. "From the type of connector, I'd say a computer. I know he has a laptop."

Ethel turned her phone camera on the open door behind the driver's. A spiderweb of cracks radiated from a hole in the window.

Jesse bent down and peered through the hole. "Someone shot him through the window. This lines up with where Jonathan must have been standing."

Ethel focused her phone on the pavement and then ran it up the inside of the rear door. "No. Although the safety glass didn't shatter, the shards made by the bullet's impact fell outside the door, not inside." She moved her phone closer to the window.

"And there are blood traces on the door's interior panel. Jonathan fired the shot and must have hit his killer's arm or shoulder. The bullet went through but created a DNA signature."

The wails grew louder.

"I saw two men running away," Jesse said. "One of them had a dangling arm."

"Brief me later. I want to check one more thing." She scooted around the rear of the Ford Escape, around the supine body, and, grasping a fistful of her nightgown to avoid leaving prints, she opened the front passenger door and popped the glove box. A black pistol and an extra magazine lay on top of the vehicle's registration and insurance papers. "There we go," she whispered. "There's the Sig."

Jesse stared open-mouthed at the petite grandmotherly woman. *Brief me later? Beretta? Sig?*

She snapped the glove box closed and shut the door.

The sirens sounded only a few blocks away.

Ethel stopped recording, grabbed Jesse's arm, and pulled him up on the sidewalk. She looked around. "The neighbors, police, and EMTs will soon turn this into a zoo until the crime scene is secured. Did Jonathan say anything before he died?"

"He whispered, 'Tell Ethel the secret.' At least I think that's what he said."

"The secret? You're sure that's what you heard?"

"Yes, although it trailed off."

"Okay, Jesse, here's what we're going to do." She stepped closer to him. "You'll give a statement to the police. So will I. They should question us separately. At this time don't tell them what Jonathan said."

"Lie to them?"

"No. If they ask, say he whispered something and you're not sure what, but he didn't say what happened or who shot him. I'll tell them I came right behind you and heard nothing. Now I'm going to leave you."

"Leave me?"

"Yes, tell the police I was overcome by what happened and went inside." She started scrolling through phone contacts.

"What are you going to do?"

"Call Cory Bradshaw."

"Who's he?"

"Head of the Secret Service."

"You know their number?"

Ethel began walking away. "Yes, but at this early hour it will be Cory's personal cell phone. So, talk to the officers and buy me a little time. I should really search Jonathan's room."

The blue glow of flashing lights pulsed across the scene as racing vehicles braked to a stop. Jesse watched Ethel retreat into the shadows, her phone already at her ear. He didn't know which stunned him more, the murder of Jonathan Finch or the actions of his seventy-five-year-old landlady.

Chapter 3

"Yes?" The single syllable stretched out from a sleep-clogged throat.

"Cory, get your butt out of bed. There's a problem." Ethel closed the front door and ascended the stairs, gripping the railing with her free hand to steady herself.

"Who is this?"

"Ethel. And you've got a dead agent in front of my house."

"Ethel." The voice was suddenly sharp and alert.

"Yes. The Arlington police are arriving. Jonathan Finch, who has a room here, has been shot next to his car. If he was on some special assignment, then you don't want the locals trampling through it."

"No," Cory Bradshaw agreed. "Not until we determine what's going on. Who else is with you?"

"I'm housing an FBI agent and another of your men. Both of them are out of town. And I have an AU student. He found the body. He's my double-first-cousin-twice-removed. I can handle him."

"I don't know what that relationship means, but do you know what he'll tell the police?"

"I've coached him. You can get his full story later." Ethel paused at the top of the stairs to catch her breath, feeling a little dizzy from the sudden exertion. Then she moved down the hall toward the back bedroom. "I'm going to search Finch's things while the police are still outside. If I find anything that we need to evaluate first, will you have my back with the Arlington police?"

"Yes. And I'll contact the police chief and tell him this is federal jurisdiction."

"And federal forensics," Ethel urged. "Get a mobile crime lab here ASAP. I think they'll find blood from the shooter on the inside panel of the door with the damaged window." She stopped at the closed door to Finch's room. "I'll be in touch."

"Thanks, Ethel. You're still on your game."

"More than a game, Cory. Jonathan Finch was a nice man. And if you don't catch who killed him, I will."

She disconnected, leaving the director of the Secret Service with no doubt that Ethel Fiona Crestwater meant what she said.

Ethel noticed that the sirens had ceased. The police and EMTs must have been in place. They would first assess the situation, establish a perimeter, reroute traffic, and then talk to Jesse. There was a good chance the process wouldn't involve her until a homicide detective arrived. The uniformed officers would have their hands full just securing the scene.

Again, she clutched the fabric of her nightgown and turned the doorknob with the tips of her covered fingernails to preserve prints. The room's overhead light was on. Finch had been in Richmond with his family and wouldn't have left the bulb burning all weekend. Either someone else had been in the room or Finch had come up and then returned to his car. He had a key but would have used the back door and stairway so as not to disturb her or Jesse.

Ethel first looked for anything out of place. The single bed was made so tightly a drill sergeant could have bounced a quarter off the taut blanket. On the nightstand lay a book titled *The Case for Cryptocurrency* with a torn piece of an envelope marking a spot about two-thirds of the way through the pages.

The small writing desk was empty. Ethel knew that Finch usually set his laptop there. The computer wasn't in the room, and the cable Jesse identified as a power adapter suggested that Finch had had it in his car. Maybe it had slid under the seat.

She checked the armoire and the dresser. Clothes were neatly hung or folded in drawers. Ethel was puzzled that it looked like Finch had simply come in and turned on the light before returning to his car. She carefully dropped to her knees beside the bed. Looking under the springs, she saw a gym bag pushed against the wall. The course of its path was clearly indicated by the trail it left through the fine layer of dust. Ethel made a mental note to admonish the housekeeper for her lack of thoroughness.

Ethel slid under the bed until she could reach the bag. She knew she must look a ridiculous sight, a seventy-five-year-old woman whose wrinkled feet scrambled for traction to pull her out again. When she'd managed to extricate herself, she sat on the floor beside the bag. A single zipper ran along the top. She opened it with one fluid motion and then used both hands to widen the opening. Rolls and rolls of hundred-dollar bills. A convention of Benjamin Franklins.

"Ethel, the police would like a word." Jesse's voice came from the front of the house.

Ethel used the bed to help her to her feet. She couldn't leave the money in the room. It must involve some case Finch was working on. The bag was heavy, but she managed to lug it down the back stairs where her own first-floor bedroom was out of sight of the foyer.

"In the bathroom," she shouted as she closed the door behind her. She pushed the bag under her bed and went into the adjoining bathroom. She flushed the toilet, and ran water in the basin. She wiped her face with a damp washcloth, brushed the tangles from her shoulder-length gray hair, and prepared to take on the role of a bewildered little old lady.

Chapter 4

Jesse had watched Ethel disappear into the shadows of the front porch and then heard the click as the door closed. He looked down at the body, at the blood-soaked robe, and for the first time he felt the chill of the night air penetrate his pale skin. There he stood in only a T-shirt and boxers, suddenly lit up by the beams of multiple police flashlights.

He held his arms out from his side like he'd seen in the movies. At least his skimpy clothing left little chance for a hidden weapon. He counted three patrol cars and one ambulance. The medical team grabbed packs and ran to Finch. Six patrolmen spread out to secure the area, with two of them keeping their lights on Jesse as they approached. They stopped a few feet away, careful not to stand too close together. One was African American, the other Hispanic. They both looked like they couldn't have been more than a few years older than Jesse, and he was only twenty-two.

"Sir, let's step away a few yards and give the medics space to work." The Black man's voice was deep and his words more than a request.

Jesse retreated as the men advanced. "He's dead. His name's Jonathan Finch. I saw two men run away."

The officers looked at each other. A speedy debrief might mean a speedy arrest.

"I'm Officer Tepper." He gestured to his partner. "He's Officer Garcia. And you are?"

"Jesse Cooper."

"Did you call this in, Mr. Cooper?"

"No. My landlady did. But I heard a shot. Very loud." He pointed to a second-story window at the front of the house. "That's my room. I saw Mr. Finch lying by his car. I didn't know for sure it was him till I got here. From the window I also saw two men running away down the middle of the street."

"Can you describe them?"

"Sorry. Not really. They were shadow figures."

"White, Black, skinny, fat?" prompted Tepper.

"Average. They stayed away from streetlights. Dark clothing. I couldn't make out ethnicity. One man carried something under his right arm. It could have been a laptop computer. The other man held a satchel or gym bag in his right hand. His left arm was loose."

"Loose?" Tepper asked.

"Yeah. Like limp. He was running slower than the first man."

"Could he have been injured?"

"Maybe. Maybe there were two shots together. There's a gun at Mr. Finch's feet."

"How do you know Finch?"

"He has a room here. He's Secret Service."

The two officers exchanged a glance. They knew the case had just ratcheted up. Everything they did would be scrutinized under a microscope.

One of the EMTs caught Tepper's eye. He gave a single shake of his head.

Tepper sighed and said to his partner, "Better call forensics and homicide."

Garcia started to leave.

"Wait." Tepper turned to Jesse. "Did you see the fleeing men get in a vehicle?"

"They were a block away, but it looked like one of those big SUVs. Black or some dark color. Throaty engine. They peeled rubber as they took off."

"Okay," Tepper said without enthusiasm. DC and the surrounding area had more black SUVs than bicycles. "Put out a BOLO for a large, dark SUV, possibly a Suburban or Tahoe. Have someone at the station alert the hospitals for a possible gunshot victim showing up at an emergency room. And tell everybody to boot up and string a perimeter. We're now a murder scene. The murder scene of a federal officer."

Garcia hurried away to radio from his patrol car.

Jesse shivered. "Can I go put some clothes on?"

"A few more questions first. That bloody robe by the victim. Is that yours?"

Jesse hesitated, remembering Ethel's instructions to hold back information that the Secret Service would want to know first. Part of that effort was Ethel exaggerating her image as an elderly woman distressed by what she'd witnessed.

"It's my landlady's. She followed me out here but then went back inside to phone for help. She left the robe with me. I tried to use it as a bandage."

Tepper's eyes widened. "So Finch was alive?"

"Just barely. His breaths were quick and ragged. I used the robe as a compress on his chest."

"Did he say anything?"

"He might have whispered something. I was focused on trying to stop the bleeding and telling him to hold on."

"But he whispered something?" Tepper pressed.

"Right before he died. A syllable or two, but he didn't say who attacked him."

Tepper studied Jesse for a few seconds. "Your landlady. What's her name?"

"Ethel. Ethel Crestwater."

"And you and Finch are boarders?"

"Yes, sir. There are two others, but they're out of town."

"If Mr. Finch was Secret Service, do you have any idea what he was working on?"

"No. He never talked about his work."

Tepper nodded. "They don't call it Secret Service for nothing. Would your landlady know?"

Without thinking, Jesse said, "You'll have to ask her."

"All right. I take it she's withdrawn to the house."

Jesse mentally kicked himself for accelerating rather than delaying the police coming to Ethel.

"She's seventy-five, Officer Tepper. She might not be up for questioning."

"If she's seventy-five, she might not be up for a murder in front of her house. I at least want to check on her." Tepper scanned the scene to make sure everything was proceeding as he'd instructed. He knew homicide detectives would soon take over the case, and they might not have it long once the feds parachuted in. Tepper didn't want to have anything botched up in the meantime, including a seventy-five-year-old woman dying of shock.

"Lead on, Mr. Cooper."

Jesse walked as slowly as he could, hoping his bare feet would explain the snail's pace. He stepped up on the front porch, found the door unlocked, and walked into the foyer with Tepper close on his heels.

"Ethel, the police would like a word."

Chapter 5

Ethel grabbed another robe from her closet. She saw a couple of canes hanging on wall hooks. She didn't need them for balance but for those occasions when she did a little pedestrian surveillance. No one was more invisible than an elderly woman shuffling along a grocery aisle or a city sidewalk.

But a cane might be a bit much, and, depending upon what Jesse had told the police, suspicious if he said she'd come running after him. Ethel hoped he'd give her some sort of cue.

She found Jesse and a police officer standing in the living room.

Jesse stepped closer. "Ethel, are you all right? Officer Tepper wants to make sure."

"Thank you, Officer Tepper. It's been quite a shock. Is poor Jonathan actually dead?"

"Yes, ma'am. Despite Mr. Cooper's efforts, I'm afraid his wound was too severe."

"Oh, my." Ethel retreated a few paces and grabbed the arm of an overstuffed chair. "Do you mind if I sit?"

"Not at all." Tepper studied the woman a few seconds. She was petite, not more than five-two, a full foot shorter than himself. As for her age, if she was seventy-five, it was a youthful seventy-five. Her brown eyes were alert and inquisitive. Still, she did appear a little shaken. Better to be careful. "Would you like me to summon one of the EMTs?"

Ethel sat and then waved her hand dismissively. "That won't be necessary. But please sit down. I'd like to help however I can."

Jesse sat on the sofa, leaving room for Tepper to join him. "We both would," Jesse said, "but I don't know how much more we can tell you. We found Mr. Finch's body. I urged Ethel to return to the house and phone for help. She lent me her robe." Jesse crossed his arms as if trying to warm himself. "I'm afraid it's ruined. I tried to use it as a bandage."

"That's all right, Jesse. I only wish it could have been helpful." Ethel nodded, signaling she was up to speed on Jesse's version of events.

Officer Tepper's voice softened. "We'll take it into evidence, Miss Crestwood. If there was a scuffle, maybe some of the attacker's fibers were transferred to Mr. Finch and then onto the robe. Do you know anyone who might have meant him harm?"

Before she could answer, a loud rap sounded from the front door. Ethel jumped like another pistol had fired. "Who can that be?"

Tepper scowled. "Probably a colleague. Don't worry, I'll handle it." He got to his feet and moved to the foyer. The door swung open as he reached for the knob.

On the other side of the threshold stood a man about a head shorter and a tad wider than Tepper. He wore a rumpled blue suit with the coat and pants slightly different hues. His white dress shirt had a curled collar where a loosely knotted red tie overlapped its edge. The man's ruddy cheeks were covered with gray stubble that pegged him as late fifties or early sixties.

"Detective Mancini?"

"Ah, Tepper. I assume you're securing the victim's room." He pushed forward, forcing the uniformed officer to retreat.

"His room?"

"Yes. In case our victim was targeted for more than a random burglary or carjacking."

"But I was just about to get statements from two witnesses."

Mancini raised an eyebrow. "Together?"

Tepper didn't answer. He knew the statements should have been taken separately.

"Well, did you get a description of the assailants?"

"Two men, in shadows, who escaped in a large, dark SUV."

"Have you called it in?"

"Yes, and asked for a check of area hospitals. One of the men might have been wounded."

"And you got this from Miss Crestwater?"

"No, sir. From her roomer. Jesse Cooper." Tepper motioned his head toward the living room and whispered, "Miss Crestwater was a bit shaken up."

"Really? There may be many things that happened here, but I assure you Ethel Fiona Crestwater being shaken up isn't one of them." Mancini stepped to one side, clearing the way to the front door. "Tell Garcia to post outside the victim's room while you coordinate the exterior activities."

"I don't know which room is the victim's."

"Then come with me, and we'll ask."

Mancini pivoted and headed for the living room with Tepper in tow.

When Ethel saw Mancini, she rose from her chair and crossed to meet him.

"Frank, I was hoping they would send you. I didn't think it would be so fast. I see you dressed in the dark."

"Actually, I heard the shot." Mancini looked at Jesse Cooper as he stood from the sofa. He noted the T-shirt and boxers and the mussed brown hair in need of a cut. The young man obviously hadn't had the chance to dress. "I live two blocks away," Mancini said. "I can sleep through a lot of noises, but my brain recognizes a gunshot, whether I'm conscious or not." He offered Jesse his hand. "Detective Frank Mancini, Arlington Police Department."

Jesse found the man's grip to be firm without trying to be dominant. "Jesse Cooper. I have a room here."

"Right. Now here's how this is going to work. I'm posting a man outside the victim's room until forensics can have a look. Which one is it?"

"The one at the top of the back staircase," Ethel said.

"And where is your room, Mr. Cooper?"

Jesse pointed up. "Right above us at the opposite end of the hall from Jonathan Finch."

"Our victim?"

"Yes," Jesse confirmed.

Mancini turned to Tepper. "All right. Pass that information on to Garcia and have him bring two sets of gloves and booties. I'd like to see the room before the team goes in."

Tepper's eyes widened. "Garcia goes in with you?"

Mancini understood the officer didn't like his seniority being jumped. "No. I simply want an extra set. Stress to Garcia he's not to enter the room but have the gloves and shoe covers ready. And you'll have enough to do managing the outside logistics. Tent off the car and body so we've got some working privacy. Tell the captain I'm recommending we double our uniform presence."

"Yes, sir." Tepper started to leave.

"One more thing."

Tepper paused, but Mancini spoke to Ethel.

"Is anyone else in the house?"

"No. Just Jesse and me. I have two other renters who are out of town. I expect them back sometime tonight. Jonathan Finch was driving in from Richmond this morning."

Mancini nodded. "Tepper, tell Garcia to come through the front door, where Mr. Cooper will be waiting for him."

"Me?" Jesse exclaimed.

"Yes. Garcia will escort you to your room, where you'll remain until I'm ready to talk to you."

Jesse looked to Ethel.

"Do as he says," Ethel said. "It's my house and only logical the detective would wish to speak to me first." She turned to Mancini. "Can we have our conversation in the kitchen? I'll put on the coffee. It's obvious you need a jolt of caffeine."

Without waiting for permission, she left the men standing in her living room.

When Mancini joined her, he found her scooping ground coffee into a vintage percolator.

"What? No French press or Keurig machine?"

"No. I call this a coffeepot. You can't beat the smell or the sound. I'm just glad I can still buy my Eight O'Clock coffee at the grocery store without having to mail order the damn stuff."

Mancini chuckled. He hoisted his rotund body onto the barstool at the island in the middle of the kitchen floor. Ethel threw a switch on the percolator and turned to the detective. Even standing, the short woman had to look up at him.

"Did you really hear the shot, Frank?"

He ran a hand down the front of his shirt. "You think I'd have come dressed like this if I hadn't? I phoned it in only a few minutes after you did, and then I followed the blue flashing lights."

"So, it's your case?"

"It's a homicide. I'm the veteran homicide detective. My

partner's on medical leave, but I'll pull a team of juniors together." He paused and studied the older woman a few seconds. "So, what did you do? Fake a swoon for Tepper?"

She ignored the question and took two mugs from an overhead cabinet. "You still like your coffee black?"

"Black and truthful. Was Finch one of your boys?"

She cocked her head. "You were one of my boys once."

"Aren't I still?"

"I hope so. If you give me some space to work."

"And I have to work my case until..." He left the sentence hanging.

"Until what?"

"Until I'm told not to. I assume you've made the call."

Ethel shrugged. "It was the second call. Jonathan was Secret Service."

"Bradshaw?"

"Why not? My father always went to J. Edgar Hoover. He taught me to start at the top."

"Not just the top," Mancini said. "Another one of your boys."

"I have girls now too, Frank."

"And this Jesse Cooper?"

Ethel shook her head. "He's family. A grad student at AU."

"I didn't realize you had family."

"In California. I'm giving him a place to stay."

"He's getting more education than he bargained for."

"He's a good kid, Frank. He doesn't know anything. Go easy on him."

"Ethel, if he shares your genes, I'll be the underdog." He reached into his coat pocket and extracted a notepad. "While we wait for the coffee, I want to get some things on the record before Bradshaw and the feds shut me down."

Mancini had Ethel detail what she did and observed from the

time of the murder until he walked into her living room. Ethel followed the script Jesse created, reiterating that she'd heard Finch say nothing, given Jesse her robe, and gone back inside to phone for help. She repeated what Jesse had said about two men running away, one carrying a satchel and the other what Jesse thought might be a laptop.

Mancini took notes without challenging the veracity of her statement. Then he asked, "Do you know what he was working on?"

"No. He'd been called up for temporary presidential detail. With the increased number of foreign trips President Tarleton's making in his last few months in office, more manpower's needed to cover the first family and the former presidents. Jonathan was an experienced agent in protective detail and was on assignment in DC. His normal station is Richmond, where he lives with his wife and son."

"So, he wasn't involved in an active investigation?"

Ethel shook her head. "I didn't say that. I said he was on temporary assignment here. I have no clue what he was doing back in Richmond."

"Fair enough. You ready to walk me through his room?"

"Aren't you going to talk to Jesse first?"

Mancini smiled. "Why? I'll get to him later. I know he'll just repeat whatever you told him to say."

Ethel feigned a frown. "Frank, how could you think I'd ever do such a thing?"

"Because you're Ethel Fiona Crestwater. Leave the coffee brewing. I'm sure I'll be back for it."

Chapter 6

Jesse Cooper waited in the foyer to be escorted to his room. As Ethel had predicted, the police were going to question them separately. At least that became clear when Detective Mancini took charge. Jesse hoped he'd given Ethel enough information so that their telling of events would be consistent. Maybe it wasn't that important. Jesse had read that eyewitness reports often vary because of the stress and trauma of the incident.

But there had been something in the brief exchange between Mancini and Ethel that signaled more was going on than met the eye. Ethel might have deceived Officer Tepper, but Mancini appeared to know better. Jesse decided he shouldn't stray far from the truth and only omit Ethel's video recording of the crime scene. They hadn't touched anything, so it wasn't like they'd tampered with evidence. He would stick with the story that she'd gone back into her house to phone for help. However, what Ethel might have done in Jonathan's room was another matter, and Jesse was happy to remain ignorant.

The front door opened, and Officer Garcia entered. "Show me to Finch's room and then go to your own."

Jesse hadn't been sent to his room since he was fourteen.

"For how long?"

Garcia shrugged. "Until Mancini calls for you. You'll probably know before me, kid."

The word "kid" rankled, but Jesse let it slide. Instead, he went quickly up the stairs, leaving the young policeman to scramble after him. Jesse passed the open door to his own room, hurried down the hall, and stopped at Finch's.

"This is it." Jesse noticed light shining beneath the door.

Garcia reached his hand for the knob.

Jesse said, "Detective Mancini said no one was to enter before him. And you're neither gloved nor booted. It would be my duty to tell him if those instructions weren't followed, *kid*." Jesse smiled as Garcia's face reddened. "If you need me, my room's at the other end of the hall. Just knock."

Without waiting for a response, Jesse pivoted and retraced his steps till he stood in his doorway. He turned to Garcia and stared at the patrolman positioned outside Finch's room. Then he made an okay sign as if approving the officer's placement and closed the door behind him.

He checked his laptop and saw Tracy had signed off from their Skype session. He thought she might be in class so he sent a WhatsApp text:

I'm safe man shot outside house let me know when you can talk.

Then he put on jeans, sneakers, and an American University sweatshirt. His first class wasn't till two in the afternoon, but he would skip it if things were still unfolding at the house. And he had questions for Ethel.

His phone chimed. Tracy texted:

OMG u r supposed to be in safe part of dc could have been u

Yes, thought Jesse. If it had been random. But Finch's dying message to Ethel suggested otherwise.

victim was secret service. i think involved a case no danger to me. May need to give police your name

He sent the message knowing she'd flip out. Tracy Lorton had been his girlfriend since their junior year at Berkeley. She'd gone on to the London School of Economics, and he'd chosen American University. The distance and time difference meant their dates were Skype, texts, and phone calls. He liked Tracy, but she would have been perfect if she had more of a sense of humor. Check that. More of *his* sense of humor. But Jesse had to admit there was nothing funny about having your name tied to a murder investigation.

WHAT???? came her immediate response.

just a formality first on the scene they'll want to know why I was up at half past 4
u r a witness? sure u not in danger?
can't ID anyone.

But the thought flooded his brain—*the killers don't know that. What if they think Finch said more than he did?* He mentally added that question to his list for Ethel. Then he texted:

got to go. u Skype at 10 my time?
yes miss u xoxox
c u soon xoxoxo

He closed the app and turned on his computer to look for any online mention of the shooting. Maybe in the greater Washington area it wasn't news.

Ten minutes later he heard the stairs creak under the heavy tread of Detective Mancini's shoes. He heard Ethel say, "Jesse's room is on the right whenever you want to speak to him. Or you can talk in the kitchen, and I'll go to the basement for my RBG workout."

Jesse eased to the door, hoping he'd be able to hear them from Finch's room.

"RBG workout?" Mancini asked as they passed.

"Ruth Bader Ginsburg. Every morning. Never miss it. If it worked for her, and she was even older than I am, then it should work for me. You could stand to lose some of that paunch, Frank. Bring some sweats sometime, and I'll show you the drill."

Mancini's silence told Jesse that Ethel had struck a nerve. After that, their voices became too faint to understand.

Officer Garcia straightened up as he saw Detective Mancini approach. He wondered why the old lady was with him. Surely the extra gloves and shoe covers weren't for her.

"Officer Garcia, I'd like you to meet Ethel Crestwater. She owns this house and should be able to tell me if anything is missing from the victim's room."

"Ma'am," Garcia said respectfully. He turned to Mancini. "Sir, I found the door closed and have kept it that way. Mr. Cooper has remained in his room at the other end of the hall."

"Good work. And you have the gloves and booties?"

Garcia pulled an evidence bag from where he'd tucked it in his duty belt. "I put them here, along with a few additional bags, in case you need them."

Mancini took them. "Thank you, Officer. You can rejoin

Tepper now. Let me know when forensics is clear to move the body. I want one last look."

Garcia gave his last look at Ethel, confused by what he considered the detective's most unusual involvement of a woman old enough to be Garcia's grandmother. "Ma'am, sorry to meet under such circumstances." He left reluctantly.

Mancini rolled on a pair of gloves. "I can help you cover your slippers."

"Why?" Ethel took the booties, squatted down on the floor, and pulled the coverings over her red suede moccasins. Then she got to her feet without assistance.

Mancini shook his head and then leaned against the wall with one hand while wrestling the booties over his black oxfords with the other.

"Need some help?" Ethel offered.

"Don't rub it in."

When Mancini was ready, he turned the knob and pushed open the door. "Who turned on the light?"

"It must have been Jonathan. I'd say he made at least one trip up here before being shot at the car. The light certainly wasn't on all weekend." She looked around the room as if seeing it for the first time. "His laptop's not here. Did you see it in the SUV?"

"No. If it wasn't taken by one of the men, then maybe it's under the seat. I'll check when I go back out. Maybe Finch first brought some hanging clothes for the armoire."

"Maybe. I wouldn't be able to tell."

Mancini picked up the book on the nightstand. "This cryptocurrency. Was that something he was interested in?"

"He never spoke about it with me. But the Secret Service deals with currency, so I guess it's an area of interest."

Mancini looked at the bed. "Blanket's tucked so tightly it doesn't look like he set anything on it or sat on it." The detective's knees cracked as he knelt on the floor. He peered under the bed. "Nothing under here now. Did he normally store something there?"

Although she didn't want her onetime roomer to get out in front of her, Ethel was pleased Mancini proved to be observant. "I can't say."

"Can't say or won't say? Something has been slid in and out, sweeping a path in the dust."

"Then there's your answer."

Mancini got to his feet. "No, there's my question. Could it have been the satchel Jesse saw? Had Finch just brought it down from the room or gone back to retrieve it and his laptop from his car?"

"It could have been a satchel of clothes."

"And it could have contained evidence. And evidence could have been on Finch's laptop. And you know more than you're telling me because that's why you called Bradshaw directly."

Ethel's eyes flashed. "Frank, I went to Bradshaw because Jonathan Finch was Secret Service. If the victim were your Officer Tepper, I would have gone straight to you. You know that's the truth."

"Yeah, I know," Mancini grumbled. "It's one thing to play second fiddle on an investigation, and it's another thing to play second fiddle if the conductor's changing the score sheet for a cover-up."

"And if it's not a cover-up but an undercover operation? Isn't it prudent to pursue justice without blowing up what could have been Finch's case, a case he gave his life for? A life that includes a wife and son back in Richmond."

Mancini stood silently chewing on his lip for a few seconds. Then he stepped closer and looked down at the woman who had always had his respect. "And that's what you think?"

"What I think is we don't know enough to rule anything out. You know the old adage. It's not what you know you don't know that kills you, it's what you don't know that you don't know. That's why both of us need to proceed cautiously. That's why, at this stage, second fiddle at least keeps you playing in the orchestra."

A smile broke through Mancini's grim countenance. "Why do I get the feeling that you're the one holding the baton?"

Chapter 7

As dawn broke, Jesse Cooper stood at his bedroom window and watched the scene below. A tent had been erected over the SUV and the spot where Finch had died. Jesse couldn't tell if the body had been removed. More uniformed officers maintained a perimeter defined by tape and sawhorses. Beyond, neighbors gathered in small clusters, neighbors who might not have spoken to each other in months or even years.

A rap on the door broke into Jesse's thoughts. Mancini entered.

"Mr. Cooper. I know you gave some information to Officer Tepper, but I'd like to go through it again." He walked across the room and joined Jesse at the window. "You saw the two men running from here?"

"Yes. Away from me. The one with the satchel was a good ten yards behind."

"And you think the other man was carrying a laptop?"

"It was the right size and shape. I'd seen Jonathan use one before. But it could have been something else."

"And you saw their vehicle from here?"

"No, I saw it as I ran across the yard. I came down the stairs and out of the house pretty fast. I could see someone had been hurt."

Mancini nodded. "That was brave of you to run to an active shooting scene."

"Not brave. I just didn't stop to think. I recognized Jonathan's car and thought he was in trouble. And I didn't see any guns."

Mancini studied the young man. He was shy of six feet by a few inches, trim but not skinny. He appeared to be in good shape with more the physique of a runner than a bodybuilder. Mancini could believe he was agile enough to get from the window to the street in under ten seconds. He looked at the unmade, rumpled bed. But could he move that fast if he'd been asleep?

"I'm impressed you reacted so quickly after the shot woke you up."

"I was already awake." Jesse pointed to his laptop. "My girlfriend's in London. She's five hours ahead. I was up at four to Skype. She heard the shot as well."

"We'll want to talk to her."

"She knows. I gave her a heads-up. Her name's Tracy Lorton, but she's in class now."

"What's she studying?"

"Economics. She's in grad school."

"And you?"

"Computer science. On the finance track. Computers move the money. Money moves the world."

"Does that involve cryptocurrency?"

Jesse smiled. "Now you're talking about a really volatile area. Yes, I'm interested in it. How it's created and protected. Tracy's interested in its economic impact."

"And you discuss cryptocurrency at four in the morning?"

"No, Detective Mancini, we do not."

"I would hope not." Mancini gestured to the open door. "Why don't we continue in the kitchen where you can buy me a cup of Ethel's coffee?"

They sat on stools across the island from each other. As the detective took his filled mug from Jesse, he asked, "How well did you know Mr. Finch?"

"Not very well. I only moved here the first of August to get ready for the fall term. Mr. Finch would be here a few days or occasionally a week. He was experienced in presidential and protective detail. He primarily filled in guarding family members when the teams were shorthanded because of the travels of the president or vice president."

"And what did he do otherwise?"

"Worked out of the Richmond office. I think he had something to do with cybercrime."

"And you never discussed cryptocurrency?"

Jesse slid his cup of coffee to one side and leaned forward. "Why the interest in cryptocurrency?"

Mancini took a sip and then held his cup in front of him. "Because there's a book in his room called *The Case for Cryptocurrency.* He never spoke about it?"

"Not to me. But it makes sense. The Secret Service deals with currency fraud like counterfeiting, right?"

"Yes."

"So, I could see them moving into fraud in the realm of digital currency as well. I wish I'd talked to him about it. I think computer science would be at the heart of his investigations."

Mancini took another sip as he considered Jesse's explanation. "Okay. I get it. Now let's get back to this morning. You ran down the stairs and across the yard in time to see a large black SUV speed off about a block away."

"Black or some dark color. I can't be sure."

"You found Finch still alive and conscious."

"Yes. I told him to hold on, that help was coming."

"You knew Ethel had called?"

"No. I just said that to keep him calm. Ethel wasn't there yet. I hesitated to leave him, but I knew I had to get help. Fortunately, Ethel came out. She gave me her robe and went back inside to dial 911. I tried to stop the bleeding using the robe as a compress. But..."

"Finch was conscious enough to speak?"

"Hardly a whisper." Jesse's stomach tightened as he formed the words of a lie. "I couldn't understand him. He might have been calling for Ethel. Then he was gone."

"Did Ethel come back out?"

Again, Jesse worried that he might be contradicting Ethel's version. "Yes, but I told her Finch was dead and she should wait inside where it was warm."

Mancini cocked his head. "Really? You gave her an order?"

Jesse felt his face flush. "I didn't think of it as an order. If she said I did, it must have come across that way."

"She didn't say anything to me about coming back out."

"Then I'm misremembering it. The police and EMTs were here very quickly. I'm afraid it's all a blur."

"Uh-huh," Mancini said, the skepticism heavy in his voice. "So, are you and Ethel close?"

"Not really. I'd never met her before coming East last month. She and my mother exchanged Christmas cards, but it had been thirty years since they'd seen each other. My mom died last May." He paused as his voice broke. "She was excited that I was coming to stay with Ethel."

"Ethel's some kind of cousin?"

"A double-first-cousin-twice-removed. My mother explained it to me, because she said Ethel would be very precise."

Mancini shook his head. "Son, I have no idea what that means. Sounds like something you'd find out from one of those ancestry DNA kits."

"Ethel's parents had siblings who married each other. A brother and a sister wed a sister and a brother. Ethel's aunt and uncle were both her blood relatives, and therefore Ethel and her first cousins were double first cousins. In other words, cousins through both sides of the family tree. I'm two generations down from Ethel—so a double-first-cousin-twice-removed." Jesse shrugged. "Doesn't mean a lot to me, but I guess since Ethel doesn't have any other family, it's her strongest blood tie."

Mancini set down his cup. "She might be two generations removed, but I guarantee you she's sharper today than either one of us ever will be. With a Secret Service agent dead on the street, she would not stay in this house without a damn good reason. So, why don't you tell me what really happened?"

The knot in Jesse's stomach cinched tighter.

"Detective Mancini?"

Mancini swiveled around on his stool to see Officer Tepper in the hall doorway. "What?" he barked.

"Chief Walpole's outside. He wants you to come immediately."

"Tell him I'm finishing an interview, and I'll be with him in ten minutes."

Tepper rocked back and forth, anxious to leave but compelled to stay. "I'm sorry, sir. He said to hold whatever you're doing and join him now." Tepper gave a nervous glance at Jesse. "There's another man with him—dark suit, white shirt, but morning stubble on his face."

Mancini slapped the counter. "Damn. My pension to a doughnut it's Cory Bradshaw." He looked at Jesse. "You see, that's why Ethel didn't come back to you after Finch died. She called Bradshaw. But I'll be back. We're not finished."

Mancini drained his coffee, slid off the stool, and pushed past Tepper. The patrolman hesitated, not sure whether to follow the detective or guard Jesse. His curiosity won out and he left.

Cory Bradshaw, Jesse thought. The director of the Secret Service came running when Ethel called him. Jesse went to the stairs leading down to the basement. He could hear a disco beat pulsating from below. Ethel and her RBG workout. He needed to talk to her. They had to get their stories straight before Mancini returned.

The sound of the music masked his footsteps. He opened the door at the bottom of the staircase expecting to see Ethel on the treadmill or stair-stepper. Instead, she was sitting on the weight bench with a gym bag at her feet. Beside her and on her lap were rolls of U.S. currency. The bills were curled and bound by rubber bands. She was removing the bands, quickly fanning through the money, and then rebinding them.

"Ethel?"

She looked up without any sign of alarm, like she was counting eggs or apples. "Where's Frank?"

Jesse walked to her. "Officer Tepper said a Chief Walpole needed to see him. And he thinks Bradshaw might be here." Jesse stared at the money. "That looks like the gym bag one of the killers carried. How did you get it?"

"From Jonathan's room. Obviously there were two, and he only got one."

"But that's thousands of dollars."

"I guess close to a quarter of a million." She swept the rolls of bills off the bench and into the bag. "It's not the amount that's so important. It's that ninety percent of it is counterfeit." She zipped the bag closed and kicked it under the bench. "Not a word to anyone, Jesse. Understand?"

"But whose money is it?"

Ethel held up a finger. "Excellent first question." She raised another finger. "The second—was Jonathan giving it to someone or receiving it? The answers will determine our next move. Are you up for it?"

Jesse felt a tingle of excitement run down his spine. "Yes. What else would you expect from a double-first-cousin-twice-removed?"

Chapter 8

Trevor Norwood swallowed a second shot of whiskey straight from the bottle and then struggled to wrap another layer of gauze bandage tighter around his upper left arm. He knew he needed stitches, but showing up at an emergency room, at least in the area, would bring the cops. His main goal was to stop the bleeding and keep the gash free from infection.

Finch's bullet had gouged a half-inch trench in his flesh. The impact had knocked him back against the inside door panel and stunned him. But he knew he'd shot Finch center chest, and the man wouldn't be testifying against him.

How could things have gone so wrong? Secrecy had bitten them in the ass. It should have been a simple operation. They arrange the peer-to-peer exchange of cash for Bitcoin in anonymity, a practice they use in all their messages. Then they follow the mark and jump him before he can examine the currency. A quick blow to knock him unconscious, reclaim the cash, and no one's the wiser. How the hell could they have known the mark lived in a nearby boardinghouse? Then that it was Finch, of all people. Somebody who recognized him.

Norwood examined himself in the bathroom mirror. Blood

stained his lower arm. His ashen face and bristly stubble made him look twenty years older than his actual thirty-five. When he went out, he'd put on a windbreaker with a hoodie. The waterproof fabric would keep any blood seepage from becoming visible. The hoodie might hide the pain in his eyes.

Seven thirty. The past three hours had been hell. He'd wait until most of the people in his Crystal City apartment complex had left for work. He'd use soap and bleach to clean the bloodstains out of his Tahoe. At least he'd been able to drive.

Norwood popped a couple of pain pills and washed them down with another swallow of whiskey. He'd sit tight for two more hours, listen to the all-news radio station, and see if he could find anything incriminating on Finch's computer. It would probably be best to just scrub its internal disk clean and then ditch the laptop in the Potomac. But Trevor Norwood was a computer whiz and couldn't miss a chance to examine a Secret Service agent's hard drive.

He returned to the kitchen, where his own laptop was logged into the tracking program. His apartment was within range of the device's GPS signal, and he saw that the second bag of currency hadn't been moved. Were the police simply taking their time or had Finch hidden it too well? For that matter, why would the police even know of its existence? Maybe the plan was still salvageable.

Things had begun to unravel when Finch stopped so soon after leaving the parking deck rendezvous. Norwood had expected the anonymous seller of cryptocurrency to be someone who had driven to the site from farther away and that there would have been time to catch up to him and retrieve the bags as they were unloaded. But Finch had already carried one bag in before they could confront him. The shooting forced them to flee immediately, grabbing only what they could find in the car and on his person.

Norwood looked at Finch's laptop and demolished cell phone lying on the kitchen counter. He'd yanked out the phone's battery and then used a hammer to reduce the pieces to the size of his thumbnail. The police would find the last cell tower ping but that was all. It was the currency that worried Norwood. The bag was somewhere in the house, and it could focus the investigation uncomfortably close.

Norwood turned his attention to Finch's open laptop. Although it had closed, the computer hadn't had the chance to go into sleep mode. Norwood had kept it active to avoid having to hack past a login password. The program for executing the Bitcoin transaction was still engaged. The history showed the virtual wallet receiving the coins, but seeing them and retrieving them were two different operations. An unbreakable private key existed for each wallet. Finch had about ten thousand dollars of cryptocurrency left. Without the private key, it might as well have been buried on the bottom of the ocean. He traced the coins back farther and saw the address for another virtual wallet, this one the source of the coins that were transferred into the first one.

Norwood stared in disbelief. The pain in his arm and the incriminating gym bag of counterfeit currency were momentarily forgotten. The coins in that second wallet had a current value of more than twenty million dollars. Where did a Secret Service agent get that kind of money? If the private key was on Finch's laptop, Norwood would find it. If not, then the key must be written down somewhere, because the string of letters and numbers was just too long to memorize. For all the crap that had gone down that morning, twenty million dollars would more than make up for it. Norwood faced a hard decision. Did he keep this knowledge to himself or did he bring in the others? One thing he knew for sure. If he didn't bring them in and they found out, Trevor Norwood would be as dead as Jonathan Finch.

Chapter 9

Detective Frank Mancini, Director Cory Bradshaw, and Ethel Crestwater sat in the living room of her Arlington home. Jesse Cooper had been sent to his room for the second time that morning.

Ethel had changed into a tracksuit and running shoes to provide credence for her workout ruse. Bradshaw looked like Officer Tepper had described him. His pressed blue suit looked out of place on a man with an unshaven face and bleary blue eyes. He was of medium build with graying hair, and he clung to his mug of coffee like it was a life raft. Mancini and Ethel sat quietly, waiting for the director of the Secret Service to lead their discussion.

Bradshaw cleared his throat. "Well, I acknowledge we all have a stake in this investigation. Frank, the murder is on your turf, and your team was first on the scene. Ethel, we know how protective you are of your roomers, since Frank and I both had that honor in our younger days. But I've got not only this murder to consider but also whatever Finch was investigating. Right now, I'm not clear on what that was. I'll be contacting the Richmond office as soon as we establish our parameters going forward."

Mancini scowled. "What parameters would those be?"

"What I worked out with Chief Walpole. That you and I share information, but I reserve the right to withhold whatever I deem might compromise another case."

Mancini shook his head. "Which means I could be wasting time going down a rabbit hole that you know goes nowhere."

"I promise to let you know if I think that's happening. I just might not be able to tell you why."

"And forensics? You've flatbedded Finch's SUV to your garage and sent his body to your morgue. Will you be sharing that information?"

"Any evidence, barring what I said might be critical to another case, will be shared. And I expect reciprocity. I know you're sly as a fox, and your department couldn't have a better man in charge, but make no mistake, if you're stonewalling me, I'll go to the attorney general. Finch was on and off presidential detail. If he was uncovering some plot along those lines, then we're talking about a whole different ball game."

"Cory," Ethel said, "I think Frank understands the gravity of the situation. My question is how much will you share with me? As you acknowledged, Jonathan Finch was one of mine. I will not be relegated to a rocking chair reading the progress of your investigation in the *Washington Post*."

Bradshaw threw up his hands in surrender. "You know you have no official standing, Ethel. But I'll keep you posted on our progress as appropriate."

"And I'll keep you posted on mine."

The two men looked at each other, neither wanting to challenge her.

After a moment of silence, Mancini asked, "Have you made progress already?"

"A little."

Bradshaw leaned forward in his chair. "You know withholding evidence can be obstruction of justice."

Ethel smiled. "Does that include withholding the interpretation of evidence?"

"What do you mean?"

"How can I be withholding evidence when it's in plain sight? You see it, Frank sees it, and I see it. Is it obstruction of justice if I form an opinion and keep it to myself?"

Mancini laughed. "Well, Cory, you want to call the AG and get a ruling because I don't know what to tell her?"

Bradshaw shook his head. "All right, Ethel. I promise to be as open with you as I will be with Frank. Now what's this evidence you're talking about?"

"The damage to the front of Jonathan's car. There are two broken headlights and a dent in the grille. But there's no damage to the bumper that protrudes beyond them and no fragments of the broken headlight lenses at the scene. So it happened elsewhere. But he didn't drive all the way from Richmond through the dark without headlights. So, something occurred before he was shot here. From the nature of the damage, I'd say he either hit some kind of railing or, more likely, ran through a crossing bar somewhere. If I were running the case, I'd look for any reports of broken railings or crossbars that happened overnight."

Bradshaw looked at Mancini. "Are you working that?"

"Hell, no. You took the damn vehicle." He turned to Ethel. "And you saw all this in the brief time you handed Jesse your robe and went back in the house to make the 911 call?"

"I saw it long enough to interpret the implications later. Now, are we going to spend the morning arguing about what I'm allowed or not allowed to know, or are we going to find Jonathan's killers?"

"I need to finish interviewing your cousin," Mancini said.

"No, you don't. You'll be wasting time. Jesse's told you what he knows. I suggest you look for where Jonathan's car was damaged. Maybe you'll luck into some CCTV footage. Unless you want Cory to get the jump on you."

Bradshaw turned to the detective. "Have you kept Finch's name off the radio transmissions?"

"Yes. I hope to notify next of kin before any ID is announced."

"Good." Bradshaw sighed. "And I guess I'd better be the one to do that. It means going to Richmond, so if you can keep a lid on his name for another two hours, I'd appreciate it. I'll call you once it's done." He turned to Ethel. "Would you be willing to go with me? I'd ask one of the women agents, but that would only delay us. I know you'll offer some words of comfort to his family."

"Of course," Ethel said. "I'll need about twenty minutes."

Bradshaw stood. "I know I look a mess, but I don't have time to run home."

Mancini and Ethel rose.

The detective smiled. "I live a few blocks from here, Cory. You're welcome to my bathroom and a razor."

"Thanks. I'll follow you." Bradshaw took a step toward the foyer. "Ethel, I'll be back to pick you up in twenty, and you can share some more of your opinions along the way."

As soon as the men left, Ethel called up to Jesse. "I'm going to Richmond. But come down. I need to talk to you."

He was there so quickly Ethel suspected he'd been listening from the top of the stairs.

"What did you hear?" she asked.

"That Director Bradshaw's going to share some things." His eyes widened. "And that he threatened to go to the attorney general."

"A bluff. He'd never make it as a poker player."

"But what about the money? That's evidence you're hiding from him."

"No. That's evidence I'm hiding from Frank. I'll tell Cory I couldn't mention it in front of an Arlington police officer. Now, let's go look at that money before I get dressed."

Jesse followed Ethel down to the basement workout room. She went straight to the weight bench and pulled out the gym bag. She sat on the bench and patted a place beside her. "Sit. I want to show you something." She withdrew a wad of bills and slipped off the rubber band. "Look at this top bill." She peeled off a C-note and handed it to him.

He held it close to his eyes, ran his fingers over the surface, and then felt the edges. "Wow, it really feels real."

She chuckled. "That's because it is real. Now look at this one." She handed him a second bill.

Jesse repeated his examination. "The ink color's a little bit darker or more saturated. The paper is a little lighter and not as, I don't know how to explain it, just not as tough. But I'd be hard-pressed to tell the difference if I wasn't holding both of them."

"Note the serial numbers of the first and second bills."

"Well, they're different."

Ethel gave him a third. "Now this one."

He needed only a few seconds to understand. "The serial numbers are the same."

"Correct. The paper and the printing are first-rate. Probably a digital photographic process, but creating a new serial number for each bill was a step too complicated." She pulled a bill from the bottom. "This is also a real hundred. Whoever pulled this money together placed a genuine C-note on top and bottom. The roll could pass a cursory inspection, especially if you were exchanging it in a hurry and in the dark."

"Do you think that's what Jonathan was doing?"

She took a deep breath. "I don't know. More likely he was the one receiving the money. He brought up one bag but was attacked when he returned for the second. I find it hard to believe some exchange was arranged in front of my house. And that doesn't explain the vehicle damage."

Jesse returned the money to Ethel, who bound the roll again, leaving out one bill and putting it in her pocket.

"What are you going to do now?" Jesse asked.

"Find the money's source."

"Through Bradshaw?"

"Not yet. I won't say anything on the way to Richmond. Maybe on the way back, depending upon things."

"Things?"

She nodded. "When you've lived as long as I have, there are always things. The unexpected masquerading as something else. Even the expected can hide secrets, so I like to be sure of my footing. Not break my metaphorical hip."

Tell Ethel the secret. Jesse wondered if Jonathan's dying sentence meant more to Ethel than she let on.

"Can you skip your classes today?" she asked.

"Yes. I just have one, and I can borrow notes. Do you need me to go to Richmond?"

"No. After I've left with Bradshaw, I want you to take this bag to the recycling bin in the kitchen. You'll find a stack of the past week's newspapers. Take them out of the bin and then remove the top layer of the money and set it aside. Put the rest of the money in the empty bin, and then hide it with a layer or two of the newspapers. Put the remaining newspapers in the gym bag and hide them with the top layer of money. Try to replicate the original weight. There are magazines in my bedroom if the newspapers aren't enough."

"I get it, but why are we doing this?"

She lifted the bag off the floor. "Because of your question, whose money is it? Jonathan could have prepped this bag with some kind of tracker sewn in the handles or the base. Or, if it's not Jonathan's money, then someone else could have done the same thing. Maybe that's how they found him if the money was a dead drop."

Jesse stared at the bag as the revelation hit him. "Then they could come back."

"They could, but if they haven't seen its location change, they may think Jonathan hid it. I don't think they'd return in broad daylight. Most likely at night or when they knew for sure no one was here. Put on some loud music. Study on the porch. But just in case, follow me."

They went up to her bedroom and she pulled back the bedspread and reached between the mattress and box spring. She offered him a pistol, butt-first.

Jesse didn't take it immediately. "What's this?"

"Well, if you have to ask, then it's not going to do you much good. It's a Smith & Wesson Thirty-Eight Special."

"Is it loaded?"

"Revolvers tend to be more effective that way, unless you'd prefer to throw it at an assailant." She released the cylinder. "It holds five shots, but I only load four cartridges, leaving an empty one under the hammer. I don't want to drop the damn thing and have it discharge. All you have to do is point, pull the trigger, and the cylinder advances so the hammer lands on a loaded chamber."

Jesse took the gun. Ethel pulled open her nightstand drawer. "Here's a box of ammo, but if you need more than four bullets you're probably in over your head and should make a speedy exit."

Jesse ran his tongue over his dry lips. "Okay. Is there a holster or something?"

"Don't fool with that. Just tuck it in your waistband and cover it with your sweatshirt. I'll be back before dark. Are we good?"

Jesse slipped the pistol under his belt in the small of his back. "Yes. If I don't shoot myself."

Ethel patted him on the shoulder. "Good boy. This weekend I'll take you to the range where you can fire some rounds. Now get out of here so I can change."

She closed the bedroom door, pulled out her phone, and sat on the edge of the bed. She speed-dialed a number.

After a few rings, a man answered, "Warren Hitchcock."

"Warren, it's Ethel Crestwater. I need a favor."

"Ethel. Good to hear your voice."

"Yeah. Glad to know you're above ground too. Listen, are you still in evidence records?"

"Yep. You know me. File without mercy. What do you need?"

"I think I picked up a bogus bill. Can you run a serial number for me and see if it's been flagged?"

"Sure. I'm in the middle of something, but I could do it later today. Will that work?"

"Yes, but as soon as you can, would be great. No need to call. Text me at this number whatever you find."

She pulled from her pocket the counterfeit bill she'd kept. She read off the serial number.

Then she thanked him and disconnected. She went to her closet and looked at the dresses on the rack. What do you wear when you're about to change a family's world forever?

———

The black Cadillac Escalade crept along Rock Creek Parkway in the midst of the DC morning commute. The driver navigated through the throng of vehicles while his passenger in the rear seat navigated through the *Washington Post*.

FBI Director Rudy Hauser first looked at any headlines that could possibly connect to or reflect upon the Bureau. If something major had transpired overnight, he would have been informed immediately. But sometimes little unnoticed stories have a way of becoming big stories if not identified and addressed early. The classic example was a bungled minor burglary at the Watergate complex that appeared as a small news article in the "Local" section and mushroomed to bring down a president. That would not happen on Rudy Hauser's watch.

The cell phone in the breast pocket of his dark suit buzzed. He glanced at the screen. Interesting. The call meant information.

"Yes."

"You might not have heard, but a Secret Service agent was shot and killed earlier this morning."

Hauser gripped the phone tighter. "And the president?"

"Not involved. The incident occurred around four thirty on North Highland Street in Arlington."

Hauser knew the street well. "Anywhere near Ethel Crestwater?"

"Her front yard."

"Jesus," Hauser muttered.

"She's okay. Bradshaw's with her."

"Got a name?"

"It's being withheld till notification of next of kin."

"Give me the name." It was no longer a question.

"Jonathan Finch. Do you know him?"

Hauser's pulse quickened. "No. But thanks for the heads-up."

The director disconnected. Having sources in other agencies was all part of the game. He knew Cory Bradshaw had his own communication lines into the Bureau. So, Jonathan Finch had been shot. A local murder with huge implications.

Hauser speed-dialed his office in the Hoover Building. One of his immediate staff would be on duty. He bypassed the switchboard, and his number was recognized.

"Sir, Agent Sims here."

"Tony, pull me everything you can on a Secret Service agent named Jonathan Finch. I'll want whatever you can get as soon as possible."

"Yes, sir."

"Tony, this is not an official request. Nothing in writing yet."

"Understood, sir."

"And one more thing. See what you can learn about an Ethel Fiona Crestwater on North Highland Street in Arlington. She rents rooms to agents, and I'd like to know if we have anyone currently staying there." He ended the call.

Jonathan Finch. A name he knew well. A man who could have the key to twenty million dollars.

Chapter 10

The gray government sedan pulled onto the concrete driveway of a brick ranch home in the Spottswood Park neighborhood of Richmond. In the carport was a green Subaru Forester.

"Good," Bradshaw said. "Someone's home." He glanced at his wristwatch. "Ten thirty. Their son should be in school."

"Maybe," Ethel whispered, "but he does have special needs." She sat in the back seat beside the Secret Service director. She'd chosen a navy blue pantsuit to look respectful, not her charcoal one that would visibly foreshadow a funeral. But now she worried she looked too much like a government agent, only missing a flag lapel pin to complete the image. She was there as Jonathan's friend.

Bradshaw opened his own door, telling the driver to stay in the car. Then he opened Ethel's and offered his arm as she stepped out.

"Thank you. I'll be fine." She turned, deciding to leave her purse with her cell phone on the seat. She didn't want any annoying vibrations interrupting what she knew would be a traumatic event.

Side by side, they walked to the front door.

"I'll first ask if we can come in," Bradshaw said. "Try and avoid breaking the news out here on the threshold."

Ethel nodded and let Bradshaw press the bell. A chime sounded from somewhere in the house.

Light footsteps drew nearer, and then the door opened.

Susan Finch smiled as her hazel eyes lit first on Ethel. She wore black jeans and an untucked, oversized white shirt with the sleeves rolled back, one of her husband's now too frayed to wear for work.

"Ethel?" The first syllable came out with delighted surprise. The second trailed off in fear. She focused on Bradshaw.

"Mrs. Finch," Bradshaw said softly, "may we come inside?"

Susan's face paled and then crumpled as she scrunched her eyes shut trying to block out the two faces, trying in vain to hold back the tears.

Bradshaw stepped forward and caught her as her knees buckled. "Help me get her inside."

Ethel pushed the door open wider as Bradshaw grabbed Susan under her arms to keep her erect.

Susan was a small woman, slim and not more than a hundred pounds. They escorted her to the living room on the right and eased her onto the sofa.

Out of the corner of her eye, Ethel saw the frightened face of a boy no more than seven peek around the corner of the adjacent dining room and then disappear.

Susan Finch struggled through sobs in an effort to speak. "He didn't take his own life, did he? Please tell me he didn't take his own life."

"No, Mrs. Finch," Bradshaw said. "But I'm so sorry to say your husband has been killed. We're not sure what happened, but we think he was conducting some kind of investigation. If he was," Bradshaw paused, seeking the right words, "then he died in the line of duty. You have my word we will bring those responsible to justice."

"Davie. I need to be with Davie. He won't understand."

"He was just here," Ethel said. "I'll find him."

"Through the den to the hall," Susan said. "His room's the first one."

Ethel left the more formal living room and crossed the foyer into a paneled den, which featured a white brick fireplace and a wide-screen television. Beyond, the hallway ran perpendicular to the den. Ethel knocked on the first door. No reply. She turned the knob, found it unlocked, and gently pushed the door open.

A single bed ran along the opposite wall. The bedspread displayed the solar system with the sun covering the pillow and the planets orbiting to the bed's foot. There was a chest of drawers with a mirror over it. Two windows overlooked the front yard. A small table was between them.

Davie sat at the table, his hunched back to Ethel. He was connecting Tinkertoys, not in a simple rectangle or tower, but an intricate three-dimensional structure with rods and hubs of different colors interconnecting in a sophisticated crystalline design. On the floor around him lay pieces of similar shapes. There were also multicolored LEGO bricks snapped together in abstract patterns.

Davie pushed away the creation in front of him, picked up two of the fragmented sections on the floor, and started dismantling them.

Ethel hoped she could come across as a kindly grandmother, a role for which she was definitely unqualified. "Davie," she said gently, "your mother needs you."

The child said nothing, just kept separating the Tinkertoy components.

Ethel walked to the foot of the bed, not wanting to crowd him. She noticed a small walker beside his chair.

Davie started mumbling as he grew more frantic in assembling and disassembling the Tinkertoys. "Mommy's crying. Mommy's crying. Mommy's crying."

An earlier conversation with Jonathan Finch came flooding back. Four months ago, Jonathan had told Ethel his son had osteogenesis imperfecta. "You might know it as brittle bone disease," he'd explained. "It's a genetic condition. His body makes poor collagen, sort of the girders of bone construction. There are varying degrees of OI, as it's known, and some can lead to an early death. Davie has Type Four, not fatal, but his physical growth is stunted, and his bones can break like glass. We have to be so careful. So does he. A severe sneeze could break a rib. Davie will always need medical care, but we're hopeful he'll be at the high-functioning end of the disease's spectrum. He's bright but withdraws into his own world because he's now old enough to know he looks different from other kids and can't play like the other kids. His mom and I do what we can to build up his self-esteem."

Ethel took another step closer to the boy. "Nice designs, Davie. Let's take one to your mother."

He turned around and looked up at her. Ethel noticed his head was larger than normal for his frame. Then she rethought that assessment. No, his head was normal, but his body was small and slightly misshapen.

Davie stared at her with brown eyes, the whites of which were tinged with blue. "Not designs," he corrected. "Molecules. Atoms can come together and break apart."

"Yes. I see that. Molecules. Come together, then break apart. Davie, your mother wants you to come together. Can you do that for her? Come together? Don't break apart?"

The boy stopped fixating on the Tinkertoys. She gently laid a hand on his shoulder. Davie flinched. "But I don't want to see Mommy crying."

"I know. But your daddy's not here, so she needs you. Come, let's go show Mommy how brave you are."

Davie pushed himself up from the chair and grabbed the handles of his walker. Ethel noticed a medical-alert bracelet on his left wrist. Engraved on it were the words, "Osteogenesis Imperfecta—Fragile Bones." Davie spun the walker around and moved toward the door, his little bowed legs taking tiny steps as he leaned against the walker for support.

Ethel took a final look around. Molecules and the solar system. LEGO creations on shelves. Jonathan Finch had been right. The boy was bright. But how would he fare without his father, the man who probably sat for hours with LEGOs and Tinkertoys, not only as Dad but also best friend?

She found Davie on the sofa next to his mother. Susan had one arm wrapped protectively around him.

Bradshaw sat in an armchair. "Do you have anyone we can call for you? A relative? A minister?"

"I have a sister in Fredericksburg. I'll call her. She can come stay with us for a few days." Her eyes welled with tears as she looked at her son. "This is going to be so hard for him."

Bradshaw glanced at Ethel, pain visible on his face. He turned back to Susan. "We'll help in any way we can. I can have an agent, a woman if you prefer, come stay with you and Davie."

"Are we in some kind of danger?"

Bradshaw raised his palms to push the thought away. "No, no. We just want to be supportive. This is a terrible tragedy, and if we can be a resource, we want to be here for you. You and Davie."

"When do you think you might release Johnny's body?"

"In a few days," Bradshaw said. "I'm afraid we have to have an autopsy and coordinate our investigation with the Arlington Police Department. They were first on the scene. But I'll assign a contact person, someone you can call day or night with any question or concern."

Susan looked up at Ethel. "Could that be you?"

Ethel said nothing. It was Bradshaw's call.

"Ethel's not part of the agency." He searched the elderly woman's face for a reaction. Ethel gave him a slight nod. "But if she's willing, we'll make that happen."

"I would like that," Susan said. "Johnny would have liked that."

"And I'll be glad to help," Ethel said. "You call me whenever you want. And if there's something I can do here, don't hesitate to ask. Let me get a piece of paper, and I'll leave you my number."

Bradshaw pulled a pen and business card from an inside coat pocket. He handed them to Ethel. "You can just write it on the back. That way Susan has both our numbers."

"My mobile is best," Ethel said. "I always have it with me."

Davie looked up at Ethel with curious eyes. "Come together?"

"Correct," she said. "I'll come back whenever you want me."

Ethel and Bradshaw let themselves out. Delivering the painful news had left both of them in pensive moods. On the way back up I-95, Bradshaw spoke of the agency's appropriate role in the funeral arrangements. Should he offer to speak? Should Susan be encouraged to have an honor guard of agents?

"I wish we knew what was going on," he said. "Why was he killed? What was in the satchel? What was on his laptop? Without answers, should we simply attend and save any honors till after we can answer these questions?"

Ethel asked herself another question. *Why was Susan afraid that Jonathan had killed himself?*

Bradshaw's cell rang, sparing her from having to respond. He spoke softly, limiting his words to "I see," "Yes," and "I'll authorize it."

He dropped the phone back into his pocket. "Well, you were right."

Ethel turned in the seat to face him. "Right about what?"

"That was Frank. He came across a report of a damaged crossing bar at the parking deck near Barnes & Noble and Whole Foods, not far from your house. He called from the site. Looks like we might have a match for the damage and paint streak on Finch's car. Also, the top deck has tire tracks where someone laid rubber in a fast exit. I've authorized our forensic team to collect a sample for analysis."

"CCTV footage?"

"Not on the deck. He's going to check the surrounding businesses. But if it was Finch, what was he doing without backup?"

Ethel thought about the implications of why Jonathan might have chosen to go it alone. "Has your Richmond office said what else he was doing in addition to temporary protective detail?"

"No. I'm going to place that call now. I'd ask you to forget whatever you hear, but I know I'm wasting my breath."

Ethel opened her small purse and extracted a pair of earbuds and her cell phone. "If it makes you feel any better, I'll leave you for the company of Tony Bennett." She scrolled to her playlist, selected her favorite album, *Tony Bennett—The Classics*, then angled the screen for Bradshaw to appreciate the album's artwork. She hit Play. When Bradshaw looked away, she paused the track, quickly activated another app, and turned her phone into an audio recorder.

Bradshaw placed his call, but before it connected, Ethel's screen flashed with a text message from Warren Hitchcock:

Serial number matches counterfeit ring busted in upstate New York last year. Majority bogus currency confiscated and held for evidence. You got a bad bill.

Ethel quickly texted:

Humor me. Check bills physical location on the QT.

She returned her screen to Tony Bennett and gathered from listening to Bradshaw's side of the conversation that Jonathan Finch had been involved in some joint operation with the FBI, an operation that involved cryptocurrency.

Bradshaw concluded with three words. "Send his report."

Ethel cut the recorder and joined Tony still longing for his heart left in San Francisco.

Twenty minutes later, the text message came from Hitchcock:

What's going on, Ethel? That counterfeit money is missing.

Chapter 11

Jesse followed Ethel's instructions by hiding the bulk of the counterfeit currency in the recycling bin, and then returning the doctored gym bag weighted with newspapers to the workout room. He didn't understand why he was doing this, but after witnessing Ethel in action, he didn't question her judgment.

He checked that the back door was securely locked, tuned Ethel's old stereo system that she called a hi-fi to a classic rock station, and cranked up the volume. Then he took his laptop out on the front porch, sat on the swing, and began reviewing class notes. He angled his back into the corner of the swing to keep the revolver from pressing against his spine.

The street was returning to normal. Jonathan's body and the Ford Escape had been removed. Officers cleared away barricades and traffic cones, and the pedestrian traffic diminished as the site lost its macabre appeal. Periodically, Jesse checked the time, and at ten till ten, he closed his laptop, left the porch, went inside, and locked the front door. He went to his room to set up for the Skype call, leaving the music playing loud enough to be heard through windows and walls.

At ten, his connection clicked through, and Tracy appeared on his computer screen. Her usually smiling face was creased with frown lines.

"My God, Jesse, what's going on?"

He told her about the meeting with Bradshaw and Mancini, their potential jurisdictional clash, and Ethel's relationship with both men, who had once been roomers at her house. Jesse omitted the discovery of the currency. If Ethel had withheld its existence from the director of the Secret Service, he wasn't going to blab about it over an unsecured internet connection.

"What do you think happened?" Tracy asked.

"I don't know. If it wasn't a carjacking gone wrong, I suspect someone wanted his laptop. We haven't been able to find it. Maybe it had evidence on it."

"So, where's his backup? Surely he backed up his data. What kind of laptop was it?"

"A MacBook Pro."

"Like yours?"

"Yeah, but newer."

"And MacBook Pros have that Time Machine feature for backing up the whole system. Don't you think he would use it to back up a machine he was shuttling between DC and Richmond?"

Tracy was right. Maybe an external drive was in his office in Richmond.

"And isn't that unusual?" Tracy continued. "I thought most government agencies used PCs."

Her question was valid. Something he hadn't considered. "I guess it would depend on the software used by each department. But there are more PC manufacturers, which the government would exploit in purchasing from competitive bidders."

"Maybe the police found it," she said.

"Maybe. But if it was a personal computer, the backup drive could be in his home. I should let Ethel know."

"She's there?"

"She went with Bradshaw to break the news to Jonathan's family in person."

Tracy shook her head. "How terrible. Ethel can't just extend her condolences and then say, 'Mind if we search through your husband's personal things?'"

"She won't. Not when the family needs space to grieve."

"Yeah, but what about the director? He might not be so sensitive."

Jesse smiled. "Bradshaw might stand up to Congress, the FBI, U.S. Marshals, and even the White House, but I don't know if he'd cross Ethel. If there's any doubt, the easiest thing is for me not to raise the question of a backup drive until Ethel returns."

Tracy nodded her agreement. "Are you going to class?"

"No. I'll skip today. Since Ethel's not here, and the other roomers are out, I told her I'd stay and keep an eye on things. Be available if the police need to come back for any reason."

"I'm worried about you, Jesse. I wish there was something I could do to help."

He felt the revolver pressing against his back. "I'll be fine. You're the one I'm worried about. You know how many Americans are run down while crossing the London streets because they looked the wrong way?"

She laughed for the first time. "They stencil 'Look Right' on the curbs at the intersections. I make it a habit of looking both ways, just to be sure."

They chatted another thirty minutes about Tracy's classes and what they would do when she came back for her holiday break. He promised to show her around Washington. They rang off blowing kisses to each other across the ocean.

He stood up from the desk and stretched. The hollow feeling in his stomach reminded him he'd not eaten since the previous night. He'd rummage through Ethel's kitchen for the makings of a sandwich or at least a bowl of cold cereal. He walked down the hall to the back stairs to the kitchen and halted at Finch's door. Tracy's point about a backup drive lingered. What if it were here instead of in Richmond? If the data had something to do with Finch's protective assignments, then it made sense he'd want to back up that information before heading home.

Even though Ethel and the police had searched the room, Jesse wanted to see for himself. No crime-scene tape stretched across the doorway; no adhesive sticker sealed the jamb. He simply turned the knob and walked in.

The room no longer bore resemblance to the one occupied by Jonathan Finch. Sheets and a blanket lay strewn across the foot of the exposed mattress. The box spring was askew as if lifted up and then allowed to drop without being properly aligned with the frame. Dresser drawers hung partially open. The door to the armoire stood ajar, and Jesse could see some of the shirts and pants had slipped from their hangers.

If Jonathan Finch had hidden a drive, it wasn't in the obvious places. Jesse eyed the ceiling. An air vent had been cut above the desk when the heating system had been upgraded from radiators to forced air. Although access to such a hiding spot wasn't convenient, the vent cover only had two screws. Jesse thought he saw faint scratches on their grooved heads. He slid the desk aside and pulled the chair underneath the vent. Cautiously, he stood up on its seat. He could just touch the screws. Finch had been about four inches taller and could easily have removed the cover, maybe not needing a screwdriver but just a thin coin like a dime. It was the kind of hiding place Jesse envisioned a spy would use. As his imagination led to thoughts of surprising Ethel with evidence proving the motive for the crime, a blast of air blew his theory away. The thermostat kicked on the heat pump, and the warm current flowed unimpeded onto his hands and face. Just to make sure, Jesse used his phone's flashlight app to shine into the slats of the vent. The duct was completely clear.

Then he heard it. The metal duct work of the heating system was like tin cans connected by a string, transmitting faint sound vibrations. A distinct creak near a downstairs floor vent could have been a footstep. Or simply a pop as the warmth caused cool wood to expand. He heard it again, and this time he suspected it came from directly below him in the short hall from the kitchen to the back door. The hall that also led to the door of the basement stairs and the gym bag of money.

He pulled the Smith & Wesson from behind his back and tucked it in the front pocket of his jeans. He covered the pistol's wooden grip with his sweatshirt and slipped off his shoes. He took the stairs one step at a time, placing his feet to the sides away from the center and near the wall where the joints were strongest and less likely to creak.

Jesse paused at the bottom and listened. Ironically, the stereo played Led Zeppelin's "Stairway to Heaven." Now he wished he hadn't set the volume so high. He noticed a vent on the baseboard of the back hall. Someone stepping beside or against it could have made the sound carried by the duct. As he turned toward the kitchen, he saw the door to the basement stairs was ajar. He knew he'd closed it after he returned the gym bag to its spot under the weight bench. He pushed it wider. The door at the foot of the stairs was wide open. Slowly he descended, tightly gripping the butt of the revolver. Halfway down, he could see the weight bench. The gym bag was still there. He breathed a sigh of relief.

Suddenly, footsteps came rushing behind him. He started to turn in the narrow stairway, wrestling the gun from his pocket. A sharp blow caught him across the back of his skull. He felt no pain. Not even as his limp body tumbled to the floor below.

Chapter 12

The pain came with consciousness, followed by a voice, distant and hollow at first, then stronger as his head cleared.

"Jesse, lie still. I've called an ambulance."

A face hovered above him and blond hair brushed his cheek. He thought it was Tracy. He was confused. Tracy was a world away.

"It's Lisa," the woman said. "I saw the window on the back door was broken. Someone threw the dead bolt. Did you see who?"

Jesse realized he must have done a complete somersault. He lay on his back, his head at the foot of the stairs. The woman knelt over him. He answered her question by shaking his head. The room swam around him.

"It's okay. I've also called the police. They can get your statement at the hospital."

Jesse raised his head enough to see the weight bench. The space beneath was empty. The bag was gone.

"Ethel," he whispered. "I need to talk to Ethel."

"She's not here."

"I know. She went to Richmond. Jonathan Finch was killed this morning."

Lisa took a deep breath. "So, it was him. We heard an agent had been shot, but the name was being withheld."

Sirens drew closer for the second time that morning.

Lisa stood. "I'll get in touch with Ethel after we get you squared away. The EMTs will want to stabilize your neck and bring you out on a gurney. I'll handle the police."

For the first time, Jesse noticed she held a pistol in one hand and her phone in the other. FBI Special Agent Lisa Draper was also one of Ethel's roomers. Lisa wasn't supposed to be back until tonight. How late was it?

Jesse brought his hand to his head and tenderly explored. He found a lump the size of a golf ball behind his right ear. Even slight pressure from the tips of his fingers elicited pain. He moved up to the crown and found a similar knot. One must have come from the intruder's attack, the other when his head hit a step or the floor. He closed his eyes and tried to recall any details. But all he remembered was the sound of quick steps behind him just before the blow.

"Promise me you'll lie still," Lisa reiterated. "I want to bring everyone through the house and not disturb the back door."

"Why?"

"Because that's where the break-in occurred. I need to preserve the scene." She left him on the floor with unspoken questions.

He stared at the ceiling. What would he tell Ethel? What would he tell the police? Everything he'd done had backfired. Had his presence on the front porch signaled the rear entry was wide open? Instead of discouraging a break-in, had the loud music masked the sound of the shattering windowpane? Had the invader come in while he was so focused on Tracy that someone had roamed undetected through the first floor? It was clear to Jesse the person or persons unknown had come for the gym bag of money. He had the misfortune to be on the stairway blocking the path. He had the good fortune not to be killed.

Heavy footsteps came down the stairs. The EMTs stopped by his side. Each carried emergency packs.

"Your name?" asked the one nearer his face.

"Jesse John Cooper. I think I'm okay. Just a couple of bumps on the head."

"But we don't really know that, Mr. Cooper. Our job is to make sure it's nothing more."

Five minutes later, wearing a rigid neck brace and strapped to a portable gurney, Jesse was carried up the stairs. As the EMTs emerged into the hallway, he managed to angle his head toward the back door. The window was shattered. Glass shards sparkled on the floor. Jesse realized he'd been so focused on checking for the gym bag, he hadn't noticed the damage. Maybe that's what he'd heard through the air duct. And for all his caution, he'd been heard coming down in his socks.

"My shoes. I don't have my shoes."

"Don't worry," said the EMT at his stocking feet. "You won't need them. Someone can bring your shoes later."

"And the—" He stopped short of saying *gun*. He no longer felt it in his pocket. Was Ethel's revolver, like the gym bag, now possessed by Jonathan's killers? Would they come back with the gun once they found newspapers instead of currency?

Lisa Draper stood on the front porch as the EMTs transported Jesse to the ambulance.

He strained against the straps, trying to signal her. "Lisa, I have to talk to Ethel."

The FBI agent smiled. "Don't worry. I will let her know. You just do what the doctors tell you."

She reentered the house, determined to delay the call until Ethel had ample time to be with Finch's family and when Lisa could give her a more definitive report on Jesse's condition. Who would care if a little time passed before Ethel and Jesse spoke? Everyone would understand Lisa was only doing what was best for both of them.

Chapter 13

Officer Tepper met Detective Mancini at the front door.

"Thanks for the heads-up," Mancini said.

"No problem. As soon as we got the call I knew you'd want to know."

"You pulling a double shift?"

"Yeah, the wife likes the OT."

Tepper stepped back, clearing a path for the detective.

Mancini stayed put, wanting first to get a clearer picture of the situation. "I understand one of Miss Crestwater's roomers phoned it in."

"Yes, sir. An FBI agent, Lisa Draper. She's in the kitchen. She also called an ambulance. The victim was the student, Jesse Cooper. We're speculating the intruder thought no one was home. Maybe thought Cooper would be in class. Anyway, he's been transported to the trauma unit at Virginia Hospital Center. He was conscious, but Agent Draper says he wasn't able to identify his attacker."

"You've secured the scene?"

"Yeah. As far as we can tell, an intruder broke a windowpane in the back door in order to reach the dead bolt. Cooper must have heard him. Draper found him unconscious at the bottom of the basement steps."

Mancini's eyebrows arched. "The basement?"

"Yes, sir. I figure Cooper confronted his attacker just inside the door and was shoved down the stairs. The tumble could easily have knocked him out. Draper doesn't know if anything has been taken. Miss Crestwater will be the best person to determine that."

"Has she been contacted?"

"I don't know."

"Any clue other than the broken glass?"

"No, sir."

Mancini took a deep breath and said nothing for a few seconds. Then he looked toward the living room. Iron Butterfly's "In-A-Gadda-Da-Vida" blared from the speakers. "The music's awfully loud."

"That's the way Agent Draper says it was playing when she arrived. She thinks it might have been turned up by the intruder to mask any sounds of a search."

"That doesn't make sense. That would only have drawn the attention of anyone else in the house. Well, let's print the back door and photograph the scene. Also, depending upon the size of the window fragments, see if forensics can lift any usable prints off the pieces. You can tell Agent Draper I'm waiting for her in the living room."

Tepper left. Mancini walked to the stereo and turned it off. He stood by the mantel of the fireplace, feeling tired, feeling his age. His thoughts turned to Ethel. She had nearly twenty years on him, and yet would be fully energized when she learned what had happened.

"Detective Mancini?"

He looked up. An attractive woman in her late twenties or

early thirties crossed the room with her right hand extended. Shoulder-length blond hair framed a tanned face. She smiled warmly but not overly effusively, mindful that they were meeting at the scene of a crime.

"I'm Lisa Draper. I found Jesse Cooper."

As he shook her hand, he quickly studied her. She wore the usual FBI blue suit and white blouse. But the creases were flat and the fabric wrinkled. He assumed she wasn't sloppy but had been on the steps and floor trying to help Cooper. And Ethel had said she was out of town for the weekend, so she might have driven in from several hours away.

"Agent Draper." He gestured toward the sofa. "Why don't you have a seat and fill me in on what's transpired?" He took the adjacent armchair and pulled his notepad and pencil from his pocket.

In an unemotional, professional manner, Lisa Draper told Mancini how she'd returned from a weekend in Philadelphia, planning to go straight to her office, but had heard news of a shooting on North Highland Street as she drew near the District. She'd called her supervisor, saying she'd be late, and he told her a Secret Service agent was alleged to be the victim.

Mancini made a note in his pad. "What time was the call?"

"Around ten thirty. I was about an hour away."

"So, weren't you already late?"

"I'd always planned to come in closer to noon. But I wanted to give myself more leeway in case I found there was a connection to this house. I doubt there are a lot of Secret Service agents on this street." She shook her head. "I was afraid it could be either Jonathan or Douglas."

"And Douglas is?"

"Douglas Gray. He also rooms here. He's new to the service. Normally, he's with the vice president's family."

"Normally?"

"The Secret Service has had to juggle schedules. The past few weeks both the president and vice president have been traveling to different destinations. A relentless twenty-four/seven demand for protection stretches manpower. Advance teams are needed before either the president or vice president arrives. As a junior man, Douglas is stateside, and he's found it easier to rent at Ethel's than to try and find a long-term living arrangement. At least until he has a more stable assignment."

"And what's your specialty?"

"Corporate fraud, embezzlement, money laundering. Think of me as a forensic accountant armed with a pencil and a pistol."

Mancini smiled. "I imagine you've brought more criminals to justice with your pencil."

"By a long shot. But my pencil wouldn't have been of much use if I'd been here instead of Jesse. Of course, Jesse had a pistol, for all the good it did him."

Mancini's eyes bored into hers. "What? Nobody said Jesse had a gun."

Lisa Draper shrugged. "I haven't told anyone yet. I was going to ask Ethel. Jesse had a .38 Special tucked in his front pocket. I removed it with a tissue and placed it on a shelf downstairs. I didn't want the EMTs to touch it."

"Mind if I ask why you're rooming here? Your job sounds much more settled."

"My job, maybe. My personal life isn't. I broke up with a longtime boyfriend this summer. One of us had to move, and a colleague suggested 'Ethel's dormitory,' as it was affectionately named."

Mancini nodded at the familiar nickname. "Have you spoken to Ethel?"

"No. Jesse said she was in Richmond. He told me she was

breaking the news to Jonathan's wife. I didn't want her worrying until we got a report on Jesse."

"She won't like that," Mancini said. "Believe me, you don't keep things from Ethel. Do you know her number?"

"It's on my phone. Do you want me to call her now?"

"Just dial her." Mancini stretched out his hand. "Give the phone to me. I'll talk to her. Then I want you to walk me through everything you saw and did."

———

The phone in Ethel Crestwater's purse vibrated as she and Cory Bradshaw passed the I-95 exit to Woodbridge. They were still about thirty minutes out from her home. The screen showed the call was from Lisa Draper. Ethel suspected the agent was calling because she'd heard about the shooting.

"I'm going to take this," Ethel told Bradshaw. "It's one of my roomers."

She accepted the call. "Lisa?"

"No, it's Frank."

Ethel cut her eyes to Bradshaw. "Oh, Frank. Cory told me you'd found the likely site of Jonathan's accident. Do you have more news?"

"Yes, but not about that."

Ethel caught the grave tone of his voice and matched it. "What's happened?"

Bradshaw became interested. "Put him on speaker," he whispered.

Ethel shook her head and pressed the phone tighter to her ear.

"Someone broke into your house. I'm here with Lisa Draper."

"What about Jesse?"

"He was knocked out. Lisa found him. He regained

consciousness but has been taken to Virginia Hospital Center. I'm going over there as soon as I finish here. At this point, we don't know the extent of his injuries. I'm hoping he's only going to be kept for observation."

"I'll meet you there," Ethel said.

"Okay." Mancini paused, and then asked, "Did you know Jesse has a revolver?"

"Yes. A Smith & Wesson. I gave it to him this morning."

"Why?"

"Because Jonathan was gunned down in my front yard, and I don't know what we're dealing with."

"But why would you think they'd come back?"

"Does it matter? Call it women's intuition. The fact is they did, and I left Jesse unprepared and unprotected."

Women's intuition, my ass. Mancini knew something more was going on. But now wasn't the time to challenge her. At least until he could get her alone.

"All right," he said. "I'll see you at the hospital. Officer Tepper will stay here until we return. Then I'll want you to go through the house and see if anything is missing."

"Certainly, Frank. Sorry if I snapped at you. It's been a difficult morning, to say the least."

"How did things go with Mrs. Finch?"

"Like I said, it's been a difficult morning."

Bradshaw ordered his driver to take them straight to the hospital. He and Ethel entered through the emergency room, and Bradshaw flashed his credentials at everyone in sight until they were allowed into a small draped-off area where Jesse lay on a wheeled bed. His head and upper torso were inclined at a thirty-degree angle. His eyes were closed; a monitor beeped softly beside him, but it appeared to be checking only his heartbeat and oxygen levels.

The staff had changed him into a hospital gown and folded his clothes into a clear plastic bag hanging from the railing at the foot of the bed. Ethel looked around for his shoes but didn't see them.

"Jesse?" she whispered.

He opened his eyes. "Ethel."

Before he could say anything further, she said, "Mr. Bradshaw is with me. We understand you were attacked. Do you know who it was?"

"No. I heard a noise. I thought it came from the basement. The last thing I remember I was on the stairs."

The privacy curtain slid aside and Detective Mancini stepped into the confined space. He said nothing.

"Was someone in the basement?" Ethel asked.

"No. I was hit from behind. I woke up and Lisa Draper was there. She called the ambulance." Jesse looked at Mancini. "And the police."

The detective took advantage of the acknowledgment. "Why did you have the revolver with you?"

Jesse glanced at Ethel, hoping for some guidance.

"I told Frank I gave you the gun this morning," she said. "When I left for Richmond."

Jesse nodded. "We didn't know who shot Jonathan or why. I offered to skip class and remain at the house until Ethel returned. She was concerned if Jonathan had been targeted because of a case he was pursuing, then maybe they thought something was still in his room. Given what happened, she was right to be concerned."

Ethel laid her hand on his shoulder. "And I was wrong to place you in that position. I'm very sorry." She turned to Bradshaw and Mancini. "Gentlemen, I think we can wait on further questioning. I'm more concerned that Jesse rest until the extent of his injuries can be determined."

"They're waiting on a room," Jesse said. "Meanwhile, I'm

supposed to have a cranial scan. They said something about a subdural hematoma, whatever that means."

"Bleeding on the brain," Ethel explained. "It can build up pressure. They might keep you in overnight for observation."

"Okay."

"Do you need anything from the house?"

"Shoes. I don't want to leave here in my socks."

"Lisa or Douglas can bring them. I'm staying here." She turned to the two men. "Frank, I can go through the house later. If something's missing, I'll let you know. Cory, I'll get a ride, so there's no sense you hanging around. If this break-in is tied to Jonathan's murder, then you'll want to compare notes with Frank."

Mancini looked at the bag of Jesse's clothes. "I want to take these. Fibers or DNA from the assailant might be present."

"Good point," Bradshaw agreed. "Since we've got Finch's clothing, why don't we run Jesse's through our lab? I'll share results." Without waiting for an answer, Bradshaw unclipped the bag from the bed.

"All right," Mancini said. "But Ethel and Jesse are witnessing that you're promising to play nice."

The men left.

Ethel waited until she was sure they were out of earshot. She leaned close to Jesse. "What else can you tell me?"

"The gym bag was there when I started down the stairs. When I came to, it was gone."

"I figured as much. They knew it was in the house. I think if Jonathan originally had the money, why would he have gone to the parking deck in Clarendon with only half of it? Makes more sense that he got both bags there and was followed and ambushed. He either gave them something or had something over them."

"That sounds like an unusual approach to an investigation. Has Bradshaw any theories?"

"No. But he doesn't know about the money. I need to tell him."

"And Detective Mancini?"

"No. I've learned the counterfeit money had been in an evidence room for the Secret Service. It's missing. I'll let Cory connect those dots, but it's his call as to what to share with Frank. If there's dirty laundry in the Secret Service, Cory won't want it aired in public. I respect that."

Jesse lay quiet for a minute.

Ethel moved to leave. "I'm going to find out how long they're going to keep you in this holding pattern."

"Ethel, there's something else. I told my girlfriend, Tracy, some of what's going on. Not the money, but the murder. I was Skyping with her when it happened. I hope that was all right."

"There's no harm in that."

"Tracy made a good point. Something of value must be on Jonathan's laptop. And if it was important enough to kill for, then it should have been important enough to back up. I think that could have been a physical hard drive. Like the way I back up my MacBook. That's what I was looking for when I heard a noise through the air duct in Jonathan's room."

He briefly described his efforts to inspect the vent. "But there's also the possibility he kept that drive in Richmond, either in his office or home. If the laptop was his personal one, then odds are any backup would be at home."

Ethel returned to his side. "Let me think about it. Don't mention that possibility just yet. If it exists, I'd like to see the data before turning it over to anyone."

"Do you not trust Cory Bradshaw?"

"Oh, I trust him. I trust him to protect his agency. We might be approaching a divergence of priorities."

"How so?"

"He'll keep things under wraps as long as he can. He'll be

after justice but on his own terms. Finding who attacked you is not his priority. But it is mine. Someone attacked my family again, and I'm not going to let that go unchallenged."

"Has someone attacked your family before?"

Ethel placed her small, wrinkled hand on Jesse's chest. "Your mother never told you?"

"Told me what?"

"My father was murdered. I was the one who tracked down his killer."

Chapter 14

Jesse stared at the opening in the privacy curtain through which Ethel had disappeared. He'd wanted to ask her about her father and the search for his killer, but she'd immediately left in search of a physician.

Lying there alone, Jesse tried to tuck the loose hospital gown under his hips. Whoever designed the butt-exposing humiliations should be forced to wear one on the DC Metro at rush hour. He tried to roll onto his side. The exertion generated a deep ache in his left shoulder. During his tumble, he must have smacked against the edge of a step. He wondered what other aches and pains awaited him.

He was still squirming to regain a modicum of modesty when the curtain split and a female nurse and a male orderly entered.

"Mr. Cooper," the nurse said, "we're here to transport you for your CT scan."

Jesse gave up and let gravity arrange the gown. "Fine. When the woman who's with me returns, could someone tell her where I've gone?"

The nurse glanced at the orderly. Both smiled.

"Oh, your grandmother knows," the woman said. "She cornered your attending physician."

Grandmother? Jesse conceded it was a far easier explanation than double-first-cousin-twice-removed.

"She's a pistol," the orderly added. "I'd want her in my corner. I heard her tell the doc that no one short of a chain saw injury is jumping ahead of you."

The nurse laughed. "So, hold on to your gown, Mr. Cooper. We're going to get you up to the imaging suite as fast as this bed will roll."

Thirty minutes later, the orderly returned Jesse to the same curtained holding area with Ethel walking closely behind. He locked down the wheels. "Dr. Kershaw will be here as soon as the scan is read. Then we'll get you to a real room."

"We'll see," Ethel said. "Thank you for your help."

The orderly left.

Jesse scooted higher up on the inclined bed. "What do you mean, 'we'll see'?"

"If the scan comes back negative, no bleeding, no fracture, then I want to take you home. You'll need rest, and I can check on you every few hours. At one time, doctors warned victims of concussions not to go to sleep till beyond the time of any complications. But with CT scans, that view's been reversed, and rest is now recognized as an appropriate and preferred treatment."

"What about my clothes?"

"I spoke to Lisa. She's bringing you something to wear. I hope you don't mind her going through your things."

"No. Of course not. Have you told Bradshaw about the money?"

"I'll do that once we get you released. Lisa's going to hang out in the ER waiting room until the doctor gives us the verdict."

Ten minutes later, Dr. Kershaw, a physician who looked like

he was ten minutes out of med school, arrived. He delivered the results as much to Ethel as to his patient. The scan was clear, and Jesse was free to leave. He recommended Jesse sit up for at least ten minutes for any dizziness to subside and then check out in a wheelchair. If there was any change in his condition, he should return immediately.

Checking out was much slower than checking in, and it was nearly three o'clock before Jesse was wheeled to Ethel's waiting black Infiniti sedan. Lisa Draper helped him into the front passenger seat.

"Do you want to drive?" Lisa asked Ethel.

"No, you got my car here safely. I'll sit in the back."

"Ethel thought my SUV would be more difficult to climb into," Lisa explained to Jesse. "Be my luck you'd fall out and sue me."

"I might need to sue somebody. We'll see how good my student health insurance is."

"How are things at the house?" Ethel asked.

"Officer Tepper's there. Detective Mancini asked him to stay on."

Ethel buckled her seat belt. "Really? That's interesting."

———

Trevor Norwood returned to his apartment with a bag from the nearby CVS pharmacy in one hand and a bag with a Big Mac and fries in the other. He'd walked to avoid anyone seeing inside his car where the blood was smeared across the seat. The interior cleaning would need to wait until his arm stopped throbbing.

He went straight to the bathroom and took off his windbreaker and shirt. Blood still seeped through the bandage and fabric of his sleeve, but the water-repellent feature of the jacket kept it from bleeding through. He dumped the contents of the

CVS bag on the counter by the sink—a topical cream with lidocaine for numbing, an antiseptic cream to fight infection, and a packet of needles and spool of strong thread.

He applied the antiseptic on the wound, ringed the flesh around it with the lidocaine, threaded the needle, and then gritted his teeth as the pain increased with each self-applied stitch.

Twenty minutes later, he sat shirtless at his kitchen table with the fresh bandage showing no signs of bleeding. He poured a double shot of whiskey into a glass of Coke and attacked his burger and fries. The pain diminished to a dull ache. He knew what he needed most was sleep, but he had twenty million reasons to stay awake.

His cell phone vibrated. A text message:

RETRIEVED BAG. DISABLED TRACKER. DON'T BELIEVE
CONTENTS SEEN. MEET TO HAND OFF?

Good news. Maybe the bills had gone undiscovered. But was returning the currency wise? Why should he run the risk now with a murder ratcheting up the stakes? Especially since the unexpected debacle with Jonathan Finch had potentially opened the door to millions. He would have to let them know the reason for the change in plans. Then admit the suspicions had been true. Jonathan Finch had a secret. A secret that explained why he'd dealt in cash. Norwood hoped Finch hadn't taken that secret to his grave.

————

Lisa Draper pulled into Ethel's driveway.

Before the Infiniti stopped, Ethel said, "That's interesting."

Lisa wondered if her elderly landlady ever found something that wasn't interesting. "What?"

"Officer Tepper's patrol car isn't here. I believe that Toyota Camry belongs to Frank Mancini."

Lisa and Jesse saw the white sedan at the curb. The detective wasn't in it.

Jesse opened his door and swiveled to get out. "Maybe he has news."

Lisa grabbed his arm to stop him. "Maybe. But let me walk with you. You could still be unsteady on your feet."

"That's a good idea," Ethel agreed. "We don't need to go back to the hospital."

The three approached the house, Lisa cupping her hand under Jesse's elbow for support, Ethel walking behind. As they neared the front porch, a slim Black man stepped out the door. The sleeves of his white dress shirt were rolled up and his blue tie was loosely knotted. The pinstripe of his pants suggested he'd left a suit coat inside.

"Can I help?" He came down the steps.

Jesse straightened his arm and made a show of moving away from Lisa. "I'm fine, Douglas. I have a hard head."

"Yeah, but I don't want you falling and that hard head cracking Ethel's sidewalk." Douglas Gray stood to one side as they passed.

He was shorter than Jesse, closer to Lisa's height. He moved with a controlled ease that might have led one to believe he'd been trained as a classical dancer. In fact, the movements came from his extensive training in martial arts. As a Secret Service agent, he not only guarded his charges with a gun, he could kill twenty-seven ways with his bare hands.

Then Detective Mancini stepped out on the porch. "Glad to see you've been released, Jesse. I'm sure you're anxious to get to your room and rest. Miss Draper, Mr. Gray, why don't you help him upstairs? I need to speak to Miss Crestwater for a few moments. In private." He retreated into the foyer but stopped to make sure the three roomers did as he ordered. When they reached the upper landing, he turned to Ethel. "Follow me back to the kitchen, please."

He led the way and stopped at the refrigerator. However, Ethel went passed him to check the back hall.

"Everything's been cleaned up," she complained.

"Well, forensics got what they needed. Actually, Tepper said Lisa picked up the broken glass and swept the floor. She told Tepper she didn't want you coming home to a mess. She also called a window service."

"But I didn't get to see it for myself, Frank."

"They'll have photographs. I'll send you copies"—he paused and stared at her—"when you start being straight with me."

She looked up at him, trying to read what was behind his deadpan expression. "What do you mean?"

"I mean, why did you give Jesse a revolver? Why did you think he'd need it?"

"I didn't think he'd need it. Not for protection. He discovered Jonathan's body. He was shaken up, and I had to go to Richmond. I thought it might make him rest easier."

"So, there was nothing here, nothing of Finch's that you thought someone might come back for?"

"No. You searched his room."

"Right, but I didn't search your room. I didn't search your Ruth Bader Ginsburg workout basement where Jesse was found unconscious." He walked back to the kitchen with Ethel close on his heels. "And I sure as hell didn't think I'd have to search this." He bent down, grabbed a handful of newspapers from the recycling bin, and tossed them at Ethel's feet. The rolls of counterfeit hundreds lay exposed where Jesse had placed them.

Ethel moved to the stove. "Let me put the kettle on, Frank. A good cup of tea will calm you down. And then I'll explain."

Chapter 15

The high-pitched trill quickly faded as Ethel removed the kettle from the stove's burner. She poured the steaming water into a teapot where two bags dangled inside. She set the full pot on the kitchen island alongside two mugs, a small pitcher of chilled cream, and a bowl of sugar cubes. "I'll let it steep a few minutes. Do you still take tea with cream and a single cube?"

Mancini nodded and slid onto the kitchen barstool in the same spot he'd sat nearly ten hours earlier. "You found that money under Finch's bed, didn't you?"

"Yes. I considered the possibility Jonathan had it as evidence in a case. It was in a gym bag similar to what Jesse witnessed one of the killers carrying. When I discovered most of the bills had the same serial number, I believed he must have penetrated a counterfeiting ring."

"And you wanted to keep me in the dark."

"I wanted to keep the investigation within the proper jurisdiction."

"So you told Cory. Why didn't he take it?"

Ethel lifted the teapot and began pouring. "I haven't told him."

Mancini's eyes widened. "What?"

"I wanted to learn what I could before Cory took possession. So I gave a confidential source in the agency the serial numbers. On the way back from Richmond, I got confirmation the bills were evidence in an upstate New York bust."

"Then these were still going into distribution," Mancini concluded.

"No, these were the confiscated bills. They're missing from the Secret Service's secure evidence storage." She pushed a mug, the cream pitcher, and sugar bowl across the counter.

Mancini ignored them. "Someone from the inside?"

Ethel shrugged and sipped her tea.

Mancini pointed to the bin with the phony bills. "Cory's got a rat in his own house. He'll be apoplectic. Those Secret Service teams are tighter than a bloated tick on a hound dog. Tighter than the FBI."

"I won't argue," Ethel said. "But you know what that means?"

"It means he should bring in outside investigators. Something he'll be loath to do."

"No. It means he's got rats plural. This wasn't a solo operation. There was a team in place. I believe several corrupt agents found each other. I'm not sure how Jonathan stumbled across them. Or why he set up a rendezvous like he did. Maybe he didn't know whom to trust. But once he got the bills, they went all out to recover them because the bills are the link to an inside conspiracy. I blame myself for not realizing that. For leaving Jesse alone."

Mancini softened his voice. "But you didn't know about the connection to the missing evidence until heading back from Richmond. Jesse had already been attacked. So don't beat yourself up."

"Well, someone knocked Jesse out for a few rolls of the bogus currency and a pile of old newspapers. They'll know we know where the bills came from. The rats will crawl back in their holes."

"But they left some things behind," Mancini said. "We have DNA from the person's blood who was wounded by Finch. We have some CCTV footage of a sedan in the area of the parking deck. The plate light was out, but the vehicle looks to be a dark blue Chevy Malibu."

"What about the SUV Jesse saw?"

"No. They must have stayed on back streets." Mancini looked at the money again. "Why'd you split it up?"

"Instinct."

"The bag was in your workout room?"

"Yes. Which is why I can't excuse my lapse in judgment. My instinct was to guard against someone taking it. I underestimated the attempt would be so soon."

Mancini poured a healthy splash of cream in his mug and dropped in a sugar cube. "Well, it's nice to finally know you're human like the rest of us."

A creak sounded from the back stairs.

Ethel swiveled on her stool. "Who's there?"

Lisa Draper and Douglas Gray stepped into the kitchen.

"Sorry," Lisa said. "We thought you'd be in the living room. Douglas and I are running out to get something to eat. We're bringing a sandwich back for Jesse. Would you like anything?"

Ethel looked at Mancini.

He shook his head. "No thanks. I probably won't be here."

"I'll fix something later," Ethel said.

Lisa looked down at the newspapers piled beside the recycling bin. Then she saw the money. "What's that?"

Ethel glanced at Mancini. He shrugged.

She turned back to her two roomers. "It might be why Jonathan was killed."

Lisa remained frozen, staring open-mouthed at the money. Douglas stepped around her and bent to pick up a roll of bills.

"Leave it alone," Mancini ordered. "I have jurisdiction over Jesse's attack. I'll be in touch with Director Bradshaw, and he and I will decide how this is handled."

Douglas straightened and moved toward the detective. "Jonathan was my friend. I won't be shut out."

Mancini hopped from the stool. "And maybe that's why you shouldn't be involved. But that's Director Bradshaw's call. You can make your case to him. Right now, I suggest you bring Jesse his sandwich."

Upstairs, Jesse sat on the edge of his bed. He hadn't moved since Lisa and Douglas escorted him to his room. His head ached but his mind raced in a thousand directions. The events of the day left him exhausted but exhilarated. Instead of being stuck in a computer lab, he'd found himself in the middle of a major crime and heard the whisper of a dying man trying to tell him a secret. Despite the attack, Jesse wanted to play a role in the investigation. Ethel was his ticket in. But he wanted more than to tag along in her shadow. He wanted to contribute something. If he were honest with himself, he'd admit he wanted to impress her.

His phone vibrated with an incoming text message from Tracy.

can u Skype now or before midnight my time? Info to share.

It was nearly ten in London. He quickly typed—

yes, but give me 5. I'll call.

Tracy didn't know about the attack and injury, and he didn't want her to know. He needed a few minutes to check himself in the upstairs bathroom mirror. To make sure he didn't look like he'd stepped off a London curb and been hit by a double-decker bus.

He ran a basin of cold water, liberally splashed it over his face, and patted some color into his cheeks. He returned to his room, closed the door, and logged in.

When her face popped on the screen, Tracy exclaimed, "You look worn out."

"It's been a long day."

"Any news?"

"The working theory is persons unknown murdered Jonathan to disrupt a Secret Service investigation. The key might be on the stolen computer, and I've shared your concern about a backup drive with Ethel."

"And with the police?"

"I'm letting Ethel determine what to tell them."

Tracy frowned. "Why would she hold back?"

"Because she has her own methods. My mother said Ethel used to work for the FBI. She knows everyone, Tracy. She's keeping her hand in the game. And I'm helping her."

"For God's sake, be careful. These people are killers."

"I will. Don't worry." He said the words as confidently as he could despite the ache in his head. "You said you have some information?"

"Yes." She glanced down at what must have been notes beside her keyboard. "I did a search on Jonathan Finch. He's not on Facebook or Twitter or LinkedIn. Maybe agents avoid personal social media. Especially ones who guard the president. I suspect on-location selfies would be frowned upon. So, I made more targeted searches of news sources, government reports, and the public affairs offices of the FBI and Secret Service."

"Any luck?"

"Maybe. There was a mention of Finch being congratulated for ten years of service and for breaking up a credit card theft operation using stolen cards to order online merchandise. That was a couple of years ago. But the most curious link to Jonathan Finch was a suicide about six months ago."

"A suicide?" Jesse opened his desk drawer and pulled out a pencil and legal pad. "Hold on. Let me write this down."

"I can send you the article. It appeared in the *Roanoke Times*. Finch was identified as a Secret Service agent who discovered the body of CEO Dwayne Parker."

"Should I know that name?"

"No. He evidently headed a tech company called KryptoFold Enterprises. It was a successful start-up that manufactured physical devices for securely storing the key to a virtual wallet."

Jesse remembered what he'd seen in Finch's room. "That fits. Jonathan had a book titled *The Case for Cryptocurrency*."

"The article said Parker's company rode the popular wave of cryptocurrency until Parker was accused of embezzling from his investors by moving funds into his personal cryptocurrency account. And you and I know without the private key, the coins in the wallet are unreachable."

"Jonathan must have been on the case because of the cyber-crime nature of the embezzlement."

Tracy nodded. "My thoughts exactly. The Roanoke newspaper article reported the death and the initial determination of suicide, but once I had Dwayne Parker's name, I was able to uncover more information from other sources. The newspaper also ran some follow-up stories. Evidently, the investigation was a joint operation with the fraud unit of the FBI. Jonathan was monitoring Parker's physical whereabouts and learned the man had gone to his mountain retreat outside Roanoke. Jonathan drove over and surreptitiously spotted Parker loading luggage in his Land Rover. Although the government had held off making an arrest, hoping to capture either the suspected virtual wallet's private key or Parker in the act of transferring coins, Jonathan feared the man was making a run for it. If he got out of the country, he could access his virtual wallet from anywhere in the world, and no one could stop him. So Jonathan called for backup and used his vehicle to block Parker's narrow mountain driveway. Jonathan said Parker saw what he was doing and locked himself in the house. There was a gunshot, and when Jonathan broke in, he found Parker dead on the floor. Forensics determined it was suicide."

"And the wallet?" Jesse asked.

"No mention anywhere. And Parker's computer had been wiped clean."

"How much money is supposed to be missing?"

"Twenty million dollars."

Jesse whistled. "Wow. And, as far as anyone knows, it's lost in cyberland?"

"Yes. Both the wallet's address and the private key. The money may as well be on the dark side of the moon."

Jesse heard the words ringing in his head. *Tell Ethel the secret.*

Chapter 16

Director Cory Bradshaw wasn't pleased with the path his investigation was taking. The murder of one of his agents could not go unsolved. But the overlap with the Arlington police, the involvement of an FBI agent, and the persistent meddling of Ethel Crestwater, who was herself a force to be reckoned with, created unwanted complications that he viewed as impediments.

The Secret Service clearly needed to be the agency in charge, especially given the uncertainty of what might be a security breach and an unexplained connection to the counterfeit currency.

The brazen attack on Jesse Cooper represented a desperate attempt to conceal the bogus money's link to his department. He was irritated that Ethel hadn't immediately told him of its existence, even if an Arlington detective had been present at the time. But she had asked for his support to withhold evidence from the police, and he had given it.

To no avail. Frank Mancini had discovered the bills and now would see Bradshaw as an impediment to his search for the truth. Aware of the simmering hostility, Ethel had interjected herself into their turf battle with a simple statement—"We're meeting at seven tonight, and we'll find common ground."

So, with two extra chairs brought from the dining room, Ethel, Jesse, Bradshaw, Mancini, Lisa Draper, and Douglas Gray gathered in the living room. A silver coffee set with six cups sat untouched on the table in front of the sofa. On either side was a plate of cookies, one chocolate chip and the other oatmeal raisin. Bradshaw and Mancini smiled, remembering how Ethel had always kept those cookies on hand when the men had been her boarders.

"Don't be shy," Ethel said. "We can talk and nibble." She sat on the sofa beside Bradshaw, leaned forward, and began pouring the coffee. Jesse distributed the filled cups and then passed the cookies.

When everyone had been served, Ethel set her cup on the end table next to her and looked at the semicircle of faces. "You all have something in common. You've shared or are sharing this house with me. From my perspective, that creates a special bond. Regardless of how long ago, or where your career has taken you, I consider you to be part of my family. Today, that family was attacked twice, and our home invaded. Circumstances and jurisdictional protocols complicate things. I understand that. Director Bradshaw has his responsibilities, and Detective Mancini has his. But I hope we agree we have a common goal—to get justice for Jonathan, his family, and for Jesse. And to uncover those who have betrayed their oath as federal law enforcement officers. It's clear to me someone inside the Secret Service had a hand in removing those bills from their secure location."

"We think that might be the case," Bradshaw interjected.

"You can think all you want, Cory, but I know that counterfeit money didn't walk out of your custody on its own. I'll agree we don't know the motive, but at this point we have to assume there was inside help of some kind."

Bradshaw didn't argue.

"And I made a mistake," Ethel said. "As soon as I learned the money's source, I should have sounded the alarm. Then maybe we could have set a proper trap, and Jesse wouldn't have landed in the hospital. All of us know what happened, and Cory and Frank will take their investigations from here. I simply want us to help by collectively sharing what we know at this point. Douglas, Lisa, Jesse, and I had interactions with Jonathan. Maybe we can prompt each other's memory by sharing any observations or conversations." She looked at Bradshaw. "I'm interested if there might be something he said or did that ties in to any case files you have."

"All right. I'm okay with this if Frank is."

Mancini held up his half-eaten chocolate chip cookie. "My cooperation is easily bought."

The tension in the room lessened.

"I'll go first," Ethel said. "Jonathan began rooming here ten years ago. I think he came out of the Philadelphia office and stayed for short-term assignments in DC. That's been the pattern over the course of our friendship. Maybe he's here for a few months every year or so. His most recent arrival was a little over four months ago, around the first of May."

"For protective detail?" Mancini asked.

"Yes. He said he'd wrapped up an assignment and would be in the protective pool for several months. I must say with the benefit of hindsight, Jonathan seemed more reserved and withdrawn. I thought he missed his family in Richmond. I know he's concerned about his son. Davie has a genetic disease called osteogenesis imperfecta, that's a fancy name for imperfect bones that are very fragile, and I think Jonathan was worried about the boy's future long-term. We discussed it one evening over a bottle of wine while everyone else was out. He hoped

Davie's condition could improve through physical therapy and genetic breakthroughs, but he admitted he wasn't very optimistic. Davie would probably always be compromised by the severity of his condition, always with a walker if not a wheelchair, and susceptible to major injuries from minor accidents. Jonathan just hoped there was an area where Davie could thrive and enjoy a productive life."

"Like what?" Bradshaw asked.

"Science. Mathematics. Architecture. I saw Davie's room; you didn't. He builds molecules with Tinkertoys, and there was a shelf filled with LEGO constructions. I think right now his mother homeschools him. He's been in and out of special-ed programs and has trouble relating to other children." Ethel shook her head. "But nothing Jonathan told me sheds any light on why he would have the currency."

Jesse hesitated and then spoke out. "Maybe he hadn't wrapped up the previous case as completely as he wanted to."

All eyes turned to him.

Lisa Draper, seated in the chair beside him, leaned close. "What case?"

Jesse glanced at Ethel. She stared at him with the same curiosity as everyone else.

"The Dwayne Parker suicide. The KryptoFold executive."

"He talked to you about that?" Lisa asked.

"No. I read about it this afternoon. When I was resting."

Bradshaw nodded. "That was a joint operation with the FBI. Were you involved, Lisa?"

"Only with the forensic accounting. Once we uncovered the missing funds and saw the bank trail end in offshore wires, Secret Service took over the cybercrime aspect. That's where everyone thought the money wound up—cryptocurrency. I believe the surveillance on Parker continued in an effort to locate the Bitcoin, Ethereum, or whatever digital currency held the embezzled funds."

Bradshaw nodded. "If you worked the case, did you discuss it with Finch?"

"Briefly. When we first met. I knew Jonathan had discovered Parker's body, and I asked if he thought the funds would ever be recovered. He told me that without the wallet addresses and, more important, the private keys to any accounts, the coins would never surface. He said there are millions of dollars' worth of coins sitting in virtual wallets because the owners lost their private keys. He compared it to having your life's savings in an impenetrable glass box. You can see it, but you can't touch it."

Mancini brushed cookie crumbs from his lap. "Okay, I get that, but how does cryptocurrency connect to those counterfeit hundreds stolen from your evidence room, Cory? That's what's directly tied to Finch's murder and the attack on Jesse."

"First step is to identify who was on that case," Bradshaw said.

Douglas cleared his throat and shifted in his chair. "Sir, I was on that case. We got a tip on ink and paper suppliers. It was a New York mob operation, but the production was upstate near Saratoga. A few notes had been floated in the area, either to test their ability to pass as genuine, or someone in the operation was greedy and ran extras for his own use. Those bills caught our attention and led to the arrests."

"Remind me," Bradshaw said, "was this before they went into mass circulation?"

"Yes. We obtained some confessions before trial. The consistent story was the money was headed out of the states for foreign distribution where the bills face less scrutiny."

"How much are we talking about?"

"A little over half a million."

"There you go," Ethel said. "I found roughly a quarter million under Jonathan's bed. The rest must have been what they carried running away."

Jesse looked at Bradshaw. "If the trial's over, why weren't the bills destroyed?"

"I don't have the facts at hand, but if not everyone copped a plea, we might have appeals at play. Or this is only the first stage of an investigation going up the food chain, and there might be more arrests. The evidence is still relevant." Bradshaw turned to Douglas. "Who ran that investigation?"

"Trevor Norwood. I was reassigned to protection and don't know if the investigation went further."

"Well, I'll look into that," Bradshaw said. "Did Finch ever talk to any of you about the counterfeiting case?"

No one answered.

Bradshaw slapped his thighs. "All right, any other ideas? Frank, what do you think?"

The homicide detective shrugged. "Counterfeiting and cryptocurrency. I'm really outside my wheelhouse. But it seems to me if we need to force a connection, what if Jonathan learned somehow that the bogus money had gone missing? It doesn't do anyone any good until you can convert it to real money, whether that's dollars, pounds, or euros. He takes Parker's playbook that converted dollars into Bitcoins or whatever and replicates it. Getting word to his suspects as an anonymous buyer that he's looking to sell. I imagine that can be done."

"Peer to peer," Jesse said. "That's what a personal, private transaction's called."

"Cash for coin," Douglas said. "And those exchanges can go bad. I know at least one case in Oslo, Norway, where a buyer was murdered. But how did Jonathan get the necessary coins?"

"Maybe he didn't," Jesse said. "Maybe he created a dummy

transaction somehow. Fooled them briefly like the counterfeit money was intended to fool him."

"I don't know," Lisa said. "Was Jonathan that sophisticated a programmer?"

Mancini sighed. "Like I said, I'm out of my wheelhouse here. It was just a thought."

"Well, Frank," Ethel said, "I think at this point all theories are welcome. Whatever Jonathan was doing, he wasn't following standard procedure. I noticed he dropped a Beretta, not his issued Sig Sauer. Cory, was his missing laptop company-issued?"

"No."

"Frank, did you find a personal phone?"

"No," the detective admitted.

"So the incriminating money, his computer, and his phone were taken, and someone was so determined to eliminate loose ends that he risked a robbery in broad daylight to retrieve the second gym bag and shut off any links to the Secret Service."

"What do you think they planned to do with the money?" Frank asked.

Ethel smiled. "Come now, Frank, isn't it obvious? It was going back in the evidence room with no one the wiser and someone richer by half a million dollars."

Bradshaw shook his head. "I don't know. A lot of speculation. But I agree with one thing. Whatever Jonathan was trying to do, he ran up against someone who was smarter and better prepared, and it cost him his life."

"Not someone," Ethel corrected. "Some team. Cory, I'm afraid you've got your work cut out for you."

That assessment brought the meeting to a close. When the house was quiet, and everyone was settled for the night, Ethel softly tread up the front stairs and lightly knocked on Jesse's door.

"Come in."

Ethel entered and found Jesse sitting at his desk, a laptop open in front of him.

She closed the door behind her. "How are you feeling?"

"My head still aches but not as bad."

"Do you think you could cut classes again tomorrow?"

"I hope to be better by then."

"Good. Because I want you to come with me. Bring your laptop and an external drive if you have one."

"Where are we going?"

"Back to Richmond. I want to test your theory about Jonathan having a backup drive, and I want to get there before Cory or Frank."

"So, we won't tell the others?"

"No." She turned to go.

"Are you good to drive to Richmond?" he asked. "I can help."

Ethel gave him a wry smile. "Who said anything about driving to Richmond? We're going by private plane."

"You've booked a pilot?"

"Jesse, I *am* the pilot."

Chapter 17

"Jesse. Jesse."

Jesse heard his name as a whisper, at first hollow and distant, and then closer with a rush of breath flowing across his ear. He felt a hand gently shake his arm, and he opened his eyes to find Ethel leaning over his bed.

"What time is it?" His voice was thick with sleep.

"Five thirty. Can you be ready to leave by six? I want to be gone by the time the others wake up."

He rubbed his eyes and saw that she was already dressed in a gray pantsuit.

She stepped back from the bed. "You can skip shaving and wash up in the downstairs bathroom. Bring your laptop and external drive."

At ten till six, Ethel quietly locked the back door behind them. Jesse paused to look at the new pane of glass that the twenty-four-hour service had installed late the previous afternoon. He hoped Ethel was correct in that now there was no reason for the intruder to return.

Ethel's Infiniti was parked in front of her single car garage. Normally, it would have been inside. Jesse suspected she'd purposely avoided the sound the power door opener would have made. He expected to hear the chirp of her keyless remote, but even that noise had been anticipated. The car was already unlocked. Ethel clearly didn't want to have to explain to anyone what actions she was taking.

Jesse laughed softly. "You want me to push us out of the driveway and down the block so no one will hear the engine?"

"I considered doing it myself, but I didn't trust your concussed brain to see straight."

Jesse wasn't sure she was kidding.

"Put your computer backpack on the rear seat floorboard," she said. "Don't let it fall against the soft thermal bag behind me. I made up some yogurt and granola for your breakfast. There's also a thermos of coffee and two sealable mugs that are full. You should be able to reach them from the front passenger seat. I'll have my coffee once we hit I-66."

Jesse did as she instructed and then buckled himself in beside her.

Ethel started the car and let its idling speed creep the vehicle out to the street. Once they were clear of the curb, she slowly accelerated to the twenty-five-miles-per-hour neighborhood speed limit.

"Don't you trust Lisa and Douglas?" Jesse asked.

"What they don't know they can't be forced by their superiors to reveal."

"I understand about Bradshaw pressing Douglas for what you're doing, but Lisa isn't Secret Service."

"No, but she'll keep her supervisor informed anyway. Jonathan's last case was a joint operation, and she'll point that out. She's smart and figures the way to stand out is to be in the know. Information is power, and she'll try to parlay that to her advantage. I did the same thing when I was her age, so I don't fault her. I just don't want to fall victim to her ambitions."

"Won't she and Douglas be curious where we've gone?"

"Yes. That's why I left a note by the coffeepot saying neither one of us could sleep, so we've gone for a morning walk along the river in Old Town. It'll also explain why I skipped my RBG workout." She glanced in her rearview mirror as she turned onto a four-lane highway. "Lisa and Douglas should report for work before our late return raises questions."

"How far is this airport?" Jesse asked.

"About forty minutes away. Near Manassas National Battlefield Park."

"A municipal airport?"

"It's private. For UFOs only."

Jesse stared at her. "UFOs? Come on, Ethel. I'm serious."

Her mouth twitched into a smile. "So am I. UFO. United Flying Octogenarians. It's a club for pilots in their eighties."

"But you're not eighty yet."

"Let's just say they consider me their adopted little sister. A little sister who owns a share of a plane. Most club members are ex-military or retired commercial. A few are like me, private hobbyists with a love of flying. My father paid for my lessons when I was eighteen. It was a great gift he gave me."

Jesse heard the crack in her voice and remembered her statement in the hospital. Her father had been murdered, and she'd tracked down his killer. He wanted to ask questions but sensed this wasn't the time.

"The grassy airstrip is on a farm owned by Curt Foster, a retired Air Force colonel. His runway only handles small craft. I've a part interest in a Cessna 172."

"But if we're forty minutes from the airfield and then have to travel from a Richmond airport to the Finch house, shouldn't we have just driven?"

"I want to log the flying hours. More important, no one can follow us through the air."

"Who would do that?"

Ethel took her eyes off the road to face him. "Who indeed? That is the question."

Jesse didn't have an answer. They rode in silence with Ethel checking her rearview mirror every few minutes. When they were on I-66 West, Jesse retrieved the mugs and thermal bag. He gave Ethel her coffee, placed his in a cupholder, opened the bag and found a spoon and reusable glass jar of granola mixed into yogurt. There were also two bananas and two protein bars.

The coffee seemed to bring Ethel out of her pensive mood. "I thought we'd save the bananas and bars for the return flight. We probably won't have time for lunch."

"Does Mrs. Finch know we're coming?"

"No. So that's going to be delicate. I expect Susan's sister might be staying with her. They'll be making preliminary arrangements, but I'm hoping they'll be based at home since things are uncertain as to when Jonathan's body will be released. Susan and I had met several times before and she asked that I be her contact with the Secret Service throughout this ordeal. That should let me ask some unofficial questions with the goal of finding this backup drive you think might exist."

"I'll follow your lead," Jesse said.

"Good. But be prepared to play with LEGOs and Tinkertoys."

The landscape along I-66 changed from glass office parks to tract houses to rolling hills. Ethel exited onto Highway 29 and then branched off onto backroads that meandered through horse country. At a silver mailbox marked "FOSTER," she turned onto a narrow blacktop bordered on either side by split-rail fences.

A farmhouse and complex of barns and stables lay a quarter mile ahead. Jesse saw fifteen to twenty horses grazing in the left pasture. The elegant animals looked like Thoroughbreds. The right-hand pasture was split in the middle with a fenced-in strip of thick, mowed grass. A windsock hung limply from a pole rising thirty feet above its anchoring fence post.

"Is that the runway?" Jesse asked.

"Yes, the horses can't wander onto it, and the grassy, level surface is nearly as smooth as a tarmac." Ethel looked at the cluster of buildings at the far end of the runway. "It appears that Curt has the 172 ready. He's such a sweetheart."

The driveway split, and Ethel bore to the right, away from the picturesque house with its wide wraparound porch. She stopped about twenty feet from the plane.

A lanky man was bent over one of the three wheels, running his fingers across the tread of the tire. He looked up and smiled. As he stood, he clutched his back with one hand, evidently feeling some pain. Then he wiped his palms on his jeans. Before Jesse could unbuckle his seat belt, Ethel was out the door and halfway to greet him.

The man must have been six-three or six-four and towered over her. His outstretched arms embraced Ethel and, despite the bad back, he lifted her off her feet. Jesse thought maybe a romance was on display and so took his time getting out of the car to join them. But there was no kissing, just a playful punch delivered by Ethel to the man's back. He winced and dropped her.

Jesse quickly sized him up. The tanned, weathered face declared hours of outdoor activity. The lines etched upon it measured time in decades. The jeans, wide belt, and boots suggested a man who was as at home on a horse as in an airplane.

Ethel stepped aside. "Curt, I'd like you to meet Jesse Cooper, my double-first-cousin-twice-removed. Jesse, this is Curt Foster."

Foster ran his right hand through his disheveled white hair in a mocking attempt to make himself more presentable. Then he offered it to Jesse. "Double-first-cousin-twice-removed. Impressive. I was only a colonel."

Jesse laughed and shook the man's hand. "I'm sure it's not as impressive as flying fighter jets."

"Are you kidding? I'd sooner be flying through antiaircraft flak again than be in this little bird with Ethel at the controls. I salute your bravery, young man."

"Don't believe him, Jesse," Ethel said. "I can fly rings around this old man."

"On a broom, maybe."

They both laughed and the teasing ceased.

"You're fueled and ready to go," Foster said. "You're going to Pete's?"

"Yes." Ethel turned to Jesse. "Pete Varner is a UFO member outside Richmond who has a strip like this."

"Pete was also my wingman." Foster looked up at the sky. "The day's clear enough. You going VFR?"

"Yes, I'll skirt the major airspaces and avoid a flight plan."

Foster shook his head. "I don't like that." He shot a glance at the plane. "I mean she's a good craft, but it's the unexpected that gets you."

"Curt, if she goes down, no flight plan is going to stop it. I'll call you when we land to set your mind at ease."

Jesse shifted nervously. "What's VFR?"

"Visual flight rules," Foster explained. "As opposed to IFR, instrument flight rules. Ethel's instrument rated, but IFR would put her under various air traffic controllers. Staying VFR minimizes her contacts. So, Ethel, I trust this is something off the books and you were never here."

"Curt, I'm so far off the books, I'm not even in the library."

"Can I offer you breakfast before you take off?"

"Thanks, but we need to get underway." She paused and looked at the farmhouse. "I'm sorry. How's Connie?"

"Good days and bad. We'll sit on the porch later if it warms up. She likes that." Foster turned to Jesse. "My wife has Parkinson's."

"Please give her my regards," Ethel said. "And thanks for having everything ready. Is it okay if I keep the car parked here? I'll leave you the keys."

"No problem. But maybe if you're not running late, we can all have a drink when you return."

Ethel dropped her car keys into his rough, callused hand. "I'd like that."

Five minutes later, Curt Foster watched from the porch as the Cessna lifted into the air. The plane circled once as it gained altitude, dipped its wing in salute, and flew south. Foster pulled out his cell phone and speed-dialed.

"Yeah," a gruff voice said.

"Pete, it's Curt. She's on her way."

"Did she say anything?"

"Not a word."

"Did you tell her you'd heard about the agent's murder?"

"It was the elephant on the runway, but since she didn't bring it up when she called last night, I saw no point in raising it this morning. You know Ethel. And she has a cousin with her, but he's pretty green. Pete, I get the feeling she's on a one-woman op that could be dangerous for someone half her age."

"What do you think I should do?"

"Offer to drive her wherever. You know Richmond better than she does."

"And when she says no?"

"Is she taking your car?"

"Yes. I offered and she accepted."

"Then figure out a way to track her. Maybe a cell phone under the seat if you've got an extra."

"You're really worried about her."

"I'm worried by our lack of information, so I immediately conjure up the worst scenario. I've done it all my life, and that's saved my life on more than one occasion. I'm counting on you to set my mind at ease."

Pete chuckled. "Is that an order?"

"You're damn straight. I still outrank you. Find out what she's up to."

Chapter 18

Douglas Gray read the note Ethel had left by the coffeepot. It was seven thirty, and he was due to relieve a fellow agent at the vice president's residence at ten. He thought he was the only one in the house, and then heard a chair squeak upstairs as it scooted across the hardwood floor. Lisa must have been working at her desk. She'd been extremely quiet, as had he, not wishing to disturb anyone. Now he realized Ethel and Jesse were gone, and Lisa could have been awake for hours.

He walked to the bottom of the back stairway and called up, "Lisa, I've got coffee ready. Want me to bring you a cup?"

"Thanks, but I'll be down in a few minutes."

Douglas poured a cup from the fresh pot and sat at the kitchen counter. He'd caught up on texts and emails and decided to enjoy a few uninterrupted minutes of peace by keeping his government phone in his pocket.

The respite was short-lived. His phone buzzed. His personal phone. The screen displayed an unfamiliar number. His first response was to send what was probably a spam call to voicemail, but it was early for spammers, and not that many people had his personal number.

"Yes?" he said cautiously.

"Is this Douglas?"

The voice sounded familiar.

"Yes."

"This is Cory Bradshaw. Can you talk without being overheard?"

Douglas immediately tensed. The director of the Secret Service wanted to speak to him, a lowly rookie agent. And on his personal phone. Had he said something during Ethel's meeting the previous night that had irritated his boss?

"Yes, sir. Lisa's in the house, but I can step out back." He moved as he spoke.

"Ethel doing her workout?"

"No, sir. She and Jesse have gone into Old Town for a morning walk."

"Really?"

"She left a note to that effect."

"Look, Douglas, I don't mean to put you in an awkward position, but I'd like you to take on a special assignment."

Douglas stepped off the back porch and looked around as if he were about to receive the nuclear codes. "Certainly. What do you need?"

"Your eyes and ears as well as your brain. Ethel is a great woman, and I have the utmost respect for her."

He paused, and Douglas said nothing, waiting for the "but."

"But she's strong-willed, and I know her well enough after thirty years to tell you she won't sit on the sidelines. Whether she has additional insights or evidence in this case, I don't know. But I want you to watch her. Jesse, as well."

"Full-fledged surveillance?"

"No. Ethel would spot that in a heartbeat. Tell her you've been pulled off protection and back into counterfeiting.

You were on the original case that generated the stolen bills and are the contact person for any that might appear in circulation."

"Will I be reporting to Norwood?"

"No. I want you to use this number from your personal phone and report directly to me. Someone completely outside the counterfeiting case will head up investigating how our evidence disappeared. In fact, you'll be questioned."

Douglas stopped pacing the backyard. "Me, sir?"

"Yes. Everyone who was familiar with the case and, more important, the existence of that bogus cash will be questioned."

Douglas shuddered at the thought of going through an interview that might turn into an interrogation. He hoped nervousness wouldn't translate as guilt. "Yes, sir. Will we start tomorrow? I'm on duty at ten today."

"You're on duty now. I've already notified the vice president's team. I've also said you'll be working away from the office for the foreseeable future."

"Anything I should do first?"

"If I were you, I'd cruise Old Town till I had eyes on Ethel and Jesse."

"Yes, sir."

"But I don't expect you to find them there." Director Bradshaw disconnected.

Douglas smiled. The director had given him the opportunity he needed to stay close to the developments, which is exactly where he wanted to be. He turned back to the house and caught a glimpse of Lisa moving away from an upstairs window, the window in Jonathan Finch's room.

———

Lisa had heard the back door close as Douglas left the house. She used the vantage point of Finch's room to see where he was going and was surprised that he was in the backyard pacing in a circle. He was on one of his cell phones. His face was tense, and his gait turned into a series of stops and starts. She couldn't tell if he was angry or unsettled by bad news. He must have left the house not to be overheard, which made her more curious. Was it a call he wanted to keep from Ethel?

Douglas suddenly pulled the phone from his ear and turned toward the house. Lisa quickly withdrew but thought he might have spotted her. Her best course of action was to go downstairs for her coffee as if nothing had happened.

Douglas was sitting at the island when she entered the kitchen. He said a pleasant good morning and pointed at a note on the counter. "Ethel and Jesse have gone into Old Town. I didn't hear them, so it must have been early."

Lisa grabbed a mug and filled it. "You on today?"

"I've been pulled into the review of how the counterfeit currency disappeared. So, I won't be traveling as much. I'll probably be tracing bills, looking for a way back to the source."

"Right," Lisa nodded. "You said you were on the original New York case."

"So?"

"So, you're one of how many who knew about the currency?"

Douglas set down his cup. "What are you getting at?"

Lisa laughed and sat on the stool opposite him. "Sorry. Didn't mean to sound accusatory. Hazard of the job."

Douglas shrugged. "Ten or fifteen of us in the field, and then up the chain of command in counterfeiting, plus the prosecutorial team prepping the case."

"You have a theory as to what happened?"

"I'd have to see the site where the currency was stored. I'd say most likely an inside job or some very sophisticated high-tech breach to get in and out."

"Maybe," Lisa said skeptically. "Or maybe lost in moving from one location to another. That's when it would have been most vulnerable. Have you checked the chain of custody?"

"I haven't checked anything," Douglas snapped.

"Whoa." Lisa drew back on the stool.

"Sorry. I've just had the assignment change, and it's been only a little over twenty-four hours since my friend and colleague was killed."

"All right. I didn't mean to press. I consider any federal agent a colleague. I guess I just want to make sure everything possible is being done to find Jonathan's killers." She reached across the island and rested her hand on Douglas's. "If there's anything I can do to help, don't hesitate to ask." She withdrew her hand halfway, but kept it poised in the air. "Friends?"

Douglas relaxed as the two agents shook hands. "Friends."

Ten minutes later, Douglas exited through the front door, heading for his car parked on the street. Lisa remained in the kitchen, sipping her coffee until she heard his engine rev and then fade away. She pulled out her government cell phone and dialed the number she'd been texted during the night.

"Director Hauser's office."

"This is Special Agent Lisa Draper. I believe Director Hauser is expecting me."

The officious voice softened. "Yes, Agent Draper. He's just finishing up a call. Can I keep you on hold?"

"Certainly."

At first Lisa was afraid the line had gone dead, but after a few seconds, a low beep sounded and was repeated about every ten seconds thereafter. She should have known a private line of the director of the FBI wouldn't be playing background music. As the minutes passed, Lisa became concerned that Ethel and Jesse would return before she'd even spoken with Hauser, let alone finished the call. Maybe she would be the next person pacing in the backyard.

"Agent Draper?"

Lisa recognized the smooth baritone voice. "Yes, sir."

"Sorry to keep you waiting. It's come to my attention that you room with Ethel Crestwater."

"That's correct."

"And it's an experience, isn't it?"

"She's a remarkable woman."

"Yes, as remarkable as she is determined. I'll come right to the point. Bradshaw is heading up the investigation of Finch's murder. That's appropriate. Finch was his man. Detective Mancini will be on the margins of the Finch case, but he has a B and E and the subsequent assault on Jesse Cooper. We don't have a dog in the case, so to speak, but with Ethel in the mix, those cases could go anywhere."

"What do you mean, sir?"

"I mean Ethel has her ways, her sources, and one of the finest minds I've ever come across. We might not have a dog in the case, but we could have a case touched by the dog. I'm talking about the Parker investigation where Finch was first on the scene. Someone, rightly or wrongly, might have thought Finch knew more about Parker's embezzled funds and pulled him into something over his head. Maybe waved that money in front of his face or threatened his family. I want you to review the Parker case. You were involved, I understand, and keep me informed about what's going on with Ethel, Bradshaw, and Mancini. I'd love for us to find that twenty million dollars. Do you think you can do that?"

"Yes, sir. In fact, there was a meeting last night of those three."

"Well, Agent Draper, I'm all ears."

———

Trevor Norwood groaned as he shifted in the recliner. The booze and the pills that enabled him to grab a few hours of restless sleep had worn off. The pain in his arm, though duller, brought yesterday's disaster back into focus.

He'd dozed without a shirt and so immediately examined the bandage encircling his upper left arm. No sign of bleeding, no red streaks warning of infection. He wiggled his fingers, raised his injured arm away from his side and then over his head. The mobility and flexibility encouraged him. Another day or two of sick leave, and he could make it through a workday.

His phone buzzed on the end table beside him. He picked it up and saw it was the third encrypted text of the day. He must have slept more soundly than he realized. He'd also slept later. It was after eight in the morning.

The earliest text had come at six thirty:

How are you? I checked my wallet.

Forty-five minutes later, another text:

Me too.

Both senders' IDs had been stripped as part of the encryption process that not only hid the message but also the source.

Then the most recent one:

SHOW ME THE MONEY!!!!

Norwood didn't need the IDs to know which of his partners had sent which text. It was always the outsider who was more suspicious, more volatile. The "How are you?" concern only went as far as "Can't you transfer our shares?"

Norwood knew he needed to get to his computer and distribute the five hundred thousand dollars in Bitcoins before the partners disregarded their plan to stay separate and came after him. But the delay would be forgiven when he told them what he'd found.

He walked to the kitchen, started coffee brewing, and then opened his laptop and logged on to the cryptocurrency site he used for his transactions. It took only a few minutes to empty the virtual wallet he'd used the previous night into the three new ones he and his team had each created. They'd shared wallet addresses but not their private keys. Once he sent the coins, only the wallet owner could access them. It was very simple and ultra-secure, but with one frightening exception—lose your key, lose your money.

Norwood sent a message of his own:

> Sorry for delay. Done. Need second satchel for return. Most importantly, I know location of Parker money.

As he expected, the response was immediate.

> Parker? Have key? Need to talk!

Then a message that shocked him:

> Secret Service has currency. Can link. Work Parker but lay low.

Norwood quickly replied:

> Nothing links us. But Parker wallet on Finch computer con-
> firms suspicions. Key might be hidden on phone or
> laptop. Or physical somewhere. Investigators might find
> first. Lay low, but be ready to move fast.

Norwood poured his coffee and assessed the situation. He wished now he hadn't destroyed Finch's phone. He'd have to go through every file on the laptop looking for a string of characters that could be the key. But that key could as easily be written on a scrap of paper and tucked between pages of a book. That meant a physical search of Finch's office or home.

He put his money on home.

Chapter 19

Although Ethel and Jesse wore headsets for communication, the noise of the engine discouraged lengthy conversation. But there was plenty to see. Unlike commercial airline pilots cruising above thirty thousand feet, Ethel maintained an altitude that kept cars, houses, and farms distinguishable, as if viewing the detailed scale layout of a model railroader. The clear fall air extended the horizon, and Jesse could make out the Shenandoah Mountain range rising up on his right.

After about forty minutes, Ethel said, "We're getting close. I'll circle the runway once before landing."

Pete Varner was mucking out a stable stall when he heard the buzz of an approaching plane. He quickly slipped out of his rubber boots, washed his hands in a work sink, and crossed the grassy runway to where he'd parked his Ford Explorer.

The red-and-white Cessna was circling so that it could land heading into the slight but steady breeze. As the plane momentarily faced away, Varner quickly opened the rear passenger door and powered up an iPhone. He double-checked it was silenced and then slid it under the front seat. He closed the door and stepped away from the SUV as Ethel began her final approach.

She taxied to the end of the runway where Varner stood waiting. With the engine killed and the propeller stopped, he hurried to help Ethel out of the cockpit. She waved him away and agilely hopped down. Then, as she'd done with Foster, she gave him a big hug.

Jesse was struck by the contrast between Foster and Varner. Foster had been tall and lanky, looking like he'd barely managed to stay under the height maximum for an Air Force pilot. Varner stood only a few inches higher than Ethel. He must have squeaked by just above the minimum. But Jesse thought once the colonel and his wingman had been in their fighter jets, height meant nothing.

Ethel introduced the two men, and they shook hands.

"Can I drive you somewhere?" Varner asked. "Richmond's my home turf."

"That's kind of you," Ethel said, "but I wouldn't want to tie you up. We'll be visiting friends. Just let us know when you need the car back."

"I've got an old Ford 150 that's my runabout truck. So, take your time. If you need to bunk over, there's room."

"Thanks. Jesse's got class in the morning, so we'll return by midafternoon at the latest. Take the Cessna up if you'd like. There's plenty of fuel to get us back to Curt's."

Varner handed her a set of keys. "Swapping an SUV for an airplane? Tempting. Maybe I'll do that."

Jesse threw his laptop backpack on the rear seat. Varner stood by the driver's window. "Know how to program the built-in GPS?"

Ethel shook her head. "No need. Jesse and his phone will handle the navigation." She turned the ignition, and the engine came to life. "And I'll do my best to avoid any crashes."

The Explorer headed out the long driveway. Varner watched

until it disappeared behind a stand of pines. He pulled out a second iPhone, activated the Find My Phone app, and grunted with satisfaction as a blue dot moved across the screen.

Thirty minutes later, Ethel pulled into the Finches' driveway. The same green Subaru Forester was in the carport. No other car was parked beside it nor along the street in front of the house. Ethel feared Susan's sister from Fredericksburg might have taken them out for breakfast.

"Bring your computer," she told Jesse. "But I might need to speak to Susan alone. Don't be surprised if I suggest Davie show you his room."

Ethel rang the doorbell. She stepped off the front porch so that she had a view of Davie's window. The closed blinds parted and the boy peeked between them. Ethel smiled and waved. The blinds snapped shut.

The front door opened. Susan stood wearing the same clothes as the day before, as if time had stopped for her.

"Ethel." She spoke the name flatly without either enthusiasm or annoyance.

"I apologize for our unexpected arrival. To be truthful, I wanted to have a conversation outside of Bradshaw and the agency."

Susan nodded, and then looked at Jesse.

"This is Jesse Cooper," Ethel explained. "He's a grad student who is helping me. He's also my double-first-cousin twice-removed."

The specifics of the relationship made no impression on Susan. She simply stepped back and allowed them to enter. They followed her into the living room, and Susan and Ethel took their same positions on the sofa while Jesse stood awkwardly, holding his computer backpack by his side.

"Did your sister come?" Ethel asked.

"Not yet. I expect her shortly. When I heard the doorbell, I thought it was her."

"I wouldn't have come if it weren't important."

"Have they found out who killed Johnny?"

"Not yet." Ethel looked up at Jesse, who was still unsure whether to take a seat or not. "Is Davie here?"

"Yes. He's dealing with his father's death as best he can."

"Do you think it would be okay if Jesse saw his room? Keep Davie occupied so he doesn't overhear us?"

"He's uncomfortable with strangers, but if I walk Jesse back and introduce him, he'll probably be all right. Especially since his room is a safe, familiar environment."

"Good," Ethel said. "I'll wait here."

As soon as Jesse and Susan left, Ethel pulled her cell phone from the front pocket of her pantsuit and activated her recording app. Then she slipped the phone back in place. The layer of fabric might muffle the conversation, but it would be intelligible.

Within a few minutes, Susan returned. As she sat beside Ethel, she asked, "Now, what's so important?"

"First, let me say I'm doing my own investigation into your husband's death. Not that I don't trust the service. I just want to make sure I get the full story and its context."

Susan's forehead furrowed. "Why would you think you'd not get the full story?"

"Because you're not telling me the full story."

Blood rushed to the other woman's face. She managed to sputter, "I don't know what you mean."

"When we showed up at your door yesterday, and you realized something serious had happened, you said, 'Please tell me he didn't take his own life.' Not 'What's happened?' or 'Has Johnny been killed?' but an immediate fear that Jonathan had committed suicide. Why would you think that?"

Susan looked away. "I don't know. I just did."

"Well, I don't buy that, Susan. Whatever your reason, it will come out, because I'll feel obligated to raise the question with Bradshaw myself. Then it will pass beyond any control I have to help you and Davie if it's something that could be viewed as detrimental to Jonathan's standing within the Secret Service."

Susan started weeping, and sniffles punctuated her words.

"Oh, it would be detrimental. He was sick. Severe headaches began about eight months ago. Unexplained bouts of nausea. His doctor scheduled a brain scan. It was a glioblastoma brain tumor. Inoperable."

"I'm so sorry, Susan. Did he decline all treatments?"

"His oncologist said radiation and chemo might stretch his life expectancy six months. Johnny called it six more months of sickness. And he'd have to go on medical leave with reduced disability pay. He said he wanted to work as long as he could, because he knew we needed every penny to provide for Davie's long-term needs."

"He told no one other than you?"

"No. But he was upset that he'd been placed on call-up for presidential detail. He'd been able to work alone more in his cybercrime role. And he was afraid if he started experiencing symptoms like blurred vision or balance problems, he'd be compromising his protection team. That was starting to depress him. Staying with you was a bright spot, as he waited for the inevitable day when he'd have to quit."

"And that's why you thought he'd killed himself? He'd succumbed to the depression?"

Susan sighed and wiped her nose. "I guess. In that moment, I felt betrayed because he'd promised he wouldn't end it that way. And there was another reason. We have a good amount of insurance, given Davie's condition. He said a suicide might jeopardize the claim, so he wouldn't risk it."

"How much is the insurance?"

"Half a million dollars."

Ethel matched the figure with the amount of counterfeit currency that had gone missing from the evidence room. Had Jonathan's depression and desperation led him to try to double what he could leave his family?

A bittersweet smile crossed Susan's lips. "I've thought Johnny's probably happy with how things turned out. He was killed in the line of duty. Our family will receive a death benefit from the service. The insurance will be paid without question." Her smile faded and tears again flowed. "But at what a terrible price."

Ethel reached out her arms and folded the grieving woman into a motherly embrace. "There, there, dear. Take comfort that everything he did, he did for his family. For now, let's keep that between us."

Chapter 20

"This is Mr. Cooper. He'd like to see your models. Mommy will be in the living room talking with Miss Crestwater." With these words, Susan Finch had introduced Jesse to Davie and left.

David sat at the table between the windows and broke apart what looked like a castle of LEGOs. His walker was by his side.

"What's your favorite thing to build, Davie?"

"Water," he mumbled without stopping the disassembly. "I like water."

"Can I get you a glass?"

Davie turned around and looked at Jesse for the first time. The boy's uncombed, straw-colored hair swirled in a cowlick and his pale brown eyes studied his visitor. "Glass?" He was clearly confused. Then his face brightened. "No. Not a glass. A molecule." He bent over and picked up a Tinkertoy construction. A larger hub connected to two smaller hubs by sticks.

Jesse laughed. "Yes. Two hydrogen atoms and one oxygen atom. Water."

Davie smiled. Then looked out the window. "That's an SUV. Where's the gray car?"

"It's being repaired," Jesse said, not wanting to get into

a discussion of government versus private vehicles. "Miss Crestwater borrowed this one."

"Miss Crest—" He held up the Tinkertoy creation.

"Water," Jesse said. "Miss Crest*water*. Very clever, Davie."

The boy beamed, now suddenly relaxed. He pointed to Jesse's computer bag. "For me?"

"No, for my work." Jesse decided there was no harm in taking out the computer. He had a few games on it that maybe he could play with Davie. He sat on the edge of the bed closest to the boy and unzipped the backpack.

As soon as the laptop appeared, Davie clapped his hands. "It's Daddy's."

"No, it's mine."

The boy became upset. "No, it's Daddy's."

Rather than argue, Jesse powered up his MacBook Pro. The display background appeared, a shot of the Golden Gate Bridge rising out of patches of heavy fog.

"No," Davie agreed. "It's not Daddy's."

"But your daddy's is like it, right?"

"Daddy's gone."

"I know. I'm sad. Your daddy was a nice man. He was my friend."

Tears welled in the boy's eyes. He looked up at Jesse and then at a bookshelf on the wall where instead of volumes, a variety of LEGO creations filled the shelves. "Daddy would build those with me. I like the cars and trucks."

Jesse crossed the room to admire the collection. One especially caught his eye. It was a vehicle about two feet long and six inches high. Jesse recognized Finch's Ford Escape. Escape. If only he had escaped. Jesse picked it up and found it to be heavier than it looked.

"No." Davie pushed himself up from the table. "That's Daddy's secret."

Secret. The word echoed in Jesse's head, but in the whispered voice of Jonathan Finch. He shook the model. Something rattled inside. "Yes. Your daddy's secret." Jesse smiled as he lied. "Your daddy told me about it. For his computer."

Davie nodded.

"I'd love to take a look." Without waiting for permission, Jesse set the model on the bedspread. The interlocking blocks appeared to be divided into three sections: the forward engine and hood, the passenger compartment, and the hatchback. He gripped the rear blocks and pulled. His pulse nearly doubled. The LEGOs proved to be an exterior shell only. From within, Jesse retrieved a silver Seagate one-terabyte external hard drive. Three words had been hand-printed on its top: "Time Machine Backup." Jesse tried not to show his excitement and paid more attention to the model. "Looks just like your dad's. And I have a drive just like this one. Can I see if yours fits?"

Davie pointed to the model. "There's more."

Jesse turned it up and peered into the cavity. What looked like a larger-than-normal flash drive was wedged in the bottom. He removed a few more LEGOs until he could extract the device. A slip of paper was wrapped around it and held in place by a rubber band. Jesse slipped off the rubber band and removed the paper. He knew immediately what the long string of letters, characters, and symbols represented—the private key to a cryptocurrency virtual wallet.

Jesse pulled two USB cables and his own hard drive from his backpack. "I just want to see if it works."

"Okay."

Jesse connected the drives to his laptop and started a file transfer from Finch's backup to his clean drive. The time indicator estimated the copy would take nearly thirty minutes. Jesse examined the smaller device with a built-in USB connector he still held in his hand. The only visible marking was a brand logo and name. KryptoFold. The company that makes hardware products for managing, storing, and using the private keys for cryptocurrency accounts. The company headed by CEO Dwayne Parker. The man whose body had been discovered by Jonathan Finch. Whatever the device was, Jesse knew he had to get it to Ethel.

"This is going to take a while to test," Jesse said. "Why don't you show me how to build some molecules?" He stood from the bed, slipped the KryptoFold into his jacket pocket, and walked to a corner of the room where a pile of Tinkertoys waited to be assembled. He sat on the floor. "I think I'll make a glass of Crestwater."

Davie laughed, sat back down at his table, and was soon lost in the construction.

Thirty minutes later, Jesse stood up and stretched. Davie was so focused on his Tinkertoys that he seemed oblivious to everything around him. Jesse went to his computer, saw that the transfer had finished, and ejected both drives. He packed up his drive and computer. He reassembled the SUV, inserted Finch's external drive, and returned the LEGO model to the bookshelf.

"Davie? Davie?"

The boy didn't respond. Jesse walked over and lightly touched him on the shoulder. Davie jumped like he'd been shocked.

"It's okay." Jesse pointed to the bookshelf. "I just wanted to tell you Daddy's secret is safe."

Davie gave a quick glance at the shelf and returned to the current project at hand.

Jesse sat on the bed, anxious to share his discovery with Ethel. A few minutes later, the bedroom door opened, and Susan and Ethel entered. Davie continued building without acknowledging their presence. While his mother went to him,

Jesse mouthed "Found it" to Ethel. She made a *shhhsh*ing pantomime with her lips.

Then she said, "Looks like you boys have been busy."

Jesse stood from the bed and picked up his backpack. "Davie's either going to be a chemist or an engineer. Either one, he's way ahead of me."

Susan smiled and tried to smooth her son's hair. "He's special. Johnny and I felt blessed. And we're going to make it."

"I know you will," Ethel said. "Now Jesse and I should head back. You call me if you need anything. And I promise to update you whenever there's new information."

Susan nodded, and her eyes filled with tears.

"Stay with Davie," Ethel said. "We'll let ourselves out."

As Ethel closed the front door, Jesse whispered, "I've got a copy of his backup drive. And I found a link to Dwayne Parker."

"Not now," Ethel said. "We'll talk when we know it's safe."

"They can't hear us."

Ethel headed for the Explorer. "See the old pickup truck pulling away from the curb a block up the street?"

"Yeah, so?"

"It's a Ford 150 and a little out of place in the neighborhood."

"That's the model Varner said he had. Do you think he followed us?"

"I don't know. If he did, I think he and Curt see themselves as guardian angels. And I don't want their concern for our safety to put them in someone else's crosshairs."

Pete Varner had started his pickup as soon as the rearview mirror reflected Ethel and Jesse leaving the house. Although they were a block away, Varner saw Jesse's attention drawn to him. "Damn," he muttered. He knew he should have simply noted the address and left. He was still looking in his mirror when he pulled out into the street.

A car horn blared, jolting him into slamming on his brakes as an oncoming Toyota Camry swerved to avoid him. The other driver glared at him. So much for slipping away unnoticed. Varner sped off, hoping to at least return home before Ethel.

The white Camry continued down the street. Ethel watched it approach, expecting to see a driver still angry or shaken by the near collision. But the man behind the wheel displayed neither emotion. He angled his face away from her. Ethel noted his short-cropped blond hair that could have been a military cut. She also noted the license plate.

———

Ethel Crestwater at Finch's house. Why?

Trevor Norwood read the text message with alarm. Then he convinced himself that she was making a sympathy call. After all, Jonathan Finch was renting a room from her. He texted that in reply.

The response was quick—

Companion has backpack.
Probably returning personal items. Were you spotted?
No. And plates clean.

Professionalism, Norwood thought. Use stolen license plates. There was no substitute for a good field operator.

He texted instructions—

Keep your eye on our new prize. Look for opportunity but don't force it. We'll cover here.

As the leader, Norwood tried to instill confidence in his teammates. But he was worried. The botched break-in at the Crestwater house had left them vulnerable. Yes, there was no substitute for a good field operative.

Chapter 21

"Are you going to confront him?" Jesse asked the question as he watched the vintage pickup turn at the next corner.

"Not until I need to." Ethel kept her eyes on the Camry as it accelerated in the opposite direction. Then she bent down and looked under the Explorer.

"What are you searching for?"

"The reason he found us. No one followed us by sight. Of that, I'm sure." She circled the vehicle, stopping every few feet to look under the chassis. When she returned to the driver's side, she opened the door, but instead of climbing inside, she looked under the seat.

Jesse opened the front passenger door and did the same. "There's a phone."

Ethel held up a hand to silence him. She walked around the Explorer and motioned for Jesse to step aside. Carefully, she reached beneath the seat and extracted an iPhone. After a brief examination, she said, "It's on but it's not connected to a current call. He must be tracking it through a second phone. So, our conversations have been secure."

"What are you going to do?"

"This." She slid the phone into her coat pocket. "We'll keep it and say nothing. Pete and Curt will know we know, and that will be enough for the moment. Now let's get home so you can analyze what might be on that hard drive."

As soon as they left the neighborhood, Ethel used her own phone to place a call using the hands-free speaker.

"Frank."

"Yes, Ethel." The detective sounded tired but not annoyed.

"You're on speaker with Jesse and me. I need a favor."

"Is this about the case?"

"It could be."

"What is it, and what's the context?"

"I need you to run a Virginia plate. QWR-5391. We just came from visiting Susan Finch, and the driver of a Toyota Camry with that tag acted a little strange as he drove by the house."

Jesse wondered what Ethel had noticed that he had missed.

"Strange how?" Mancini asked.

"He went out of his way to hide his face. Maybe it's nothing more than a man having an affair where he shouldn't be, but I'd feel better if you got a name and address."

"Okay. Did you learn anything more from Mrs. Finch?"

"No. She has no clue as to who would want to murder her husband. And nothing about the counterfeit money. Has Cory shared an autopsy report?"

"Not yet. But it's pretty clear a shot to the chest will be the cause of death."

"Push for a more thorough report, Frank."

There was a brief silence as Mancini weighed her words. "What are you not telling me?"

"I have a hunch, is all."

"Have you shared this hunch with Cory?"

"No. But ask him for more than just a description of the chest wound. And call or text when you know something about that tag."

"Okay. Listen, Ethel, we're releasing Finch's name to the media this morning, but Bradshaw's handling the press relations."

"Richmond press?"

"Not specifically. Bradshaw and I are trying to keep it local, although some enterprising reporter will probably go for the next of kin. They always do."

"And always will. On-camera grief means ratings. You and Bradshaw won't change that, but thanks for trying." She disconnected.

Jesse studied her. He saw the determined profile and furrowed brow. Her mind was running on all cylinders. "This autopsy thing. It's more than a hunch, isn't it?"

Ethel nodded. "Much more. Jonathan had terminal brain cancer. Only his wife and doctors knew. And it explains a lot."

"Like what?"

"Like why he was carrying a personal Beretta instead of his issued Sig Sauer. If he had to use a gun, he didn't want the slugs traced back to him."

"So he was part of the team that stole those bills?"

"I don't think so. Why would they fight over counterfeit money? I think Jonathan might have been selling something that he didn't want traced. He didn't know the money would be counterfeit."

"Then there must be two corrupt elements in the Secret Service?"

"Maybe one corrupt and one desperate. One greedy and one trying to provide for a special-needs child."

Jesse fingered the KryptoFold device and slip of paper in his pocket. "I think it goes back to Dwayne Parker, KryptoFold's embezzling CEO." He showed Ethel what he'd discovered hidden in the LEGOs along with the external drive. "Jonathan could have easily slipped this in his pocket since he was first on the scene of Parker's suicide." Then the full ramification struck him. "You don't think Jonathan murdered Parker for this key to his cryptocurrency?"

"No. But I think he went after Parker without backup, well aware he could be shot. Killed in the line of duty would have meant more money for his family. But Parker did commit suicide."

Jesse followed her train of thought. "And Jonathan found this device and possibly something else that went on his computer."

"Yes. Parker had his luggage packed to flee the country. He would have kept both the hardware device and his computer close."

"If we're lucky, Jonathan made his last backup right before he left Richmond Sunday night so that we're not missing any information."

"If we're lucky," Ethel repeated. "Do you know how this KryptoFold thing works?"

"The slip of paper contains a long sequence that sure looks like a private key. I'm hoping all I have to do is back up my internal drive and then restore Jonathan's in its place. There should be an app that recognizes when the KryptoFold is plugged into a USB port and we go from there. It could be as simple as typing in that sequence at the appropriate time."

Ethel gave him a smile. "Ah, the optimism of youth."

Jesse examined the KryptoFold again. Then he used WhatsApp to send an encrypted text to Tracy in London.

Found a KryptoFold model 7-HVX. Research how to activate.
Tell no one.

Ethel's cell phone rang. She took her eyes off the road just long enough to check the screen. "It's Frank." She handed it to Jesse. "Put him on speaker."

He accepted the call. "You're on speaker, Detective Mancini."

"Ethel, you say that license plate was on a Toyota Camry?"

"Yes. White like yours. I couldn't give you the exact year."

"Did you see both front and back plates?"

"Yes. They matched."

"Well, the tag number is registered to a silver Hyundai Santa Fe. For your information, Ethel, that's an SUV. Even you couldn't confuse those two vehicles."

"Hey, I'll have you know I was memorizing car models when Studebakers were on the highways."

"Anything else I should know before I pass this along to the Richmond PD and Highway Patrol?"

"Do what you have to, but I'd prefer you pass the info to Cory Bradshaw. Someone could be casing Finch's house, and our best bet might be not to jump them prematurely."

"But the wife and boy?"

"Cory should get an agent from the Richmond office to the house immediately. I'll call Susan Finch and urge her to leave the house until she gets word from Cory that her protection is in place."

"Do you want to tell Cory?" Mancini asked.

"No. You and he are officially on the case. Besides, I'll be in the air soon."

There was a long beat of silence. "You flew to Richmond?"

"Yes, Frank. *I* flew to Richmond in *my* plane. And I'll be flying back. Why so shocked? I'm only seventy-five." She winked at Jesse and gave him the cut sign.

He disconnected before the detective could reply. He offered her the phone but she waved it away.

"I've entered Susan's number in the contacts list. Scroll to it and keep the speaker on. I want to warn her what's coming."

The phone rang twice. "Ethel?" Susan asked.

"Yes. Listen. I've just made arrangements for the Secret Service to come to the house. They've released Jonathan's name, and I suggested it might be good to have someone run interference if the press descends upon you."

"But I'm not at home. My sister, Rebecca, came a few minutes after you left. We're taking Davie to IHOP."

"Good. Stay away from the house until you hear from Director Bradshaw. He'll move quickly."

The phone was silent a few seconds. Then, a stifled sob broke through. "Thank you, Ethel. I don't know how I can ever repay you."

"You and Davie be strong. We'll get justice for Jonathan. You know he'd be doing the same for his fellow agents. I'll be back in touch."

Ethel nodded for Jesse to end the call.

He sat quietly for a moment and then said, "You're really good with her. I can't imagine what she's going through."

"I can't imagine what she will go through if Jonathan turns out to be complicit in whatever happened."

"And you? Won't you feel betrayed?"

"Maybe. Or maybe I'll be sympathetic. But we won't know till we find out the truth."

Jesse felt the moment had come when he could broach the question that kept surfacing in his mind. "Ethel, you said in the hospital your father had been murdered and that you had tracked down his killer. How did that happen? My mother never told me."

For a few moments, Ethel kept her eyes on the road, and Jesse thought his question was going to be ignored.

Then, with a quick glance at him, she said, "No, I guess

she wouldn't say anything." She focused back on her driving. "Murder was something that was viewed as a scourge on the family. On two families, really. Given the double blood ties, the family endured a double suffering. When my mother died in childbirth, it was the loss of a wife and a sister. When my father was murdered, a brother and widower were gone."

"So, no one would talk about it?"

Ethel gave a mirthless laugh. "Unpleasantness was something my aunt and uncle avoided at all cost. To discuss it was to admit that it had happened."

"Didn't you see them growing up?"

"In the summers, my father and I would go out to California for two weeks, and I would play with your grandmother, my double-first-cousin. I had a nanny in DC, but when I was older and started school, I'd take the bus down to the Department of Justice building every afternoon. Mr. Hoover wasn't known for being fond of children, but my father was one of his key agents, and even Hoover had to respect his efforts at being a single parent. When I was fourteen, I was allowed to work after school in the fingerprint department. I'd examine and label cards of ink-stained whorls and ridges for classification and then match the records when crime-scene prints came to the department for identification."

"Pre-computers," Jesse said.

"The tools of the trade were a magnifying glass and a bright light. I was good at it. When I graduated, my father wanted me to go to college, but back then a woman's best career options were teaching or nursing. I was fighting crime. I went to Mr. Hoover and told him I wanted a job. I was eighteen and knew my mind. No one knew the fingerprint department better than me. And I said if he ever needed a woman for field investigations, I was that woman."

"What did he say?"

"He was amused. But he gave me a full-time job with fingerprints. Back then, I couldn't be a special agent. Mr. Hoover didn't allow women in the role. He said I could consider myself his special asset. As a consolation prize, my father paid for flying lessons as an outlet for what he called my overly adventurous spirit. After a while, I graduated to surveillance work, mainly playing the role of a young wife or older daughter paired with an appropriate male agent. Strictly assignments with minimal risks. But I leveraged that into full field agent training, claiming it would be of benefit so that if something unforeseen ever happened, I could at least defend myself. When Mr. Hoover died in 1972, the policy toward women changed, and I became a full-fledged FBI special agent."

"And your father's death?"

"That happened when a field operation went bad. An organized crime gang had moved into hijacking tractor-trailers. When they drove them across state lines, the FBI got involved. This was back in 1967. I was twenty and definitely barred from any mob-related cases. My father had an inside informant. Word was passed that a shipment would be jumped one night along one of the lonely stretches of West Virginia. The informant didn't know exactly where, so my father decided to set up a roadblock just beyond the likely stretch of highway. They were ambushed. The gang knew precisely where they would be positioned and three cars came up behind them. Six agents died that night, including my father. One survived long enough to say what had happened."

"Your father's informant double-crossed him?"

"The informant's body was discovered the next morning in the rear of the hijacked trailer. The betrayer had to have been someone in the Bureau. No one outside the on-the-scene agents knew that location."

"And you found him?"

"Yes. Ironically, through fingerprints. My father kept a file box in his desk drawer with active cases. He had some topographical aerial photos of the targeted stretch of the West Virginia highway in order to select the best interception site. He'd circled the exact spot. Access to those photos would have provided everything needed for a surprise attack. The mob didn't just want to stay with the original hijack plan, they wanted to cripple the FBI's investigation. I dusted that file box and the desk drawer handle. In addition to my father's prints, I found those of an agent who worked bank robberies. I kept agent prints on file so that they could be ruled out if they happened to contaminate a crime scene."

"Wouldn't he claim your father had authorized him to review some other case in the file? The prints could have been left at any time."

"Yes, but the agent had recently cut his thumb. There was a raised scab where it was healing. That showed up in the fresh prints and narrowed the time frame to a day or two before the ambush. And some of the prints were clearly laid over my father's. I knew without a doubt the man had jimmied the locked drawer, reviewed the file, and passed the information along to the mob. And the worst of it was that the agent was my godfather. He not only betrayed the Bureau, he betrayed a friend."

"Did you take your findings to Hoover?"

"A woman's word against a man's? Even Mr. Hoover might have viewed my theory as unfounded if the agent concocted some other explanation."

"What did you do?"

"I confronted him one evening."

"At the office?"

"No. Outside his home in Chevy Chase. I told him what I'd

found, suggested he turn himself in and cooperate in building the case against the men who killed my father."

"Did he?"

"No." Ethel fixed Jesse with a hard stare. "He pulled a gun. So I shot him."

Jesse took in a sharp breath. "You killed him?"

Ethel shrugged and concentrated on the road ahead. "Well, technically, the bullet killed him. It was from the gun I gave you yesterday. Mr. Hoover wasn't happy, but when he found payoff funds in the dead man's bank account with links back to the mob that led to arrests, he got over it."

"And your status?"

"Let's say shooting an agent doesn't exactly win popularity contests, no matter how much the son of a bitch deserves it. But shortly afterward, I started renting rooms to new agents, and life went on. The suspicion faded away."

"What suspicion?"

"That I shot the bastard in cold blood."

Jesse said nothing, trying to reconcile the little old woman skillfully maneuvering the SUV through heavy traffic with a gun-toting avenger.

"And you know, Jesse, if he hadn't drawn, maybe I would have."

Chapter 22

As the Ford Explorer neared the long driveway to Pete Varner's horse farm, Ethel retrieved his phone from the pocket of her pants suit.

"Power this off so there's no tracking possibility."

Jesse took the iPhone and started the shutdown process. "I can't get to the battery, so I'm not completely sure the phone can't be still located."

"That's a low probability," Ethel said. "There would have to be a Trojan app or extra chip installed, and that would be done by the NSA. I doubt Pete's on their terrorist watch list."

"Okay. Done."

"Stick it in your computer backpack. We'll return it if Pete asks for it. But I'll bet he'll not want to admit to tracking us."

As they walked up to Ethel's plane, Pete emerged from the stables. "Everything go okay?"

"Yes, but let me give you some gas money." Ethel pulled out her wallet. "I should have stopped and filled up on the way back."

Pete waved it away. "Your money's no good here. It was my treat to see you. Why don't you come in the house for a drink?"

"Love to," Ethel said, "but I don't want to get pulled over for an FUI."

Varner laughed and turned to Jesse. "She means flying under the influence. All right, then lemonade."

"Thanks, Pete, but I really need to get back. Next time."

"Well, I can speak for Curt and say if you need help, you know where to find us."

She gave him a mischievous smile. "And if I need help, you'll know where to find me."

They said their goodbyes, and five minutes later the Cessna was airborne and heading northwest.

Varner checked for his phone beneath the Explorer's seat. "You sly little vixen," he whispered to himself.

———

Ethel and Jesse were in the Infiniti on I-66 when her cell phone rang. She glanced at the screen before handing it to Jesse. "It's Frank. Put him on speaker."

As soon as the call connected, she said, "You've got Jesse and me. What's up?"

"We've found the Malibu, and we're nearly positive it was the same car we saw on CCTV near the parking deck."

"Where?"

"In a lot by William Ramsay Elementary School near the activity field. The car had been reported stolen in Falls Church on Sunday afternoon, but whoever took it also stole another set of plates. They could drive fairly confidently that they wouldn't be spotted."

"Probably the same modus operandi as our Richmond driver. I doubt if you'll find anything like prints or DNA."

"No, they know what they're doing. I notified Cory, and

he's checking if other vehicles or plates in the region have been reported stolen. He also told me they've moved Mrs. Finch and her son to her sister's in Fredericksburg."

Ethel nodded her approval, even though Mancini couldn't see her. "Better to take the extra precaution."

"It's more than that. When Cory's agent accompanied Mrs. Finch, her son, and her sister back to the house, they discovered it had been broken into and searched."

Ethel and Jesse exchanged worried glances.

"Anything taken?" she asked.

"She doesn't think so. Cory said it looked like they were after some paperwork. Finch's home office was tossed, as were the bedroom and kitchen drawers."

"The boy's bedroom?"

"He didn't say one way or the other." Mancini paused a beat, and then a wariness crept into his voice. "Is there a reason you think the boy's room would be searched?"

"I was concerned about the effect on Davie. It would be traumatic enough seeing the rest of the house turned upside down, let alone his own room."

"Cory made no mention of the boy's reaction, but he was only summarizing what his agent reported."

"Thank you, Frank."

"It's a two-way street, Ethel. I expect reciprocity."

"Sometimes I can only point you in the direction the street's headed."

"Like the autopsy and the brain tumor."

"So, you got the complete report. I couldn't tell you because I'd made a promise to Susan Finch, and she'd made a promise to her husband. It was terminal and he'd refused treatment. That might have led him to take chances on his own without endangering others. He didn't care if he died in the line of duty."

Mancini was silent a moment. Then he said, "All right, I appreciate what you did. I'm not sure how it affects my case."

"It could shed light on why Jonathan acted as he did and stirred something up that cost him his life. But I suspect that's a line of inquiry Cory will keep for himself. Now, you were going to give me copies of the crime-scene photos of where Jesse was knocked out yesterday. Can you scan and email?"

"Yes. Sorry I didn't ask earlier, Jesse, but how are you feeling?"

"Good, sir. A little tender where I was struck."

"You were lucky. The blow was well placed. My guess is you were also lucky you didn't see your assailant."

Jesse paled. "I hadn't thought about that."

Ethel kept her eyes on the road but angled her body toward the phone. "Back to the stolen car... Are you thinking what I'm thinking?"

"You mean about logistics?"

"Yes. Jesse saw two men, but there had to be at least a third accomplice in the Malibu. The men at the murder scene couldn't have driven the car to the school and been in front of my house at the same time."

"That's what I figure," Mancini agreed. "Two men may have been able to shuttle vehicles prior to the attack, but the time-stamp on the CCTV footage, the time Jesse places the killing, and the distance to the school demand a third person. Cory has come to the same conclusion."

"Has he concluded they're all within his agency?"

"If he has, he's keeping a tight lip. But I'd expect nothing less. Give me your email address, and you'll have the photos by the end of the day."

Ethel thanked him and said goodbye.

Jesse took a deep breath. "Do you think whoever broke in found the hard drive in Davie's room?"

"No. I think they were looking for that KryptoFold device or the scrap of paper you found. They might have done a cursory search of Davie's room, but the odds are they saw that LEGO construction as a solid toy."

"Shouldn't we tell Director Bradshaw about it?"

"Probably." She gave him a conspiratorial smile. "But we don't know what we've found, do we? Let's determine that first so we don't waste Cory's valuable time."

He grinned. "Cousin Ethel, your consideration of others is truly awe-inspiring."

It was midafternoon when they pulled into Ethel's driveway. To their surprise, Lisa's and Douglas's cars were both parked on the street.

"What do we tell them?" Jesse asked.

Ethel opened the driver's door and got out. She turned back to Jesse who remained in his seat. "That we went to Richmond after our walk. I wanted to check on the Finch family. The first rule of undercover work is to stay as close to the truth as possible. Now you'll tell them you're tired and going up to rest. How long will it take you to re-create Jonathan's computer?"

"It depends upon how much data needs to be transferred. It could be an hour or two."

"Fine. Stay in your room until you have something to show me. Also, charge Pete's phone, and I'll get it from you later."

Jesse followed her through the back door and took the rear stairs. As he walked down the hall, Douglas and Lisa emerged from their rooms as if they'd been waiting for him. Their casual clothes indicated they both had the afternoon off.

Douglas eyed the backpack. "You okay? The note said you and Ethel went for a morning walk." He looked at Lisa. "We were afraid you'd developed some complication and had gone to the emergency room."

"We went to Richmond. Ethel wanted to check on Jonathan's wife. I didn't want her driving alone." He thought how ludicrous that sounded given she'd been "driving" at 4,000 feet, and he would have been no help whatsoever.

"How is Susan?" Lisa asked.

"As well as can be expected. Detective Mancini said Jonathan's name was being released today, and Ethel wanted to be there till her sister arrived from Fredericksburg."

"To stay with her?"

"Actually, Mrs. Finch and Davie are going to stay with her sister. That way they can avoid the press."

Lisa nodded her approval. "Admirable of Ethel, but I hope the trip wasn't too much too soon for you."

"I am a little tired and a little sore."

"Any developments on who attacked you?" Douglas asked.

"No."

"Let the man rest," Lisa said. "And you know the counterfeit money was lifted from your agency, so there's the pool of suspects, your own people."

Douglas scowled and his voice dropped to an intense growl. "One of my people, Jonathan Finch, was the man shot dead. I might be new to the service, but I know enough that this murder will not stand, even if Director Bradshaw pulled the trigger himself."

Jesse left them to make their peace. Both were correct. Solving Finch's murder would be all-consuming, but the likely suspects were inside the agency. With Mancini's discovery of the stolen Malibu and the CCTV footage, the conspiracy had to involve three people, and one of them would surely have slipped up somehow.

He closed his bedroom door, set his laptop on his desk, and began transferring the contents of his internal drive to his own Time Machine backup.

His phone buzzed. WhatsApp notified him of a new text from Tracy.

> have researched the KryptoFold model you found. serves to manage both private keys and virtual wallets. BAD NEWS. requires two stage process to access. fingerprint is read like on iPhone and sends a ten digit code to your computer. enter code at prompt and then KryptoFold directly applies private key. you can bypass both stages if enter private key manually. good luck. talk later?

Jesse stared at the text for a moment and then replied:

> THX talk tomorrow.

He picked up the KryptoFold. The texture of the black surface changed at one end. Here was where the print would be read. If Jesse could create an exact clone of Finch's computer, then the ten-digit code generated by the device should appear as a message. But that stage would be unattainable without first unlocking the device with a fingerprint—the fingerprint of a dead man.

Chapter 23

Ethel turned on the computer atop the small desk in her bedroom. An email had arrived from Frank Mancini with a zip file attached. She noticed he'd sent it from his personal address and realized he was counting on her to keep the materials to herself.

Uncompressing the attachment revealed ten photos taken the previous day. They showed the outside of the back door with the broken pane, the inside hallway with shards of glass on the floor, and the basement stairs taken from multiple angles. Forensics had marked the spots where Jesse's feet and head had landed. The placement suggested he'd tumbled from a high enough step to turn one hundred eighty degrees. Ethel deduced his assailant used more than a roundhouse punch. The blow was precise and powerful, not necessarily because of the attacker's size but rather his skill and technique. She reviewed the photos carefully for a second time, then made a phone call.

"What is it, Ethel?" Director Cory Bradshaw sounded exasperated.

"I wanted to thank you for the speed with which you got an agent in place for Susan and Davie Finch."

"You're welcome. And I understand from Frank Mancini that you alerted him to the suspicious activity."

"We were fortunate to have gone down to check on her. Sorry I didn't get a good look at the driver, but I have a suggestion."

Bradshaw laughed. "I'm sure you do."

"There's no way around the fact that at least some of the participants in this counterfeit theft are Secret Service agents. And they could have been on the original bust. If I could see their photographs, I might be able to make a partial identification."

"Based on what?"

"Hair color. Ear shape. He had close-cropped blond hair, and his ear stuck out a little."

"I don't know, Ethel. I'm moving forward in that area, checking alibis and access. Let me narrow the field and then we'll reevaluate."

"All right. You know I won't interfere."

Bradshaw laughed louder. "Did we just pass into an alternate universe?"

Ethel ignored the gibe. "Frank told me about the brain tumor the autopsy uncovered."

"Yes. That must fit somehow. We'll need to follow up with his wife and his doctor."

"I can help with Susan if you like."

"Thanks, but this will be a more formal interview. Anything else? I've got a staff meeting I'm late for."

"Just one thing, and it's about the attack on Jesse. Did you find anything useful on his clothing?"

"I had the lab share the report with Frank. I'm afraid it doesn't help him. There was nothing at all to show Jesse came in contact with his assailant."

"Nothing?"

"Nothing. His clothes could have come straight from the wash."

Ethel rang off and closed the crime-scene photos. She wouldn't interfere, but she'd not stand idly by. Suddenly, she felt tired. She'd been up before dawn, driven to Manassas and back, flown to Richmond and back, and kept her mind racing the entire time. Just a few minutes of rest would be refreshing. She slipped off her shoes and lay down on top of her bedspread.

———

Jesse heard the chime signal his computer had been restored from Jonathan's backup drive. The first thing he noticed was the screen photo was no longer the Golden Gate Bridge but a picture of Susan and Davie sitting side by side on swings in a city park.

A cursor blinked in a space named "Password." Jesse groaned. Hacking past the password of a cybercrime investigator could be a real challenge. But if this was a personal computer, even a family computer, just maybe. He typed "Davie." A circling icon appeared and suddenly the screen was populated by three folders: DAVIE, PHOTOS, and DOWNLOADS. A warning message appeared in the upper left corner—"No Internet Connection." Since the internal drive no longer held the data from Jesse's computer, it couldn't automatically join the house Wi-Fi. He quickly entered Ethel's Wi-Fi password and saw the connection restored.

Jesse picked up the KryptoFold device and plugged it into a USB port, hoping that he wouldn't take a misstep that might cause the program to self-destruct. A small blue light on the device glowed. A new window appeared on a quarter of the computer screen, first as an animated wallet opening to release icons of various cryptocurrencies—Bitcoin, Bitcoin Cash, Ethereum, and others Jesse didn't recognize—and then a text prompting him to use touch ID to sign in. Jesse knew that was a dead end and waited. Less than thirty seconds later, the program linked to an internet site that securely handled manual transactions. He was asked to enter his virtual wallet address and currency type. He checked the slip of paper he'd found wrapped around the KryptoFold. The long string of numbers and characters most resembled the format used by Bitcoin, but that was a useless guess unless he could find the wallet.

Jesse focused on the possibility that the address might be somewhere on the computer itself. A search of the key words, "wallet," "virtual wallet," "Bitcoin," and "cryptocurrency," yielded nothing. The prospects for discovering the address significantly narrowed. He moved to the individual desktop folders. DOWNLOADS was empty. It was probably just a destination folder with content moved elsewhere. PHOTOS had subfolders of various activities: Susan's birthday, Williamsburg trip, Disney World, and family gatherings at Christmas and Thanksgiving. One of the women bore a striking resemblance to Susan, and Jesse assumed she was the sister from Fredericksburg.

The DAVIE folder was also subdivided but by age categories: INFANT, TODDLER, 4–5, 6–7, MISC. They too contained JPEG photos. Jesse opened a few from each. They chronicled the boy's life from the hospital NICU to the present. As an infant, he seemed to be in a specially designed stroller and car seat. More recent photos showed him in either his walker or a small wheelchair.

Through all the photos, Jesse noticed Davie never had a normal physique. His legs were the most deformed, but his arms and torso also looked abnormal. Yet every photo made clear that Jonathan and Susan loved their little boy. How difficult it must be to worry that he was always only one fall, one inadvertent stumble from a catastrophic health crisis.

MISC turned out to be photographs of Davie's LEGO and Tinkertoy creations. Sometimes only the finished model was visible. The replica of Jonathan's Ford Escape was one. In the picture, it sat on Davie's bedroom table where Jesse had seen the boy work. A sheet of computer paper protruded from underneath the LEGO wheels. A few lines of text were visible. Jesse enlarged the image until they were legible. The first line read "the secret." Beneath it were three lines of numbers and characters. Virtual wallet addresses. Jesse's hand trembled as he zoomed in until the print began to blur. Was he seeing what Jonathan had whispered? "the secret?"

He wanted to let out a whoop and run down to get Ethel. But a realization tempered his enthusiasm. If he had found the addresses, surely the people who had taken Jonathan's computer had as well. Furthermore, Lisa and Douglas were in the house. Ethel would want to keep things quiet until she knew exactly what he'd uncovered. *Tell Ethel the secret.* Did that mean tell no one else?

He wrote down the three addresses in the Notes app on his phone. Then he returned to the internet site for manual transactions. A cursor blinked on a blank space. Beneath it was the label WALLET ADDRESS. Carefully, Jesse entered the first one on the list and hit enter. The screen changed to a new page with the address as the header and various options offered beneath it. He clicked CHECK VALUE and a number of currency choices appeared including euros, pounds, Canadian dollars, and U.S. dollars. He selected U.S. and stared at the screen in astonishment. The virtual wallet contained Bitcoins currently worth $20,005,623.17. And that was after Bitcoin's value had decreased three percent in the previous twenty-four hours.

Recent activity showed the transfer of over half a million dollars to the second wallet address on the list. He checked that wallet. Only ten thousand remained, but the activity report showed half a million transferred out between 4:10 and 4:15 Monday morning—the estimated time of Finch's rendezvous at the parking deck. Jesse entered the third address. The wallet had no value, but the half a million had passed through it late Monday afternoon. The events became clear. Jonathan Finch had taken funds from CEO Dwayne Parker's embezzled stash and used it to buy the cash, cash that turned out to be counterfeit. Was the private key he'd found written on the scrap of paper the one that would open the lock to over twenty million dollars?

Jesse forced himself to take a deep breath before trying the key. He returned to the prompt marked ACCESS ACCOUNT. Carefully, he entered the long chain of characters. He hit Enter and red letters appeared in a screen banner. KEY NOT RECOGNIZED. He was positive he'd made no error. He tried the key on the wallet with the ten grand. A blue-lettered banner. CLEARED FOR TRANSACTIONS. Jonathan had set up this wallet. But how had he accessed the multimillion-dollar account?

Jesse checked the time. Five thirty. Ten thirty in London. Odds were Tracy was still awake. He texted her a message:

need to talk asap via WhatsApp. no Skype.

He knew she'd understand he wanted the most secure connection available.

Five minutes later, she called.

"Something's happened, right?"

"Yes. Something big. I re-created Finch's computer and was able to link to virtual wallets."

"You were able to use the KryptoFold?"

"No. I found wallet addresses and worked manually." He explained the actions he'd taken and what he theorized had transpired. "I'm going to share this with Ethel, but I want you to have the same information. Get ready to write. I'm giving you the addresses and the private key to the smaller account. Set up your own wallet and transfer all the funds from the one we can open. Our killers might be trying to do the same thing. And try and trace the coins that Finch gave them. Do that as quickly as you can while I cover Ethel."

"Jesse, you know they'll see someone has taken the ten grand."

"I know. But they won't know who I am. Or you. We'll talk in the morning. Meanwhile not a word to anyone."

———

A gentle knock roused Ethel. She opened her eyes to a darkened room. Still foggy with sleep, she fumbled for her phone and checked the time. Seven thirty.

The knock repeated. She got up and switched on the overhead light. "Who is it?"

"Jesse. I've got something to show you."

She opened the door. He stood smiling and gripping his closed laptop like someone might rip it from his grasp.

"You recovered Jonathan's data?"

"Yes," he whispered. "You won't believe what I found."

"A link to KryptoFold's CEO Dwayne Parker."

His smile vanished. "How did you know?"

"It has to be why they searched the Finch house. They found what you found and are looking for the private key. So, how much are we talking about?"

"Over twenty million."

Ethel nodded slowly. "Few people would be immune to that temptation."

"What are you saying?"

"Just that we know the initial conspiracy involved at least three people. Were they at the same level, or does this thing go higher?"

"How much higher?"

"How high can you stack twenty million dollars?" She put on a pair of slippers. "Let's not talk here. The workout room would be better."

Jesse followed her down the basement stairs, acutely aware of what had happened the last time he was on these steps. They sat together on the weight bench and he opened the laptop to show her the various wallets and their values. Then he told her about contacting Tracy to be a backup resource out of the country.

"Probably a good idea," Ethel agreed. "Moving what money she can will at least keep us a step ahead. You say she can tell the history and present location of these coins?"

"Yes. That's the beauty of cryptocurrency. Each coin is created with its own unique code. It cannot be duplicated. Even though it's virtual property, just like a physical dollar bill, it cannot be in two places at once. Its location and movement through transactions are recorded by the blockchain, which are simply ledgers written by people called miners who independently confirm the accuracy of the data and create the records. They are paid in coins for their efficiency. The whole system is completely decentralized, which is why governments with central banks and taxing agencies are leery of them."

"And you think Tracy can follow the coins into the future as well?"

"Yes, but that may not be of benefit for long. I expect the Bitcoins to be converted at an exchange into another cryptocurrency that provides greater anonymity. The original coins would then be held in the exchange until someone else bought them."

"Why wouldn't the embezzler Parker have converted them himself?"

Jesse shrugged. "Good question. My guess is that since Bitcoin is the oldest, he considered it the most stable."

"And the prospects for finding the key to the wallet with Parker's fortune?"

"Not good. I'll go back through the photos and files on the laptop to see if Jonathan hid it in a similar manner, but I'm not optimistic. Our other option is to search through Davie's LEGOs and Tinkertoys again."

Ethel looked at the glowing KryptoFold device still plugged into the computer's USB port. "There's one other option."

"What's that?"

"We get Jonathan's finger."

———

Trevor Norwood had read the text with disappointment.

searched house. no key. what now?

His all-caps, one-word response:

WAIT

Wait for the woman and boy to come home. Wait for the internal furor over Finch's death to subside. He knew he'd be questioned, maybe even by Bradshaw himself, but nothing linked him to the counterfeit bills and certainly nothing linked him to CEO Dwayne Parker. Let things play out. Then he would find out what the woman knew.

He'd fixated on Finch's laptop, watching the values of the untouchable wallet change as the price of Bitcoin fluctuated. That was when he noticed the other wallet change. The ten thousand dollars in coins was disappearing before his eyes as it was transferred to a new account. Someone had that private key. It had to be the wife. And she would tell him what he wanted to know.

Chapter 24

Ethel knew Lisa Draper usually came down to the kitchen every night for a banana before going to bed. It was a ritual Ethel had introduced to her. Thirty years earlier, a nurse from the Philippines had told Ethel the fruit had soporific powers. For the past three decades, she had never had trouble falling asleep after taking the advice.

Now Lisa insisted on restocking the banana supply. Although Ethel's roomers didn't eat full meals there, they had always been good about replacing whatever they did eat or buying their own favorites.

At a few minutes past ten thirty, Ethel heard Lisa's soft footsteps on the back stairs. She started slicing a banana on a small plate so that Lisa wouldn't realize she'd been waiting at the kitchen island to make sure they crossed paths.

"Ethel, why are you still up?" Lisa stopped by the refrigerator, surprised that her landlady hadn't already gone to bed. Wearing a white terrycloth robe loosely cinched over aqua silk pajamas, Lisa was clearly ready to go to bed herself.

"Lots of thoughts ricocheting around in my mind. But don't let me stop you if you were going to take your banana back to your room."

"No. I'd like to join you, if that's okay." Lisa took a banana from the fruit basket on the counter and eased onto the stool across from Ethel. "How many conversations have you had around this island?"

"More than I can count and more years than you've been alive."

Lisa snapped off the stem and stripped the yellow peel halfway down. "You should have a reunion. Make up T-shirts. 'Ethel's Army.'"

Ethel laughed. "I'm afraid a lot of my army has mustered out of this mortal coil and the rest lead lives too busy to include this old woman."

"Nonsense. You're a legend. I can't tell you how many people are envious that you rented me a room till I find more permanent accommodations."

"No rush. I assume you and your ex-boyfriend have come to terms."

"I moved the last of my things into storage over the weekend. We're done."

"Still planning to go back to the Philadelphia office?"

Lisa nodded as she chewed banana. Then she swallowed and said, "I suppose I could stay in DC, especially since we have some loose ends in the Parker case."

Ethel picked up a slice of banana and popped it in her mouth.

Lisa filled the silence. "You know Jonathan and I talked about the case a little. He suspected Parker had hidden his millions in cryptocurrency, but no one ever found a web address or private key."

"How thorough was the search?"

"Down to pulling out the inserts of his shoes to see if anything was written under them."

"What about a computer or a laptop?" Ethel asked.

"As far as I know, Parker had a laptop but the hard drive had been completely scrubbed by some destructive program. Maybe he had the necessary information stored somewhere we can't trace."

"So, what do you think happened?"

Lisa finished the banana and folded the peel in her hand. "I think he converted the embezzled money into cryptocurrency and probably moved it through multiple coins—Bitcoin, Bitcoin Cash, XRP, Ethereum—and then maybe back to Bitcoin because it's the most widely circulated. From there it could have gone to an offshore or Swiss account after creating a convoluted crypto trail impossible to follow. Parker may have arranged to have the codes physically stashed in a safe deposit box in some bank out of the country."

"So, whether in a bank account or virtual wallet, that money is lost?"

Lisa hopped off the stool and dropped the banana peel into the trash. "That's where I see this ending up." She turned on the sink faucet and washed the residue from her hands. She dried them on a paper towel. "Do you think there's any connection?"

"To what?"

"To the Parker case and Jonathan's murder."

"I don't know. What do you think?"

Lisa thought a moment. "I think Jonathan suspected something wasn't kosher in the counterfeiting division but didn't want to say anything till he had some proof."

"I wonder what tipped him off?"

"Somebody must have said something that made him suspicious. That's my guess."

Ethel picked up a banana slice and then put it down. "Douglas was on that team that busted the New York ring, the one where the bogus money came from."

Lisa's eyes widened. "But you don't think Douglas was involved, do you?"

"No," Ethel quickly answered. "Of course not. I'm confident he won't be a match."

"A match for what?"

"The shooter's DNA from the blood in Jonathan's SUV." Ethel put a finger to her lips and peered down the back hallway as if she thought someone might be listening. Then she whispered, "Bradshaw's going to require everyone on that team to give a DNA sample. He wants to rule out an inside job."

"Really?"

"Yes, but don't say anything. I shouldn't have told you."

Lisa stood quietly for a second.

"What?" Ethel asked.

"You really are amazing. I can't tell you what an inspiration you are to me and so many other women in the Bureau. The trails you blazed for us."

Ethel shrugged. "I was just stubborn enough to stand my ground. And when the boys gave an inch, I took a mile. Not for me, but for the Bureau and all it stands for. That's my advice to you. It's about integrity, fairness, and justice indiscriminately applied. Make those your goals and you'll blaze your own trail."

"Thank you." Lisa turned to leave, then stopped. "As for your racing mind, treat yourself to a second banana and sleep well."

Later, Ethel sat on the edge of her bed, more troubled than she'd been before the conversation with Lisa. Had she given the impression that she considered Douglas Gray to be a suspect to be investigated? Would Lisa take that on herself? Or would Lisa tell him what Ethel said about the mandatory DNA sampling? She'd thrown a stone in the pond to watch the ripple effects and weigh the consequences.

But what weighed heaviest upon her was the advice she'd

given Lisa. Integrity, fairness, justice. How did concealing Jesse's discovery of Jonathan's hard drive, and the existence of the multimillion dollar wallet, square with those values? The Secret Service or FBI might be able to hack past the private key, but other than accessing the money, it would only remove the carrot that might keep Jonathan's killers in the game. She thought about what her father would have done. What he would have prioritized. Three words sprang to mind and she heard them in his long-silent voice: "Solve the case."

She and Jesse had Jonathan's KryptoFold device. If they couldn't get that to work, then they would be at a dead end, and she would turn over everything they'd discovered. She knew that would reflect badly upon Jonathan Finch at a time when his wife and son needed an honorable memory to cling to. The revelation of the backup drive could wait till after the funeral.

She checked her watch. Twenty minutes after eleven. Late but not so late to keep her from calling. She picked up her phone and speed-dialed.

Cory Bradshaw's voice rumbled. "What now?"

"I'm anticipating an inquiry from Susan Finch first thing in the morning regarding the status of her husband's body. I'm hoping you can give me something to tell her."

Without hesitation, he offered, "We're releasing the body tomorrow. I planned on notifying her first thing."

"Good. That's good. Do you know anything about a funeral service?"

"Just that we received a call from a funeral parlor in Richmond. Walker or Walthers. They said when the body was released it should come to them. Why?"

"Just an address to send flowers, but I can ask Susan in the morning."

"Do me a favor and ask whether she now has a funeral date. I'd like to have as many of Finch's colleagues attend as possible."

"Certainly. Thanks, Cory."

"Anything else to tell me?" he asked before she could disconnect.

"Like what?"

"Like anything else?"

Ethel smiled to herself. His curiosity was the price she had to pay for calling him so late. "No progress on who attacked Jesse Cooper, if that's what you mean."

"I mean we all know you're not sitting on the sidelines. I want to make sure we're on the same team."

"We're on the same team, Cory, but even a team has players with specialty skills."

"And yours would be?"

"Being underestimated on the one hand and being a pain in the ass on the other."

Bradshaw broke out with an unrestrained laugh. "Well, I don't underestimate you. I guess that's why I'm stuck with your second attribute. All I ask is if you find one of my guys is dirty, you give me a heads-up. I don't want to be blindsided."

"All right. You know I'm not one to jump to conclusions, but if I find someone in the service is clearly dirty, I'll come to you first. Fair enough?"

"Fair enough. Good night, Ethel." He rang off.

Ethel held on to the cell phone and called up her video app. She replayed her recording of the crime scene of Finch's murder. The light was low and the footage grainy, but she watched as the camera moved across the body lying faceup, over the Beretta, and around the SUV's damaged grille that had led them to the shattered parking deck bar. The camera continued to the second rear passenger door with the glass shards visible on the pavement outside the door and the red stain of smeared blood on the inside.

She froze the image and whispered to herself. "It will come down to the blood."

———

Trevor Norwood was asleep in his recliner when the buzz of his phone woke him. At first he was disoriented, thinking his alarm had sounded. He'd set it to allow time to apply a thinner bandage and freshen up before going out of the apartment to meet Director Bradshaw. If he could survive the director's questions, he would be home free.

But the buzzes had been two text messages sent almost simultaneously. The first one—

we need to meet before Bradshaw usual place

The second text—

RIP 3 Handoff bag

He looked at the current time. A few minutes after one in the morning. He'd told them that someone had raided one of the wallets. So, whatever was shaking, it must be important that he be briefed before his meeting. And he understood he was being summoned to take charge of the remaining money. RIP threw him for a second, then he connected it to "usual place." Roosevelt Island Park off the George Washington Memorial Parkway. He pulled himself out of the chair and got his jacket and keys. "There'd better be a damn good reason," he muttered.

Chapter 25

Ethel stopped the treadmill when she heard her cell phone ring. A glance at the exercise machine's odometer showed she'd only gone one mile of her targeted two.

Despite her lack of sleep, she'd risen early to get her workout done before the day brought new surprises. The call at six fifteen promised to be the first. It certainly wouldn't be someone wishing her a good morning.

She recognized Mancini's number. "Frank. What is it?"

"Another dead Secret Service agent. This one's Trevor Norwood. Do you remember the name?"

"The agent that Bradshaw said headed the team on the New York counterfeit bust."

"The same. One of our night patrols found him at Roosevelt Island."

"Roosevelt Island? But that's in the District. And as a national park, the rangers have jurisdiction."

"Yes, but the parking lot is in Virginia, and our guys caught sight of a vehicle from the G.W. Parkway."

"When was this?"

"A little before four. It was a black Tahoe and must have circumnavigated the gate. Rather than bother the park service, they thought they'd check it out in case it was just an abandoned vehicle. Norwood was dead in the driver's seat, a gunshot wound to his left temple."

"Left-handed?"

"To be confirmed. The patrol team called me, and I called Cory. I've just left the scene where he's wresting control away from the rangers."

Ethel walked to the weight bench and sat. "So, this is a courtesy call to me?"

"If you want to call it that. I consider it living up to our bargain to share information."

"Thanks, Frank. Sounds like the Tahoe could be the vehicle Jesse saw driving away from Finch's murder."

"Could be," Mancini agreed. "But the real tie-in is what they found on the floor of the passenger's seat."

"A written confession?"

"Better than that. Two gym bags, one filled with bogus bills and the other filled with the mix of bills and newspapers that was stolen from your house. Trevor Norwood was a trained agent. He could have knocked Jesse out with one hand while holding a drink in the other."

"Where are you now?"

"Heading back to the department to write up a report. My case is still the attack on Jesse."

"What would you say to my fixing you fresh coffee and a ham-and-cheese omelet?"

"Ethel, I thought you'd never ask." He disconnected.

Ethel stood up quickly, then felt the room swim. She sat down hard, her knees weak and her head tingling. Had she gotten up too fast or stopped her workout too abruptly and her body hadn't reset? *I'm not a girl of eighteen.* She took some deep breaths, and the dizziness passed.

She expected Mancini to be no more than ten minutes away. She returned to her bedroom, changed out of her tracksuit, and went to the kitchen to start the coffee percolating. She decided to wait for him in the living room where she could see the front door and meet him before he knocked or rang the bell. No one was stirring upstairs, and she didn't want to wake them. At this point, she hoped to keep the conversation between the two of them.

A few minutes later, the Arlington detective parked his Camry at the curb in front of the house. Ethel had the door open before he reached the porch.

"They're all asleep," she whispered. "Let's talk in the kitchen."

Mancini chose his customary stool and watched Ethel close the kitchen door for greater privacy. She brought him a mug of coffee, and then she busied herself with the omelet.

Mancini cut to the chase. "So, what do you want to pry out of me with this food?"

Ethel whisked the eggs in a bowl while keeping her back to him. "Well, if you've told me everything you know, then I'd like to talk through some questions I hope are being asked."

"Like what?"

"Like why the hell would Norwood go to the trouble to drive to Roosevelt Island, when he could have more easily killed himself at home?"

"Maybe he didn't want someone he knew finding a mess. Better to be discovered by a total stranger than a loved one."

Ethel looked over her shoulder. "Did he have a loved one?"

"I don't know. I'm sure Cory's delving into his personal life."

Ethel reached into a bottom cabinet and retrieved a large cast-iron skillet. "Which means he should get to Norwood's house or apartment as soon as possible. As Jesse witnessed, two men ran off with Jonathan Finch's computer, phone, and the second half of the stolen counterfeit money. Norwood might have killed himself, but we've deduced that at least three people had to be in on the scheme for the logistics to work."

Mancini took a healthy sip of coffee and sighed. "I'm confident Cory's following up on all those points."

Ethel turned on a stove burner and set the skillet on it. Then she grated cheese and diced slices of ham onto a small cutting board. "My questions are simply my due diligence for Jonathan and Jesse because at least two suspects are out there, and for some reason, they're still interested in Finch's family. I'd like you to talk to Cory about my questions, including whether he'll do a DNA match of Norwood's blood to what he found in Jonathan's SUV."

"Why don't you ask him yourself?"

She poured the beaten eggs into the skillet. "I think he's sick of hearing from me."

Mancini laughed. "And I'm not?"

Ethel turned around. "Oh, I didn't realize you didn't want the omelet after all."

He raised his hands in surrender. "Okay. You win. Anything else?"

"Yes. Ask Cory if they found keys on Norwood's body."

"Keys?"

"More specifically, a house key. I think Cory's going to find someone has beaten him to Norwood's home."

Mancini considered this. "Then maybe I should ask him now."

"Your call, Frank. You know I'm not one to tell you how to do your job. But if you get him, remind him to send me photos of the agents who worked with Norwood on the counterfeiting case. I might be able to match one to the man I partially glimpsed cruising by the Finch house. The man who probably broke in and searched it."

Mancini pulled out his cell phone. "You know, a little chopped onion in that omelet would be nice."

Upstairs, Lisa Draper sat on the edge of her bed, fully clothed, but not ready to leave her room. She'd cracked her door and could hear muffled voices from downstairs. Maybe Jesse was up. She didn't think it was Douglas. His car hadn't been parked overnight. Then she heard Jesse's footsteps padding down the hall to the shared bathroom. Hers was the only upstairs bedroom with its own bath, which Ethel reserved for any female roomer.

One of the voices grew a little louder, and she recognized it as Detective Frank Mancini's. She checked the time. Six forty-five. He had to be bringing important news to show up so early. Her curiosity tempted her to tiptoe to the top of the rear stairway where she might overhear the conversation, but the possibility of Jesse discovering her when he emerged from the bathroom nixed that action.

Then she had another thought. Ethel probably wouldn't tell her what was going on, but she might tell her something-cousin Jesse. He seemed to be the one the elderly landlady was confiding in.

Lisa rose from the bed and checked herself in the mirror hanging over the bureau. Her eyes looked puffy from lack of sleep. Her white blouse was no longer crisp. More makeup and a change of clothes might have the desired effect on a grad student whose girlfriend was across the ocean. Not that Lisa would be a seductress, just a charming woman interested in engaging him in a flirtatious conversation, a conversation she would guide to the questions she hoped would yield information. Now that she had the ear of the director of the FBI, she wanted to keep that inside track and protect the access that could serve her so well.

Maybe she already had something to report. She grabbed her

phone and scrolled back through her call log. She found the private number Director Rudy Hauser had used.

"Yes?" The word was snapped short, no trace of sleep but rather the tone of someone with too much to do in too little time.

"It's Agent Draper, sir. Lisa Draper."

"Sorry. I didn't recognize your number. What's going on?"

She didn't want to start a report with "I don't know," even though she shouldn't know. Instead, she said, "That Arlington detective, Mancini, is here. I think he's been here a while."

"Do you know why?"

"I assume he's had a break in the case. I don't think Ethel called him because she could have done so last night. I just wanted to give you a heads-up in case you have sources that could provide more details."

"Thank you, Draper. I do."

There was a beat of silence as Lisa hesitated to say anything further.

"It's okay," Hauser said, "you can ask me."

"I'm only asking what I might need to know to be your eyes and ears here."

"Another Secret Service agent was shot last night. Arlington police found the body in a Tahoe parked in the lot for Roosevelt Island Park."

Lisa let out a gasp of air. "Wow. Mancini must be here to see if it ties in to Finch's death."

"Or the attack on the student, Jesse Cooper. Bradshaw has pretty much tightened control of the investigation into Finch's death. Now he's got another one. He'll be consolidating them into one case, a case that will cross over into our Parker case."

"How so?"

"The agent in RIP was Trevor Norwood. RIP, damned ironic."

"That name's familiar."

"It should be. Norwood headed up the bust of the New York counterfeit ring and netted the evidence haul that Jonathan Finch brought into Ethel Crestwater's house. And you know Finch was the man who found Dwayne Parker's body."

"I know, sir. I was also on that case."

"So, this thing could be mushrooming. Don't get me wrong. Half a million in bogus bills is nothing to sneeze at, but my gut tells me the focus of the case is shifting, shifting to the twenty million Parker squirreled away somewhere. I want that money."

The way Hauser stated the demand, Lisa wasn't sure it was personal or professional.

"Yes, sir. I'll keep my eyes and ears open."

She heard Director Hauser take a deep breath.

"How well do you know Douglas Gray?" he asked.

"Well enough to speak to. We've shared wine and tea with Ethel. We're both on crazy schedules. Why?"

"Because he was on Norwood's team. Pay attention to how he reacts to this news."

Lisa saw the chance to interject what she hoped would catch Hauser's attention. "I don't think Douglas came in last night. He was out when I went to bed, and I don't think he's here this morning. At least I haven't heard him, and I've been up for a while."

"Interesting," was all Hauser said. "Very interesting."

———

At a few minutes before seven, Douglas Gray drove his silver Honda Accord slowly down North Highland Street. The faint light of the pending sunrise enabled him to cut off his headlights, and he hoped he would find curbside parking within a block of Ethel's house.

Although she and the others were used to his crazy hours, he wasn't returning wearing his customary dark blue suit but rather the black jeans and tan fleece of the night before. The problem with living with fellow agents was they were so damned observant. With luck, he'd enter through the back door unobserved.

As he approached Ethel's, he saw Lisa's and Jesse's cars parked in front. If his fellow roomers were up, he'd say he'd crashed at a friend's apartment. But as he passed the house, the front door opened, and Detective Frank Mancini stepped out on the front porch. Ethel stopped on the threshold behind him. Both looked his way. Well, he was an adult. He didn't owe them an explanation. Maybe better than the friend excuse, it would be more plausible if he claimed he'd been on overnight surveillance.

Maybe it was good he'd been seen. It gave him a reason to ask why the Arlington detective had made such an early call. Whatever he learned, he'd parlay that information into a need to contact Bradshaw. He wanted to have the director's ear and stay in the loop.

His phone buzzed, and he glanced at the screen. Speak of the devil. "This is Gray, sir."

"Are you up?" Bradshaw asked.

"Yes, sir."

"Come to Roosevelt Island Park immediately. No questions and don't talk to anyone." A click and he was gone.

Douglas Gray felt a knot tighten in his stomach. Bradshaw's tone had been ice cold. Suddenly, he wondered whether getting close to the director had been such a good idea after all.

Chapter 26

The alarm clock on Jesse's phone chimed softly, waking him at the desired time of six forty-five. It took a few seconds for him to fully emerge from what had finally become a deep sleep. He rolled out of bed, stretched, and exchanged his sleeping wardrobe of T-shirt and boxers for a clean T-shirt, clean boxers, and yesterday's pair of jeans. Then he walked barefoot down the hall to the bathroom.

He noticed Lisa's door was ajar, but the only sound was the faint murmur of voices from below. Probably Ethel talking to Douglas or Lisa. Maybe all three were up. He had no desire to join the conversation.

As soon as he used the toilet, he returned to his room and fired up the clone of Finch's computer to check the status of the virtual wallets. The one Tracy had drained was still empty. She'd sold the ten thousand dollars of Bitcoin at an exchange where she'd either bought U.S. dollars or another cryptocurrency. He smiled, thinking he had to trust her to eventually return the money because he had no way to retrieve it. Likewise, the half a million from Finch that had been split three ways had also been exchanged or sold, effectively ending the transactional trail.

Yet, the big prize still sat there—twenty million in Bitcoin—visible to him, to Tracy, and to whoever had Finch's computer. Jesse knew they would be desperately trying to access it as much as he and Ethel were. But he had the KryptoFold device and Ethel's audacious scheme for the unlocking fingerprint.

The click of the front door latch broke his concentration. He went to the window in time to see Detective Mancini get into his car. His had to have been one of the voices he'd heard. Something significant must have happened to bring Mancini out so early. Jesse sat on the bed and put on his socks and shoes. As he tied the final knot, there was a soft knock on his door.

He quickly moved to the desk where the laptop displayed the wallets' information. There was no time to power down, so he simply closed it. Then he cracked the door expecting to see Lisa or Douglas. Ethel pressed a finger to her lips and then whispered, "Come to the kitchen."

He nodded, stepped across the threshold, and closed the door behind him.

In the kitchen, Ethel handed him coffee and asked, "Would you like some breakfast?"

Jesse noticed a dirty mug and plate in the sink. "I'll have the same as Detective Mancini."

Ethel gave no indication that his comment surprised her. "Good. He had a ham-and-cheese omelet with a little dash of onion."

"Perfect. Are you considering changing into a bed-and-breakfast?"

"If it means getting information, then yes."

"What information?"

"The agent who headed this counterfeit bust, Trevor Norwood, was discovered shot in his Tahoe in the parking lot of Roosevelt Island Park. The missing currency was found with the body."

Jesse gave a soft whistle. "What's the theory?"

"Suicide. But no note. Just the incriminating bills."

"What's your theory?"

Ethel started cracking eggs. "Norwood was part of the team, maybe the mastermind. But he was the person Jonathan wounded, and he became a liability to the others. They killed him to break the link. You said the half million from Jonathan wound up being migrated to three wallets. That's got to be Norwood and two accomplices. I assume the coins have been exchanged?"

"Correct. For either dollars or another currency. The wallets are empty. So, what happens now?"

Ethel whisked the second batch of eggs and poured the mixture into the heated skillet. "Bradshaw will scrutinize everyone around Norwood. He'll go through his apartment with a fine-toothed comb. What he won't find is Jonathan's computer because that still offers the potential of a huge payday. They won't walk away from that."

"What are you going to do?"

"You and I are going to eat breakfast. Then you're going to go to class and carry on with your normal schedule, whatever that might be. Tomorrow we leave early for Richmond. Jonathan's body is being released this morning to the funeral home. I've looked them up. Walthers. Not too far from the Finch house. I want us there when they open. I'll say I'm coming ahead of the family and ask to see Jonathan. Maybe make sure there's no disfigurement that would shock Susan and Davie. If I can create a distraction, you get your computer out with the device and find the correct finger. Odds are it's either an index or a thumb. You think the device will then send a ten-digit code to Jonathan's Message app?"

"That's how Tracy said it works."

"Well, we not only want the wallet unlocked, we want that key visible so that you can screen capture it or something."

"There's probably a settings app once I get through the security levels," Jesse said. "Or I can put the coins in a new wallet with a new private key."

Ethel shook her head. "Wouldn't those holding Jonathan's computer see that happen?"

"Yes," Jesse admitted.

"I don't want to tip our hand yet. Not if we can devise a way to lure them into the open."

"But as we take this farther on our own, aren't we courting an obstruction-of-justice charge?"

Ethel dropped bits of ham, cheese, and onion into the skillet. "To make an omelet, Jesse, you have to break a few eggs."

———

Douglas Gray turned off the G.W. Parkway onto the access road for Roosevelt Island Park. A short distance in, he came to a barricade manned by a uniformed ranger.

Douglas lowered his window. "I'm here at the request of Secret Service Director Bradshaw." He flashed his ID.

The ranger studied it and then pulled a walkie-talkie from his utility belt. "I have a Secret Service Agent Gray to see Director Bradshaw."

"Copy that," came the reply. "Wait for confirmation."

The two-way went silent for a few minutes. Neither Douglas nor the ranger made small talk.

A crackle of static, then, "Wave him through. Tell him to park at the end of the lot opposite the crime scene."

"What's happened?" Douglas asked.

The man just motioned for him to drive ahead. A second

ranger directed him to a back corner where several marked and unmarked vehicles stood. He got out and started walking. Strands of fog drifted across the open lot, probably part of the morning mist that often hung over the nearby Potomac. He saw that a black Tahoe was partially covered by a white tent. The forensics team buzzed around the scene like bees around a hive.

Bradshaw stood to one side. As Douglas drew closer, he noted that the director was in his dark suit, white shirt, and red tie. Did the man sleep in those clothes? Douglas was conscious of his wrinkled fleece and jeans. Well, the choice had been to come suited or come fast.

Bradshaw walked toward him, his face grim as an executioner's. "Agent Gray, thanks for coming so quickly."

"Yes, sir. Ready to help any way I can."

Bradshaw studied the rookie agent. Douglas was tempted to fill the silence but realized it would be nothing more than prattle.

"All right," Bradshaw said. "I've had a chance to review the reports of the New York counterfeit bust. It looks like Agent Norwood was the person who signed the evidence in and out. Does that square with you?"

"I don't know, sir. I was there for the sting, but I had no dealings beyond that. Norwood and others on the team worked with the prosecutors."

Bradshaw nodded. "And unofficially?"

Douglas shifted uncomfortably from one foot to the other. "Unofficially what, sir?"

"Did you see Norwood or the other team members?"

"Yes, sir. We met a couple of times for beers at the Dubliner."

"Social gathering?"

"Yes, but you know how it is. We'd rehash the operation. Try to reconstruct what happened. Norwood, and maybe some of the more senior team members, would be called to testify."

"As the new guy, did they always include you?"

"I wouldn't know. But I wouldn't expect so. And I went over to protective detail, where those hours and locations fluctuate. That's why I took a room with Miss Crestwater." Douglas took a deep breath and looked at the Tahoe. "May I ask what's going on?"

"Come see for yourself." Bradshaw led him to the driver's side and pushed aside the tent flap. He kept his eyes on the young agent.

Douglas gasped. The driver's window was down, but the passenger-side window looked like a red-and-gray Rorschach inkblot had been smeared on it. Smeared with blood and brain. He looked down. Sprawled across the console on his side lay the body of Trevor Norwood. A red circle surrounded by burned flesh marred his temple, the mark of a pistol barrel pressed in direct contact with the skin.

"Jesus," Douglas muttered. He searched Bradshaw's face for a clue as to what he was thinking.

The director's expression was as dead as Norwood. "Have you seen those bags before?" He cut his eyes back to the SUV's interior.

Douglas looked again and saw two gym bags on the floor in front of the passenger's seat.

"No, sir. Is it the missing money?"

"Yes. Do you know if Norwood was left-handed?"

Douglas pivoted to put his back to the grisly scene and closed his eyes. He didn't conjure up an image of Norwood holding a pistol or even a pen. No, he saw Norwood raising a pint of Guinness at the Dubliner, toasting the team for a job well done, lifting the glass high in his left hand. Douglas opened his eyes. "Yes, definitely."

"Good." Bradshaw stepped away and signaled for Douglas to join him.

They walked side by side, and Bradshaw didn't speak until they were out of earshot of the others.

"Do you know anything about Norwood's personal life?"

"No. Other than he was divorced."

"Girlfriend?"

"None that he mentioned. But he would be on his phone a lot. His personal, not his agency one."

Bradshaw halted and turned to face Douglas.

"Did you ever overhear anything?"

The younger man looked away. "Nothing specific. Just snatches of his side."

"Okay. So make an educated guess. Could it have been a girlfriend? Even a boyfriend?"

"Bookie," Douglas whispered. "I think Norwood was a gambler. A serious gambler."

"Umm. That can make a man desperate for cash." Bradshaw stepped closer. "Where were you last night?"

The question caught Douglas completely off guard. "Me? I was...I was at a friend's house."

"Name?"

Douglas's dark skin turned darker and his mouth went dry. "Cassandra Richards. *Mrs.* Cassandra Richards."

"And the night Finch was killed?"

"The same."

"And she'll vouch for your whereabouts?"

"I don't know, sir. She...she has a husband. He's out of town a lot."

Bradshaw's eyes narrowed. "Not in the agency, I hope."

"Oh, no, sir. I would never do that."

"Yeah?"

"I swear. Sandy's someone I've known a long time. Her marriage isn't a happy one."

Bradshaw said nothing.

"Do you want my resignation?"

"No. I want your eyes and ears on this case. You know how I learned you were out all night?"

Douglas shrugged. "I guess Ethel told you."

"No. Detective Mancini. He saw you drive by. He called me with a list of questions that had to come from Ethel. If you'd been in position in the house, you might have learned more than what he shared."

"Yes, sir. I understand."

"Good."

"Can I ask what Ethel's questions were?"

"Did we find another wound on Norwood? Did we find a house or apartment key? How many rounds were left in the pistol? Could I send her photos of Norwood's team? Had I checked your alibis?"

"Me? She suspects me?"

"Of course she does. And with good reason, I'd say. But if you're innocent, you've got no one better covering your back. Remember that."

"And the answers to her other questions?"

Bradshaw smiled for the first time. "Norwood has a separate, earlier wound to his shoulder, and it looks like the interior of the vehicle shows older traces of blood that someone attempted to clean. His keys were in the ignition, but there's no house or apartment key on the ring or on the body. Two rounds are missing in the pistol, but Norwood was shot only once. And Ethel might be able to ID a suspicious driver who was casing Finch's house, and that's why I'm sending the photos of your case team to her."

"Well, she would have recognized me. I'm the only Black agent on the team."

"Right. But we now figure Norwood had two accomplices, and odds are they both are part of that team. Your team. So the best way to prove you're not one of them is to find them."

———

Jesse realized he hadn't thought through the consequences of turning his laptop into a clone of Finch's. That became clear when he went to review his class notes and saw Finch's screen instead. Backing up Finch's data and reinstalling his own would run the risk that something could go wrong with the transfer. Better to leave everything in place until after the next day's visit to the funeral home.

In the meantime, Jesse's study options were reduced to his iPhone and the documents that were backed up in the cloud. He found taking notes on his notes improved his recall of the information garnered through his professors' lectures. He was in the process of distilling key concepts into a notebook when someone knocked on his door.

"Come in." He didn't bother to get up from his desk.

Lisa Draper entered, flashing a big smile and a cheery "Good morning."

Jesse slid back his chair.

"Don't get up. I don't mean to disturb you." She made the claim as she closed the door and sat on the unmade bed. Springs creaked.

"My. Rather noisy." She bounced up and down. "Mine are much quieter."

Her coy look flustered him, and he was embarrassed for feeling embarrassed. "I'm a sound sleeper," he managed to say.

"Not that anybody's getting much sleep. You know Detective Mancini was here before seven. What was that about?"

"Another Secret Service agent was shot. I didn't talk to Mancini, but Ethel said the victim was the agent who headed up the investigation into the New York counterfeit ring."

"Trevor Norwood?"

"You know him?"

"No. Just the name in regard to the money Jonathan had. Has a motive been determined?"

Jesse shook his head. "Suicide seems to be the prevailing theory, although Ethel thinks his own partners might have silenced him."

"Contain the problem," Lisa said. "I'd like to know the real reason behind Jonathan's murder. I can't help but think it ties in to my Parker case. Someone might think Jonathan held back information about the circumstances surrounding Parker's alleged suicide."

"Do you?"

She looked out the window for a second, and then gave Jesse a hard stare. "I don't know what to think. Please don't tell Ethel, but I've worked myself into a position where Rudy Hauser's pushing me to discover if and how this all ties together. Me, reporting only to the director of the FBI. It's like he wants to keep everything a secret until I can hand him those funds Parker embezzled." She lowered her voice. "I hate to say this, but I'm not sure what he intends to do with them. I mean, I'd be tempted, wouldn't you?"

"I'd have a better chance of winning the lottery."

She shifted her gaze to Jesse's closed laptop. "But you're a computer guy, right? Someone who creates the codes is the best person to hack the codes."

"Except cryptocurrency encryption is written by the best in

the world. No, I think your only chance is to discover Parker's private key."

She laughed. "Right after you win the lottery." She bounced up and down squeaking the bedsprings. "Well, I'd better let you study before Ethel thinks I'm corrupting her double-first-cousin-twice-removed." She glanced again at his closed laptop. "For a computer scholar, why are you studying using your iPhone?"

Jesse looked at the laptop like it had just appeared out of nowhere. "Umm, it's in the middle of a download. Software upgrade. I wanted to complete it before I head to class."

She stood. "Well, thanks for listening. It's nice to talk with someone who is not and never has been in law enforcement. Talking shop isn't a way to make friends." She opened the door, then turned back. "Although if you learn anything that involves my case, I'd appreciate a heads-up." She left, closing the door behind her.

Jesse sat there. Had she just shared more than she should have? Was there a chance that the director of the FBI was somehow keeping an operation off the books? He wanted to ask Ethel, but Lisa had taken him into her confidence. Lisa of the quiet bedsprings.

———

Ethel heard Jesse leave for campus. Douglas hadn't returned since he'd driven by early that morning, and she wondered what that was about. She thought Lisa was working upstairs on her FBI computer, one that could be used securely in the field, but she suspected Rudy Hauser had told her to stick close as his eyes and ears. Neither Rudy nor Cory Bradshaw were the subtlest of agents to pass through her house.

She unfolded a small stepladder she kept in the back of her bedroom closet and climbed three steps to where she could reach the top closet shelf. Remembering her brief dizzy spell, she leaned against the doorjamb for extra support as she lowered an old leather-bound scrapbook, the kind with protective plastic sleeves and a binder that allowed pages to be added.

She sat on the bed and ran her forearm across the cover to wipe away the dust. She wasn't sure how long ago it was that she'd last looked at it. Not since Douglas and Lisa moved in. Maybe six months. Maybe a year. She smiled as she recalled one of the older agents who had taken her under his wing. He'd told her, "Life is like a roll of toilet paper—the closer you get to the end, the faster it goes." At the time it was funny; at the present it was truth.

She opened the book to the first page of pictures. They were black-and-whites. The oldest was of her and her father. He wore a double-breasted pinstripe suit. She was in a frilly dress and bonnet. Her aunt had to have picked it out. A penciled date in the white border read, "Easter—1949." She was two. The motherless child of the family. They would have gone out to the cemetery after church. Although she didn't remember that trip, she remembered the other times. The stone had been scary. Accusatory. Her mother's death date was her birth date. She and her father had always celebrated her birthday one day early.

She flipped forward through the years. Her favorite picture was of her and her father standing in front of the little single-wing Cessna 195, vintage 1951, but fourteen years old at the time. She was eighteen and had just soloed. From their grins, it was harder to tell who was prouder, father or daughter.

She skipped the photos some kind soul had sent her of her father's funeral. He'd obviously been trying to curry Mr. Hoover's favor, as J. Edgar appeared in most of them. Ethel looked through the years of faces of those who had lived in this house. She stopped at Frank Mancini. He was a little thinner, his hair a little thicker. Then came Rudy Hauser, ambitious from the start, destined to one day lead the Bureau. Bradshaw overlapped him by a year. He was Secret Service, but just as ambitious. Anything that hinted at competition pitted the two against each other. Some people, like some things, never change.

She stopped at Jonathan Finch's photo. The color had yet to fade. He was young and thin. She remembered the day he'd told her he'd become engaged. She brushed the protective sleeve as if trying to stroke his face, trying to touch his forever smile. She came to the end, where a fresh page was ready. When this was over, she'd have to add Douglas and Lisa. And, of course, Jesse. She had the feeling he could hold his own with any of them.

She flipped back to the photo of her with her father and the old Cessna. His death was as real to her as the book in her hand. Integrity, fairness, justice. She'd lived long enough to know they aren't absolutes. Context cannot be ignored. Her father would understand.

At least she hoped he would.

Chapter 27

Ethel carefully slid the scrapbook back onto the top shelf, folded the stepladder, and closed the closet door. Again, she felt a little dizzy, but not to the extent she had earlier.

Other than her abbreviated workout, she hadn't been physically active. Yet her mind had been racing since Detective Mancini's dawn phone call. The scrapbook had been a brief diversion from the troublesome events of the past few days until her final thoughts about her father brought them back again. Fifty-five years ago, the Bureau had hushed up the fact that an inside betrayer had caused her father's murder on that lonely West Virginia road. Then they'd hushed up the fact that Ethel had killed that betrayer. J. Edgar Hoover didn't like the Bureau's dirty laundry being made public. Would the same thing happen again?

Ethel checked the time. Two o'clock. Jesse wouldn't be back from class till after four. Maybe she'd rest on the bed and close her eyes for a few minutes.

She'd just laid her head on the pillow when her computer chimed that a new email had arrived. She moved to her desk. The sender was Cory Bradshaw with a short message:

Here they are. Get back to me immediately.

She downloaded the zip file, decompressed it, and discovered Bradshaw had provided the photo IDs of eight agents. Two were women, one was Douglas Gray, and the remaining five men looked like they ranged in age from thirty to mid-forties. Other than Douglas, the names meant nothing to her. She was surprised Bradshaw hadn't included Trevor Norwood.

Her cell rang. It was Bradshaw already.

Ethel answered. "Hi. I just got the photos. I can't get back to you till I have a chance to view them."

"Well, look at them now," Bradshaw said. "I'll wait on the line."

She enlarged each to fill her computer screen. She ruled out Douglas as she would have noticed his darker complexion. The two women had shoulder-length hair, and unless one of them had gone to a much shorter style, they couldn't have been the driver; the profile Ethel had seen included an exposed ear. And she was pretty sure that person's hair color had been blond. One man was blond, but hair can be dyed. Another had brown hair, and the third man was of Hispanic descent with coal-black hair.

"Well, I'm better at ruling out rather than identifying," Ethel said. "I see three possibilities." She read the names aloud. "Carver, Ellison, and O'Hara. I suggest you check them for alibis. This would have been yesterday morning around eleven in front of the Finch house."

"Okay."

"Why didn't you include a photo of Trevor Norwood?"

"Because it couldn't have been him. We found a receipt for a bottle of bourbon from a nearby liquor store with a time stamp that eliminates the possibility he was in Richmond."

"Unless someone made the purchase for him," Ethel said.

"We are checking for CCTV footage, but a credit card in his

wallet matched the one used for payment. And he was wounded in the upper left arm. Looks like he dressed and stitched it himself."

"Imagine that."

"Yeah, I know. You told me to check for a wound. His apartment key was also missing. The super had to let my team in. The place was sterile. He'd been living there about six months."

"Alone?"

"As far as we can tell. Norwood was divorced, although his ex is still on our records as next of kin."

"Have you contacted her?" Ethel asked.

"Not yet. I want to keep his identity quiet for a few more hours while we focus on who might have been his accomplices."

Ethel weighed Bradshaw's information. "I'd be interested to know why and when that marriage broke up."

"Douglas Gray thinks Norwood might have had a gambling problem."

"That would create a money motive," Ethel said. "Douglas still on your suspect list?"

"Not really. But don't tell him that."

"No, I wouldn't want to kill his incentive to report back to you on every breath I take."

Bradshaw chuckled softly. "That obvious, huh?"

"I've got nothing to hide," Ethel lied. "But I don't know if I'd discount him as a suspect, not unless he has an ironclad alibi. He wasn't here at the time of either death."

"His alibi is a little shaky. There's a married woman in the mix."

"Oh, dear, and she won't confirm, will she?"

"That's about the size of it," Bradshaw admitted.

"What about Jonathan Finch's laptop and phone? Were they in Norwood's apartment?"

"No. Maybe he never had them. Maybe they're in some garbage dumpster."

"Or maybe the phone and laptop are keys to what's still going on. Why someone broke into Finch's house looking for something more. I think you didn't find Norwood's apartment key because he was murdered, and someone took that key to get into the apartment ahead of you. I believe Norwood had the computer and the phone."

"And something on the computer is more than incriminating evidence," Bradshaw speculated. "Something they want."

"I don't have a gambling problem," Ethel said, "but that's where I'd place my bet."

"If it's the Parker case and the embezzled millions, then that casts a shadow over Jonathan Finch. Had he found more than he claimed?"

"Maybe. Maybe he was bluffing in an attempt to bring the rats out of the shadows. Willing to take a risk because he knew he was dying."

"It also explains why Rudy Hauser is so interested. You know he showed up at Roosevelt Island, allegedly offering the FBI's help?"

"And you don't think the offer is genuine?"

"Oh, it's genuine, especially if it links back to Parker."

"Any proof that Norwood's death wasn't a suicide?"

"You inquired about the cartridges in the magazine. There was room for two more. We found only one shell casing. So, I figure Norwood knew his attacker or attackers. They held him at gunpoint and forced him to give up his own pistol. They immediately used it to shoot him through the temple before he could react, and then they wrapped his dead hand around the grip and fired a shot in the air to create the expected powder residue on his skin. They picked up the second shell casing, quickly dressed the scene, took the apartment key, and left. Everything could have transpired in a matter of minutes."

Ethel studied the three photos again. "So, it comes down to Carver, Ellison, and O'Hara. Maybe two of the three were involved. Don't forget to see who has an alibi for when Jesse was attacked. And just because I saw one suspect doesn't mean any of the eight couldn't be the third accomplice, the person who attacked Jesse."

"Ethel, you're not going to let me forget anything, are you?" She disconnected. It was time to bring in Pete Varner.

He answered on the first ring. "Is this Amelia Earhart?"

"No, I'm not lost yet. And if I am, you'll find me, right?"

"I don't know what you're talking about."

"Where are you, Pete?"

"In the hayloft. Why? Are you looking for a roll in the hay?"

"You old flirt. Where were you fifty years ago?"

"Flying over North Vietnam."

"All right. That's an acceptable excuse. But what I'm looking for today is your email address. I'm going to send you some photographs."

"Of you?"

"Of the person you nearly rammed when you tried to slink off from your surveillance of me yesterday morning."

Silence. Then Pete sighed. "Guilty as charged. Guess I wouldn't make a very good spy."

"Let's just say your ground game isn't your air game. But I am interested in identifying who was in that other car. Did you get a good look?"

"You mean considering I nearly ran straight into him? Yes, if the photo re-creates an expression of surprise and panic, I should be able to recognize the poor bastard."

"Good. I'm sending you eight photos total, including two women on the off chance they had their hair pulled back or cut short. It's okay if you can't be sure. You can prioritize your maybes."

"You want to tell me what this is all about?"

"You want to tell me why I now own an extra phone?"

He laughed. "Curt and I were foolish enough to think you might be getting into something over your head. I was your unwanted backup."

"I'm touched. I really am. Look at the photos and we'll talk."

Twenty minutes later, Pete Varner called back. "I think the man matches the picture labeled Ed O'Hara. I can't be completely sure, but both he and the man I saw in Richmond have an angular face and thin eyebrows."

"Thanks, Pete," Ethel said. "That's very helpful."

"These certainly aren't police mug shots you sent. These look like official ID photos."

"They are, which is why I'm proceeding cautiously."

"Which means you're crossing dangerous paths, circumventing someone's authority."

She couldn't insult his intelligence by arguing. "Is this the phone you always keep with you?"

"Every place but the shower."

"Then take a shower tonight and keep it with you after that. I'll text you instructions if there's a way to help me."

"And a way to find you, Amelia?" he asked.

"Well, isn't that the point? Goodbye, Pete."

Ethel next placed a call to Agent Warren Hitchcock. The phone rang a long time before he answered it.

Without a hello, he said, "Sorry. I saw it was you and was talking to someone. After your last call to me, I didn't dare answer where I could be overheard. This place has gone crazy since those bills disappeared."

"Are you in trouble?"

"Nah. Fortunately, it appears the funny money most likely went missing during an archival move a couple of months ago. Thanks for keeping my name out of it, by the way."

"Sure. But I'm afraid I need another favor."

"Uh-oh."

Ethel could hear his wariness through the phone.

"Nothing big," she assured him. "But I need you to keep what I'm asking confidential. I want you to find out what you can about an agent named Ed O'Hara. He was on the original team for the New York bust. Anything at all."

"You think he's good for it?" Hitchcock asked.

"More likely he knows someone who knows someone. That kind of thing. His name popped up in an off-the-record conversation, and I don't want to trigger something official if there's nothing there."

"Okay. I can ask around. How soon do you need it?"

"Sometime tomorrow afternoon would be great. You can call me, or if the info's not too long, just text me."

"You got it."

"Great. I owe you, Warren."

"Then I'll collect at my favorite pub."

"It's a deal." She disconnected. There were no more calls to make, and she finally managed to get that elusive nap.

Later, as night fell, Ethel invited Lisa and Douglas to join her for a nightcap in the living room. Jesse declined, saying he had a paper to write. When he heard the steady stream of voices from below, he did as Ethel had instructed. But only after texting Tracy not to try to reach him until he contacted her first. Then he stowed his computer in the backpack, pleased that Ethel's revolver fit snugly underneath the power cord.

Chapter 28

Lisa Draper lay on her bed fully clothed. Although it was only six in the morning, she wanted to be ready in case Ethel made some kind of move. The woman seemed to have myriad connections in both the Secret Service and the FBI, and a maestro's skill to play those connections to her advantage. No doubt she had Norwood's team members identified and was probably even running a step or two ahead of Director Bradshaw.

Lisa's own boss suspected Ethel knew more than she was sharing. He seemed obsessed with the Parker case, and that put her under his micromanagement. She felt like a bug under his microscope.

But she sensed that today would be a turning point. With Norwood's death, the investigation would either permanently stall or make a breakthrough. And if a breakthrough, then she needed to be in the room where it happened. She also wanted a look at Jesse's computer. His "downloading software" comment had rung false. Clearly, he didn't want her to see what was on the screen. Maybe if he took a shower, she could sneak a few minutes in his room.

She heard the squeal of a hinge. Either Jesse or Douglas had opened his door. She sat up, ears tuned for any other sound. Distant footsteps drew nearer. It had to be Jesse. She thought he was heading for the bathroom, but the steps went past her and down the back stairs.

Lisa moved to her door. As she reached for the knob, she heard a second set of footsteps. These started closer. From Douglas's room. He moved even more quietly than Jesse. Mr. Martial Arts. Ninja Warrior. His footfalls faded as he followed Jesse downstairs.

Lisa checked that the hallway was clear and then quickly tiptoed to Jesse's door. She turned the knob. Unlocked. She opened the door wide enough to see his desk. The laptop and backpack were gone. Lisa hurried to the window in Finch's room, where she had a view of Ethel's car in the driveway. Jesse was putting his backpack on the rear seat. Ethel held a thermos and a small picnic basket. She handed them to Jesse, and he set them on the floor behind the driver's seat. Then Ethel held the car keys out to him. He looked surprised.

Lisa returned to her room and got her own keys and a leather bag she kept ready for unexpected events. Whether Douglas saw her or not, she didn't care. She knew Rudy Hauser would want her to follow Ethel. That was authority enough for her.

Standing by the Infiniti, Jesse stared at the keys in Ethel's hand. "You want me to drive?"

"Yes, if you don't mind. There are things I can do along the way."

"You've got the address?"

"Programmed in my phone GPS. ETA is a little before eight. I'm anticipating someone will be at the funeral home by then. According to their website, Walthers is still family-owned. Some of them might even live upstairs." She tossed him the keys and walked around the car to the passenger door.

Jesse slid behind the wheel. He noticed Ethel had already

stuffed a large handbag on the floor beneath her feet. "What else did you bring?"

"I printed out the eight photos Cory sent yesterday. I might need to show them to Susan. She could have seen someone in her neighborhood before the break-in, or worse, someone since she relocated to her sister's in Fredericksburg."

"Wouldn't the Secret Service agent guarding her recognize another agent?"

"Not necessarily. There are over three thousand agents."

"Not all on the East Coast," Jesse argued.

"No. But enough that I don't want to assume one agent would recognize another." She snapped on her seat belt. "Let's roll. We can review the case on the road."

Lisa stepped out onto the back porch as soon as she heard the car leave. She ran down the driveway in time to see the Infiniti turn left. She also saw Douglas pull his Accord away from the curb, clearly following Ethel.

As she rushed to her own car, Lisa checked the extra magazines she'd dropped in her blazer pocket and felt the reassuring weight of her shoulder-holstered Sig Sauer. Douglas Gray could be off the reservation. She may have to stop him.

Traffic was already heaviest coming into DC. Although Google Maps directed Jesse on a route that went against the plethora of commuters, I-395 South was still congested with ancillary traffic without express lanes to alleviate the flow. He and Ethel rode in silence until he'd traveled beyond the beltway and merged onto I-95 South. From the corner of his eye, he saw that Ethel was texting a long message and waited till she dropped her phone in her lap before speaking.

"Any word?" he asked.

"We've got two shadows, and they're so close together, we don't know which is which."

"Do you think Bradshaw or Hauser would have put a tracker on this car?"

"Possibly. And maybe off the books."

"Isn't that illegal?"

"Jesse, you have to realize there are two dead agents and twenty million dollars at play here. Frankly, I hope it is an unauthorized tracking. I can use that to negotiate away our own sins."

"I know. Break the eggs to make the omelet."

"And we don't have to be the ones breaking all the eggs. We just have to know how many chefs are in the kitchen."

Jesse shook his head. "I'm not much of a cook. Sorry I brought up the omelet metaphor. Can you tell me in plain English what you think is going on?"

"Yes, but be careful. Facts drive the theory, not the other way around. We're still gathering facts."

"Okay. And what is the theory your facts are supporting?"

Ethel held up two fingers. "Two key facts underpin what I see has happened. First, about six months ago, Dwayne Parker, the crooked CEO of KryptoFold, tried to make a run for it. Jonathan Finch showed up in time to thwart that plan, and rather than engage Jonathan in what would have become a shoot-out or make an attempt to escape on foot, Parker shot himself."

"So, the suicide happened?"

"Yes. The wound, the body, the single round, and shell casing all support that interpretation. But given the remoteness of Parker's mountain home, it took close to thirty minutes before other federal law enforcement arrived. Jonathan was well aware that Parker had siphoned off a substantial sum of his company's funds. Maybe Parker was leaving his computer to be packed last. He would have also kept the KryptoFold device near or on his person. With the device and the computer program, Jonathan could have quickly accessed the virtual wallet and transferred the funds into his own account, all using Parker's computer. I imagine there was a way to even reprogram the KryptoFold device."

"Wouldn't it look suspicious that Parker's computer was wiped clean?"

"Not really. Jonathan said Parker had done it to eradicate incriminating evidence. I expect Parker had some kind of sophisticated program to destroy the drive. Jonathan simply activated it and then waited for reinforcements."

"Why would he risk a peer-to-peer transaction with fellow agents?"

Ethel sighed. "That's an ironic twist. We know the basic fact that Jonathan got access to Parker's virtual wallet. As I said, that's key fact number one. We know the basic fact that Norwood and others got access to half a million dollars in counterfeit bills. That's key fact number two. I think they planned to sell those bills to a buyer, rip the buyer off, and then return the bills to evidence without anyone knowing they were gone."

"Jonathan meeting Norwood is a big coincidence," Jesse argued.

"Really? We have Jonathan wanting to sell Bitcoins, and Norwood wanting to buy. This so-called Dark Web would provide a means to arrange a transaction, right?"

"Yes."

"And probably some kind of filter for geographical locale and size of transaction. If Norwood puts out an offer of cash for Bitcoin, how many DC-area takers do you think he would have for a half a million dollars?"

"Not that many," Jesse conceded.

"You see, I think neither Jonathan nor Norwood knew they were dealing with another Secret Service agent. That didn't become evident until Norwood tried to reclaim the counterfeit dollars."

"So Jonathan's final words to me were cut off. 'Tell Ethel the secret' was meant to be 'Tell Ethel the Secret Service.'"

Ethel took a moment to answer. "Maybe. Or maybe he was going somewhere else with that whisper. Why didn't he say, 'Tell Ethel it was Norwood'?"

"Then what?"

"I don't know. Speculation would put the theory ahead of the facts. What we do know is Norwood and company took Jonathan's laptop. Probably to make sure nothing incriminating was on it. A link to whatever dark site they used to set up the anonymous exchange. Then they discovered what you found on the backup drive. And now they want the Bitcoin treasure that makes their half-a-million scam look like chump change."

"Why murder Norwood?"

"His blood was on the door of Jonathan's SUV. No explaining that away if he were required to provide a DNA sample. So he had to go or else he might have ratted out his accomplices."

"Was he required?"

"The real implication is if he wasn't."

With that cryptic comment, Ethel went back to checking text messages on her phone. Jesse wondered how high up this conspiracy could go. Bradshaw? Or Hauser, based on what Lisa had told him about the FBI director? He thought of Ethel's admonition not to get ahead of the facts. Stick with the plan. He mentally braced himself for what lay ahead, beginning with his grasping the hands of a dead man.

Walthers Funeral Home was located on the outskirts of Richmond only a few miles from the Finch house. The two-story structure looked like its white sideboards had been freshly painted, and the yard was nicely landscaped with lawn intermixed with flowerbeds. A circular driveway looped through a porte cochere that extended from a wraparound porch. A small, empty parking lot was on one side, and a triple garage on the other. Mounted in a stone wall terracing a raised bed of colorful fall pansies was a bronze plaque reading "WALTHERS— SERVING RICHMOND SINCE 1925."

"Park in the side lot," Ethel said. "I don't want to advertise our presence."

Jesse pulled to a stop next to a handicap space. He retrieved his backpack and carried it by one strap.

"Pop the trunk," Ethel said.

Jesse used the remote key fob, and the release clicked.

Ethel reached in and removed a wooden cane. The black sheen of its finish contrasted with the ornate silver handgrip. "Gives me a certain dignity, don't you think?"

"Definitely."

She winked. "And I want to be seen as future business. Make them a little more malleable to our request."

Jesse closed the trunk. "And I'll say as little as possible. Other than I'd appreciate a moment alone with my mentor, or should I say father figure?"

"Stick with mentor. Jonathan's too young for a father figure."

"Like an older brother," Jesse suggested.

"Sounds good. So, let's do this." She walked up the handicap ramp to the porch, tapping her cane in time.

A sign covered by a plexiglass shield hung over the glowing button of a doorbell. It read, "Please ring for assistance."

Ethel nodded her approval. "The Walthers must be available for grieving families day or night." She pressed the button and held it a few seconds. A buzz sounded from inside the door and also from the floor above. "They must have multiple units throughout the house."

Footsteps drew closer. The door opened, and a young woman greeted them with a warm smile. She wore a blue pantsuit not unlike an FBI agent's. "Good morning. Please come in." As she spoke, her eyes swept over them from head to toe. "What a beautiful cane, ma'am. Is it a family heirloom?"

"Future heirloom. I'm afraid I'm older."

The woman stepped back and gestured for them to enter. "I'm Evelyn Walther. How can we help you?"

"Ethel Crestwater. My grandson, Jesse Cooper. We're helping a dear friend."

Evelyn's countenance conveyed concern. Ethel thought if it wasn't genuine, the young woman was a good actress.

"I see. Why don't we step into the office and you can tell me what you need? Has there been a death in your friend's family?"

"Yes. But you're already handling the arrangements."

Evelyn looked confused. "The only family we're currently serving is the Finch family. Has there been a death overnight?"

"No. It's the Finch family. Susan is a dear friend." Ethel nodded to Jesse. "And Jonathan was a mentor to my grandson."

"He was like an older brother," Jesse said.

Evelyn clasped her hands together in front of her. "I see. I'm so sorry for your loss. But I had a good conversation with Mrs. Finch yesterday. I thought everything was worked out."

"Oh, it was, dear. And you have a wonderful reputation. You live here?"

"My family takes turns staying overnight. We want to be responsive."

"Yes, I can see that. And I don't mean to imply there's anything wrong. It's just when you reach my age and have attended so many funerals, well, you don't get a chance to make a second first-impression. Susan doesn't know we're here. We've come on our own initiative. It was a shock the way he died, and I just want to make sure everything is perfect when Susan walks in."

Evelyn Walthers took a deep breath and dropped her hands

to her side. "Mrs. Finch is supposed to come later today. But I was up early getting things ready. Some flowers arrived yesterday afternoon, and I've set those out. You're welcome to make changes in their presentation. Mrs. Finch said our smaller parlor would be sufficient, but any overflow can be accommodated by the whole first floor." She started walking. "If you'll follow me."

Ethel stayed close to the woman as the three left the foyer.

"We'll have the 'Those Who Called' book on a stand right outside the door." Evelyn led them down a short hallway. "It's here on the right."

"What suit did Susan decide on?" Ethel asked. "I assume she sent one down yesterday."

Evelyn Walthers stopped in mid-stride. She turned around, and her face was as pale as bleached chalk. "Suit? There must be some mistake. Mrs. Finch was very specific about the arrangements and what she wanted from our stock."

The woman stepped aside so that Ethel and Jesse could enter the room ahead of her.

There was a nice oak pedestal that could support a casket. Except there was no casket. Simply a display of fresh flowers forming a backdrop for a shiny bronze urn.

"See." Evelyn pointed as if they needed her instruction. "It's the John Keats Grecian model. Mrs. Finch said her husband loved poetry."

Ethel forced the words across her lips. "It looks lovely, dear."

Chapter 29

Jesse banged the palm of his hand on the steering wheel. "Cremated. Of course, he had to be cremated."

He and Ethel sat in the car still parked in the funeral home lot.

"Well," Ethel said, "it was a long shot, at best."

"Now it's an impossible shot."

Ethel seemed unperturbed. She checked her phone, texted a brief message, and then reached into the back seat for the thermos. She pulled two mugs from the handbag at her feet. "Have some coffee."

"I'm keyed up enough as it is. What do we do now?"

"The backup plan. Since we're stymied, we let the resources of the government either unlock the KryptoFold or circumvent the key somehow."

Jesse looked at her with alarm. "But they'll know we held on to that evidence."

"They might suspect, but they can't prove it."

"And the ten thousand dollars Tracy has?"

She smiled. "We cross that bridge later. I suggest we go to the Finch house straightaway. The sooner we get there, the sooner we find."

"We find?"

"Yes. I'll call Susan and Davie and tell them we're going to straighten up the house, and this time you'll uncover what everyone else missed—Jonathan's backup drive and KryptoFold."

"How do we find it if the house is locked?"

"I'll unlock it. Now drive, before Evelyn thinks one of us has died and needs her services."

———

Lisa Draper couldn't risk getting any closer than the far end of a strip mall's lot. Douglas had parked at the other end closest to the next cross street. That told her he was able to keep eyes on Ethel and Jesse without getting near enough to be seen or be trapped facing the wrong way whenever they went mobile again.

She checked her phone map and learned Walthers Funeral Home was located a half block down the cross street. It had to be the destination. Were they checking on arrangements as a favor to Finch's wife since she was still in Fredericksburg with her sister? Lisa could think of no other reason. And why would Jesse have brought his computer?

Her phone beeped. The text message from Hauser read:

What's on tap for today?

She wanted to say, "Beer, go have a few." The man was obsessing over the case. If he thought there was a legit connection, why weren't there more agents on it? It was like he wanted the search for the twenty million not to go beyond her. If she found the code and gave it to him, would she be in danger?

Then there was Douglas sitting in his car less than fifty yards away. Was he working for Bradshaw or for himself? She envisioned a scene where she might have to protect herself. Actually take him out. Her defense would be he'd been on Norwood's team. Maybe he'd come to Ethel's to be close to Finch. She'd remind any review board that Douglas had the skills to have knocked Jesse out with one well-placed punch. His hands were lethal weapons.

Lisa sent Director Hauser a reply:

Followed her and Jesse to Richmond. At funeral home and they must be helping with arrangements.

She decided not to mention Douglas or Jesse's computer. Hauser could overreact and blow things prematurely. If she were to succeed, she had to do things her way. She was in the field; he was behind a desk.

Douglas's car eased onto the street. Lisa started her SUV. The caravan was on the move.

———

Jesse turned onto Finch's street "Where do you want me to park?"

"Might as well park in the driveway like we're supposed to be here. And neighbors might recognize the car from before and think nothing of it."

Jesse stopped behind the green Forester still in the carport. "She must have ridden to Fredericksburg with her sister."

"Or her Secret Service escort." Ethel bent over and rummaged through her bag. "Bring your backpack."

"What are you getting?"

She held up a small leather pouch. "Our ticket in."

———

Douglas Gray stopped a block behind them. He'd not been in the neighborhood before, but he assumed Ethel and Jesse had gone to the Finch home. Maybe the wife and boy had returned from Fredericksburg, and Ethel was running errands for them. First the funeral home, then something for the house. He pulled a pair of compact binoculars from the glove compartment and trained them on Ethel's car. He saw the old lady get out with a large wallet or small purse. Jesse had his backpack. Instead of going to the front door or the door from the carport, the two walked around back and out of sight. Maybe Mrs. Finch was resting and had left the back door open for them. But where was the assigned agent? Where was that agent's vehicle?

A block behind Douglas, Lisa used her own binoculars. Fortunately, the street arced slightly left so she had a clear view of the house. The risk lay in her being exposed to both Douglas and Ethel. The rookie agent was probably so focused on his quarry that he neglected to check his own tail. Ethel would not be so naive. For that matter, she'd probably already made Douglas. That could work to Lisa's advantage. Ethel might not look beyond one follower. The downside was she might try to lose him and lose her in the process. Lisa hoped Douglas would cool his jets and keep his distance until she could figure out what was going on.

———

Ethel stepped up on a small deck. There was a barbecue grill; a wrought-iron, glass-topped table; and four matching all-weather chairs. A pair of glass-paned French doors enabled direct entry into the kitchen.

"Good," Ethel said, "I was afraid there'd be sliding doors with a wedge blocking the inner track. We would have to risk either going through a window or opening a door within sight of the street." She set the pouch on the table and untied the leather strap keeping it folded closed. She flipped it open to reveal a set of fine-pointed and thin-bladed instruments. It looked like a portable dentist's kit.

Jesse peered over her shoulder. "Are those picks?"

"My father's pride and joy. He'd lock me out of the house with only these tools and a flashlight." She selected two of the picks and went to the door. "Once I had to shelter in the garage during a thunderstorm. Didn't get in until three in the morning."

"How old were you?"

"Ten."

"You were ten, and your father locked you out in the rain?"

She bent down and examined the lock. "Now, before you go reporting a sixty-five-year-old incident to Child Protective Services, you need to know I wouldn't have gone in the house any other way." She looked back over her shoulder. "I don't give up, Jesse."

"So your father taught you how to break and enter and then fly off in a getaway plane."

She chuckled. "Every girl should be so lucky. Now stand back and give me a little room."

Ten minutes later, they were inside. The kitchen stood in disarray. Drawers were pulled out, cabinets left open. A walk into the living room where Ethel and Susan had sat a few days earlier found the sofa and chair cushions cut open with pieces of stuffing scattered everywhere. The same scene existed in the den, the master bedroom, and a bedroom converted into an office.

Here, they found a file cabinet with its drawers so extended that the whole thing had tipped forward.

Davie's room hadn't been spared. Boxes and tubes of Tinkertoys and LEGOs had been dumped on his bed. A toy chest had been overturned, spilling a variety of action figures, crayons, and puzzles onto the carpet. Books had been pulled from the bookshelf. The items that appeared to have had the least scrutiny were the completed LEGO and Tinkertoy models on the display shelves, but even they seemed askew.

Jesse remembered how neat Davie had kept everything. Seeing his room so ransacked had to have been traumatic. Jesse picked up the model of Jonathan's SUV. "You were right. Whoever went through this room saw these as solid. Do you think the police have searched as well?"

Ethel stepped next to him. "I think Bradshaw locked this place down as soon as he got word of the break-in. He wouldn't involve the local police if he could avoid it. Bradshaw probably sent a forensics team through, but they made the same mistake. Still, you'd better make sure the drive's still there and then put the KryptoFold back in the replica with it. I'll call Susan and tell her we'd like to help get the house in order. Then you can make your discovery. Meanwhile, I want a few more hours to gather some information on the man Pete identified."

"This Ed O'Hara?"

"Yes. He's our main suspect. By the end of the day, we'll hand the KryptoFold, the backup drive of Jonathan's computer, and O'Hara's name over to Cory Bradshaw in one package."

Jesse retrieved the KryptoFold device from his backpack and returned it to the hiding place. "You know, I stopped searching Davie's room as soon as I found what was hidden here. 'Daddy's secret,' Davie called it." He put the replica back on the shelf and studied the others. Most were smaller. "What if I missed something?" His eye caught the model at the far end of the shelf. "This looks like their house."

With Ethel close behind, he picked up the replica of the Finches' home. The roof wasn't peaked correctly, but Davie had done the best he could with the available LEGO sizes. Jesse removed the top, one piece at a time. He found Davie had even constructed internal walls to create rooms. Yet it wasn't a dollhouse. There was no furniture or a family of LEGO figures. The only loose item was a strip of curled paper about the size of what Jesse had found wrapped around the KryptoFold. It was in the space approximating Davie's bedroom. Jesse's heart raced. Could this be the private key to the virtual wallet holding twenty million dollars of Bitcoin?

Ethel wedged in beside him because she was too short to see over his shoulder. "Well, for God's sake, unravel it."

But it didn't unravel. The curled paper turned out to be looped with the ends taped together in a half twist. Actually a Möbius strip with the phenomenon of technically having only one side. If the surface was traced by a finger or pencil, one never came to the strip's end but rather traversed both sides as if they were one. Jesse held it up for Ethel to see. In a child's block script, someone had scrawled a message in red crayon. It wasn't numbers or special characters. Simply all cap letters. "DAVIES SECRET."

"That's touching." Jesse gave it to Ethel. "The boy saw his dad put his secret in the model of his SUV, and so he put his pretend secret in his room in the model house."

Ethel studied the handwriting. "That's the logical explanation."

Jesse set the LEGO house back on the shelf.

Ethel handed him the note. "Better put this inside and replace the roof. Otherwise, someone could see the hollow interior and discover the other hiding place."

"But I thought you were going to offer to straighten up the house so that we can legitimately find these things?"

"Not till we talk to Davie. A change in plans. His secret is now our secret. We need to be in Fredericksburg, and we're an hour away."

———

Douglas Gray wondered why Ethel and Jesse had come to the house. Jesse had told him and Lisa that the mother and boy were staying at her sister's with agent protection. What did they hope to find here that everyone else had missed? More important, what did Director Bradshaw expect them to find? Was a confrontation imminent? He dialed the private number he'd been given.

———

Lisa saw Ethel and Jesse return through the carport. She grabbed her binoculars for a closer look and determined they were carrying the same items they'd originally taken out of the car. There were no toys for the boy, no changes of clothes, no toiletries— the kinds of things you would think a displaced family would want. Lisa had no way of knowing whether they'd left anything in the house or whether they'd picked up something small that fit in what they already carried. Something that explained why Jesse had his computer backpack with him. If the actions were part of Ethel's unofficial investigation, then there was a reason for each stop they'd made that morning. Where they went next could clarify everything.

Time to call Director Rudy Hauser.

No hello. Only an abrupt "Where are you?"

"At Finch's house. I think they're running errands. First, the funeral home and then their home."

"I thought they were in Fredericksburg."

"They are. Ethel may just be checking on things for Finch's wife. There's been another development. Douglas Gray is also following them. I don't believe he's seen me. I guess he's working for Director Bradshaw."

There was a moment of silence. Lisa knew Hauser was weighing the implications of Gray's presence.

"Maybe." Skepticism laced the word. "Or maybe he's working on his own. Remember, he was part of Norwood's team."

"Good point, sir. Should I stay clear of him?"

"Yes, but follow as best you can. Let things play out, unless, God forbid, there's some unexpected escalation. Then get to me immediately. Till then, we need to keep this off the books, or Cory Bradshaw will go to the AG and accuse me of meddling in his case. But we're taking a risk with this approach. I have an inside source who told me Bradshaw sent Ethel photos of the agents on Norwood's team. If Ethel finds someone who can ID Douglas Gray as the man who broke into Finch's house, then Gray might try to take that person out, even if it's Finch's wife or son."

"Surely Gray knows they're in protection."

"But who better to get closer than another agent? Look, I'm leaving you solo on this, so stay in the shadows. You need to watch Gray as much as you do Ethel."

"And the Parker money?" Lisa asked.

"Parker's still our connection to Finch. We'll let Bradshaw deal with the rats in his house. Your goal is to find twenty million dollars."

"Understood, sir. I'll be in touch."

FBI Director Hauser disconnected. Lisa started her engine.

She'd gotten what she'd wanted from her boss. She just wished she'd been able to record his comments about being off the books. Insurance, if things went sideways. Ethel's possession of the photos of Norwood's team told her that Ethel had something to offer Director Bradshaw, some compelling reason he would go outside his own investigation and share those photos. Something that could be a problem.

Chapter 30

A light rain began falling as a storm front moved into eastern Virginia. Jesse and Ethel crept along I-95 North with headlights and wipers engaged. As they neared the exit to Fredericksburg, Ethel's cell phone vibrated.

"It's my contact in the agency. He won't want to go on speaker." She accepted the call. "You're earlier than you anticipated."

Warren Hitchcock laughed. "That's because I'm scared of you."

"Anything to share?"

"I have a contact in HR who gave me some info without asking too many questions of her own. However, it's going to cost you a bottle of Scotch."

"For her or for you?"

"You raise a good question. Fortunately, that dilemma has an easy answer."

"Okay. A bottle of Glenfiddich single malt for each of you."

"Well, if you insist. Ed O'Hara is thirty-eight and a ten-year veteran. He's primarily worked in currency and credit card fraud. As I'm sure you know, he was part of the bust of the New York ring and testified at the trials."

"Trials?"

"Yes," Hitchcock said. "Some of the perpetrators were prosecuted separately. A tactic to encourage plea bargaining and turning defendants into federal witnesses. The classic climb-up-the-food-chain maneuver."

"Do you know where O'Hara was based?"

"Philadelphia had been his longest residency. He had a wife and a house there. He lost both in a divorce several years back. Four months ago, he requested a transfer to Richmond."

Ethel glanced at Jesse and arched her eyebrows. "Richmond? Does your source know why?"

"No," Hitchcock said. "And I also asked about his current assignment, but that's not in the HR database."

"And the counterfeit currency?"

"It moved around, according to trial date and location. Probably in conjunction with O'Hara's relevant testimony."

"Is it conceivable that it could have been held out for a day or two without anyone being the wiser?"

"It's not inconceivable. I'm grateful it doesn't appear to have happened on my watch."

"Yes, you're only guilty of accepting a Scotch bribe."

Hitchcock laughed again. "Bribe? I consider it an early Christmas gift."

"Then Merry Christmas. And thanks." Ethel rang off.

Jesse gave Ethel a quick, curious glance. "Merry Christmas?"

"That's because we were given a present. Looks like O'Hara moved to Richmond, where he and Norwood would be closer. I expect they hatched their scheme after the arrests. Once they found a buyer, all they needed was access to that currency for twenty-four hours."

"But some of those hundreds were real."

"Which they also planned to get back."

"Did Bradshaw check to see if the real hundreds had been removed?"

Ethel turned in her seat and gave Jesse an approving nod. "That, my cousin, is a very good question. If so, then it's one more clue that Norwood was murdered." She started a text.

"Are you contacting Bradshaw?"

"I'm checking to see if our tagalongs are still in place."

———

Douglas Gray began to worry. The death of Trevor Norwood, the summons to the scene by Bradshaw, and the clear mandate to report back on Ethel's actions played upon his mind. And he knew he was a suspect because Norwood had tainted their whole team. Concern for all of these factors had made him overlook one basic rule of mobile surveillance—always start with a full tank of gas. He had been at three-quarters. Now, after the drive to Richmond, the fuel gauge hovered just above a quarter. The Honda Accord got good mileage, but it was a known phenomenon that the second half of a tank always burned faster than the first. A stop for gas would mean losing sight of the black Infiniti, especially in the rain. He hoped Ethel was heading home.

Ethel's right turn signal blinked. A half-mile ahead was the exit for Fredericksburg. Was she stopping for gas? Then he remembered Susan Finch's sister lived there. That was probably the destination. He reached for his phone. Bradshaw would want an update.

———

Jesse drove slowly through the Braehead Woods neighborhood of Fredericksburg. The homes looked like they'd been built in the 1960s and '70s. A mixture of brick ranches and split-levels.

Ethel had her eyes fixed on her phone GPS. "It should be coming up on the right."

The house wasn't much different from the Finches'. A carport with a red Hyundai sedan, boxwoods neatly trimmed beneath the front windows, and a lawn with a dormant sprinkler attached to a hose that ran across the cement walk to a spigot near the home's foundation.

Jesse parked in the driveway. "Her sister's Rebecca, right?"

"Yes. Rebecca Tyson. She's divorced."

"Why is there only one car? Shouldn't an agent be here?"

Ethel got out without answering. Without a raincoat or umbrella, she darted up the walk, leaving Jesse to keep up.

Rebecca Tyson opened the door as they stepped onto the shelter of the porch. Compared to her sister, she was a little older and a little heavier, but with the same hazel eyes. Those eyes studied her visitors with surprise. "I saw you drive up. You must be Ethel and Jesse. You just missed Susan."

"Was she headed back to Richmond?"

Rebecca's brow furrowed. "She was going to meet Director Bradshaw. We thought you knew."

"Did the director call?"

"Yes, not more than twenty minutes ago. He spoke to the agent, who told Susan that she and Davie needed to go with him."

Ethel touched Jesse's arm, signaling him not to say anything. Then she forced a smile. "I must have missed a call. Do you know where they're meeting?"

"No. I assumed Washington. The agent just said that the director was very busy and they needed to leave right away if they wanted an in-person update."

"And Davie went too?" Ethel asked.

"Yes. They took his walker and his portable wheelchair. Is something wrong?"

"No. There's just a lot going on. Do you mind if we come in for a moment?"

Rebecca threw up her hands. "I'm sorry. Where are my manners? Can I get you coffee or tea?"

"No, thank you." Ethel turned to Jesse. "Why don't you bring those photos? The ones we were going to show Susan."

"No problem." He hurried to the car.

"Just let yourself in," Rebecca called after him. "We'll be in the living room."

Jesse found the living room was just off a small foyer. Both women were still standing, and he handed the eight photos to Ethel. She indicated for Rebecca to sit on the sofa, and she then took a seat next to her. Jesse stood beside a wingback chair closer to Ethel. His clothes were damp from his dash through the drizzle.

Ethel set the stack of photos facedown on the coffee table in front of her. "I brought these pictures to show your sister. People that Jonathan might have been in contact with shortly before his death."

Rebecca shrugged. "I don't know how I can help."

"They might have been watching Susan's house before you came here or been in your neighborhood since."

Rebecca paled. "Are they who broke into Susan's house?"

"We're just ruling out some remote possibilities." Ethel flipped over the first picture. Douglas Gray.

Rebecca shook her head.

"You're sure," Ethel prompted.

"If I saw him, he didn't make an impression."

"Okay." Ethel flipped the next photo, and heard the catch in Rebecca's throat.

"Why, that's Agent O'Hara."

"Have you seen him before?"

"Seen him? He's the agent who just took Susan and Davie to meet Director Bradshaw."

Before Ethel could reply, her phone buzzed with an incoming text. She quickly glanced at it, struggling to keep her expression calm.

SAY NOTHING OR THEY'RE DEAD!

Chapter 31

Susan Finch felt the tension building in the pit of her stomach. Something wasn't right. Her unease had been heightened by the sound of locking doors as soon as the Secret Service agent had gotten behind the wheel of the dark sedan. Then he'd asked her to give him her cell phone. Avoid potential tracking, he'd said. Director Bradshaw was meeting them at a safe house, and policy dictated that its location remain secure.

There was also the way his mood had suddenly shifted. He'd been friendly enough when he'd arrived at Rebecca's at eight that morning. The agent who had stayed the night was surprised that his relief wasn't whom he'd been expecting. The new agent had flashed his ID, Ed O'Hara. He said it was a last-minute schedule change. Susan thought nothing of it. She knew from her years with Johnny that schedules were created only to be changed. But then the agent had gotten the phone call. They were to leave immediately. She'd asked if there had been a break in the case. He'd said Director Bradshaw would explain, and then he'd hustled her and Davie to his car.

Susan looked at the passing landscape. The rain intensified, peppering the windshield with greater ferocity. Instead of the expected I-95 North route to Washington, O'Hara was taking them on rural backroads. Without the sun for a reference, she couldn't determine the direction they were headed.

She leaned her body against the seat belt so that she could see O'Hara in the rearview mirror. "Excuse me, but when will we get to this safe house?"

He cut his eyes to the mirror. He didn't bother to hide his annoyance. "In about twenty minutes."

"It's just that we should soon be eating lunch." She stretched out her hand so that her son could clasp it. "Davie doesn't do well if the routine is broken. And I have medicine in my purse that he shouldn't take on an empty stomach."

"Well, when we get there, I'll send out for some food."

"Thank you." She heard a phone buzz. Hers had been powered off.

O'Hara pulled a phone from his suit coat. Susan noticed it wasn't the kind issued by the Secret Service.

O'Hara pressed it to his ear. "Eighteen minutes out." He listened a moment. "Yes, I have it with me."

It. Not them. Not Mrs. Finch and her son. *It.*

Davie squeezed her hand. Was he picking up the same vibes? She fought down her panic for his sake. *Johnny, what have you done?*

———

Ethel showed Jesse the threatening text as soon as they were back in the car.

"Oh, my God. Are you going to call Bradshaw?"

"Yes, but only to let him know Ed O'Hara was the duty officer, and he said Bradshaw was meeting them. That claim is already out there. We can honestly say we don't know where O'Hara is at the moment. Nothing about this text."

"But the resources Bradshaw can bring. The trained negotiators if this turns into a hostage situation."

Ethel reached out and squeezed Jesse's forearm. Her grip was strong, almost painful as she forced him to focus his attention on her words. "They sent this message to us for a reason. I think they've determined Susan and Davie know nothing about Jonathan's actions. Yet they saw the ten thousand dollars disappear from the smaller wallet, proving that someone has access to the clone of Jonathan's computer, and we're the likely candidates." She released his arm. "At least I hope that's the case."

"Why?"

"Because they'll keep Susan and Davie alive, as long as the mother and son have value. The fact that O'Hara has openly disclosed his culpability tells me their game is drawing to the final stage. They must have an exit strategy, and there's still the half million they've already collected. With Norwood's death, maybe that's now split only two ways. They might have run other scams or shakedowns and have a nest egg somewhere offshore or in virtual currency."

Jesse's hand trembled as he gave Ethel her phone. "But we don't have anything to give them."

"They don't know that. They'll contact us again. We'll admit we have Jonathan's backup drive, his KryptoFold device, and the private key to the smaller wallet, where we'll return the ten thousand dollars. We'll exchange everything for Susan and Davie. Nothing virtual, a face-to-face meeting. No involvement by the Secret Service or the FBI."

"Not even as backup?"

"Jesse, I learned a hard lesson when my father was betrayed. We don't know where the tentacles of this conspiracy are reaching, so we can't trust anyone beyond our own team. That means you text Tracy to put the Bitcoins back as a sign of good faith that they can verify. Then you drive us to Richmond, and we reclaim what we left there. I expect O'Hara to settle somewhere soon and be in contact. Somehow, he'll use burner phones or route untraceable messages."

"Probably a Virtual Private Network," Jesse said. "With a VPN, he could be in Virginia but appear to be in Mexico City or anywhere else in the world."

"That's your area of expertise, not mine. As long as our phones are working, we should be good. I'll call Bradshaw and share that O'Hara has gone somewhere with Susan and Davie. He can figure out how O'Hara got that assignment."

"Unless it was Bradshaw that made the switch," Jesse said.

Ethel shot him a sharp glance. "God, I hope not. But I won't bet Susan and Davie's lives on him. Now text Tracy and let's get to Richmond. It's time we became the hunters, not the hunted."

———

When Lisa saw Ethel and Jesse emerge from Rebecca Tyson's house, she made a U-turn and headed away. She didn't want to risk being spotted. She wished Douglas Gray weren't still involved and wondered again if he was on assignment or tailing Ethel for his own purposes. She had to admit he'd been impressive in his surveillance.

Lisa picked up her phone and speed-dialed Hauser's private number.

He answered immediately. "Anything happening?"

"They're at the sister's in Fredericksburg, where Mrs. Finch and her son are staying. I still think they're just running errands for them."

"What about Douglas Gray?"

"He's pulled off," she lied. The last thing she wanted was for

Hauser to tie her up tailing Douglas. "So, I can hang here or return to DC."

"Come on in," Hauser said. "I'll send you the names of the agents on Trevor Norwood's team. See what you can dig up on them."

"Surreptitiously?"

"Do you have to ask?" Hauser was clearly annoyed.

"No, sir. I'll get on it as soon as I can."

He disconnected without another word. Lisa suspected her lack of success was cooling his interest in the case. That was good if it kept him off her back for the remainder of the day.

———

"He said he was bringing them to me?" Cory Bradshaw's voice rose to a near-shout.

Ethel moved the phone away from her ear. "Yes. Susan's sister made a positive ID and said O'Hara got a call that he claimed was from you."

"This is bad. Really bad."

"So, this is news to you?"

The near-shout rose to a crescendo. "Of course it's news to me. Does the sister know anything else? What was he driving? Did she see which direction he took?"

"She didn't see anything. It had started to rain, so she lent them umbrellas. Davie was in his portable wheelchair. The car was down the block. She really didn't see it, because she closed the door as soon as they started down the walk."

"O'Hara must think Susan knows something. Whatever he was looking for in the house. And I'm going to have someone's head for changing that schedule."

"Probably he innocently offered to swap for the shift," Ethel said. "You hadn't put any restrictions on Norwood's team, had you?"

"No. And that's my mistake."

"Jesse raised a question about the counterfeit money you found with Norwood. Were any of the hundreds real?"

"No. That's why I'm nearly certain Norwood was murdered. Killed in cold blood."

"What are you going to do?" Ethel asked.

"Do a search of wherever O'Hara was living in Richmond, plus any desk or computer files he kept in the office. As soon as we hang up, I tap into the highway patrols of Virginia and neighboring states. Not that it will do much good when all I can say is 'be on the lookout for a man, woman, and child traveling in a nondescript vehicle.'"

"A man with a woman and child riding in the back seat," Ethel added. "Susan would want to belt him in but not risk his being hit by the airbag. And she'd want to stay beside him."

"Good point," Bradshaw conceded. "What are you going to do now?"

"Wait. Hope. Even pray. But I think whatever happens will happen soon."

"You'll keep me posted if you're doing more than that?"

"Cory, isn't that why you have Douglas Gray spying on me?"

Silence.

"It's all right," Ethel said. "I would do the same. But tell me this. Did Douglas approach you with an offer to watch me or did you seek him out?"

"I contacted him."

"And has Rudy Hauser been in touch again?"

"Just to offer the Bureau's assistance. I guess I should take him up on it."

"Don't."

Another pause, and then Bradshaw asked, "Why not?"

"Because his case isn't your case. He's still got the Parker suicide sticking in his craw. We have an agent's widow and child to protect. That's what the Secret Service is known for, protecting the lives of others, whatever the cost. So, to hell with the twenty million dollars, Cory. Saving Susan and Davie is the only priority now."

Chapter 32

Ed O'Hara turned onto the single-lane road that had degenerated into water-filled ruts and potholes.

Susan clutched Davie's hand tighter. "Why are we way out here?"

"Safest place to be. Just a little farther, and then we can explain everything." He drove another hundred yards until a metal gate barred the road. "I need to unlock this. Stay put."

He fished through his suit coat for a key and then reached under the seat to retrieve a black umbrella. He opened the door, released the umbrella's catch, and bolted into the rain. The car idled, wipers running full speed and headlights illuminating the agent fumbling with a chain and padlock.

Susan tried the door handle. It was locked. O'Hara must have set the doors to childproof status. She thought about crawling over the seat back and getting behind the wheel, but O'Hara kept glancing at her. He swung the gate on squeaky hinges, dodged puddles on his return, and shook the umbrella before collapsing it. Then he dropped it on the passenger seat. He drove forward, leaving the gate open behind them.

The road curved through a copse of trees and then widened

into an empty asphalt parking area large enough for about ten cars. Patches of grass and weeds had broken through the pavement. A large Quonset hut sat at the far end, its steel surface brown with rust. Vines grew up the sides and onto the arched roof.

Susan looked beyond it to what she first thought was another road. She wondered why O'Hara hadn't driven them there on what appeared to be a straighter, smoother alternative. As they neared the hut, she realized the road was actually a runway, plagued by the same splotches of invading grass. At one time, the hut must have been an airplane hangar.

O'Hara stopped in front of a normal-sized door adjacent to two others large enough to admit a small aircraft. He killed the engine and turned to face Susan. "There's an office where we'll be more comfortable. I'll need to start a generator for power, but we'll have lights and heat. Do as I say and we'll get along fine."

He took the umbrella. Susan watched him disappear around the side of the hut. A few minutes later, the murmur of a gasoline engine rose above the rain. O'Hara returned, opened the smaller hut door, and turned on an interior light. Then he came to the car.

He double-clicked the key fob and Susan's door unlocked. "I'll get the wheelchair from the back. Then hurry inside. I'll be right behind you."

Susan unsnapped her seat belt and helped Davie out of his. Pulling him close, she tried to shield him as she assisted him into the chair and then wheeled him through the rain.

The office wasn't a separate room but simply a cluster of old battleship-gray furniture in an area of about twenty by twenty feet. Three metal desks, three beat-up rolling chairs, two vertical filing cabinets, and two waste bins, one of which was overturned. Bare bulbs dangled from an overhead power strip running to the back corner where built-out perpendicular walls and a door created a room not much bigger than a closet. A second power strip ran a few inches above the floor providing multiple outlets. A space heater was the only thing plugged into it. The unit rotated two hundred seventy degrees as its fan blew hot air across the cool concrete floor.

Beyond the throw of the lights, the rest of the interior faded into a murky, empty gloom.

Susan heard O'Hara close the outside door.

"I'm afraid the heater won't do much in this open space," he grumbled as he set a backpack on one of the desks. "But we won't be here long."

"Are we waiting on Mr. Bradshaw?" Susan asked.

"He won't be coming. You'll be dealing with me. But if you and the boy want to use the bathroom, it's over there." He pointed to the walls jutting out from the corner. "There's no toilet paper, so…"

Susan rolled Davie across the open space, anxious to have a chance to think without being under O'Hara's scrutiny. They entered the bathroom and discovered there was no ceiling, just the eight-foot-high partitions shielding a sink and toilet from view. She cringed at the disgusting sight of dirty porcelain and a broken toilet seat. Davie shook his head, refusing to step out of the chair.

"Come on," she whispered, "you have to try. We might be here a while and you know you'll get uncomfortable. You go first, then I'll go." She turned her head to give the youngster some privacy and noticed there was no lock on the inside of the door. If they took too long, she had no doubt the agent wouldn't hesitate to enter.

When they'd finished, Susan rolled Davie back to the desks. O'Hara had rearranged the chairs so that one faced an open laptop.

"You sit here, Mrs. Finch." O'Hara pointed to the chair at the desk. "Leave your son where he's out of the way."

Davie clung to his mother's arm.

"Out of the way of what?"

O'Hara took a deep breath. "We know what your husband did. We have his computer, and we have the wallets. He broke the law, but you can set things right and everyone will be happy. No charges will be pressed and your husband's reputation and good name preserved."

"Wallets? I don't know what wallets you're talking about. Johnny only had one."

"I'm talking about virtual wallets." He tapped the computer screen. "The ones your husband used to steal millions of dollars from the agency. The ones you accessed on a duplicate computer."

Susan stared at the laptop. It looked like Johnny's, but they all looked alike.

"Daddy's computer." Davie rolled his wheelchair toward the desk. "Daddy's computer."

O'Hara grabbed him roughly by the upper arm. The boy squealed and tried to pull away.

"Leave him alone," Susan Finch shouted. "You'll break his arm." She started forward, ready to claw her son free.

With one swift motion, O'Hara yanked his pistol from its shoulder holster with one hand while lifting the boy out of the chair with the other. He pressed the muzzle against Davie's temple. The child froze, fear disintegrating into a catatonic paralysis.

"You're going to give me the key to that money or breaking his arm will be the least of your worries."

O'Hara tightened his grip, and Davie's arm went limp, the unheeded Medic Alert bracelet dangling from his wrist.

"Please. Please." Sobs strangled Susan's words. "I don't know what you're talking about." She fell to her knees, not feeling the pain of the concrete. "We don't have another computer. We don't have any wallets. You've got to believe me. Just don't hurt my child."

O'Hara looked down at the woman. The Secret Service had

taught him to read faces. Taught him to make an assessment that could spot a potential assassin with only seconds to react. He saw the flooding tears, the quivering lips, the draining of the blood from her cheeks, and he knew she was telling the truth.

He gently lowered Davie back into the chair and released his grip. "Stay here. I have to make a call."

———

The warning light flashed on the gas gauge. If he was lucky, Douglas Gray figured he had fuel for about thirty miles more. He'd hoped Ethel would head back to Arlington, but she and Jesse appeared to be retracing their route to Richmond. Back to the funeral home? Back to the Finch house? Had Jonathan's wife asked Ethel for a favor, another errand? As they neared the Finch neighborhood, Douglas eyed several gas stations. He might be able to make a quick break and fill up.

When the Infiniti turned onto the Finches' street, Douglas wheeled the Honda around and headed for a Circle K two blocks back. His phone started vibrating. He glanced at the screen. Bradshaw again. Douglas hated to admit his fuel problem, but he couldn't ignore the director.

Without a hello, Douglas answered, "They've returned to Finch's home, sir."

"Anyone else there?"

His throat went dry. "I can't see anyone." That was technically true.

"We've had a major development." Bradshaw gave a brief update on how O'Hara arranged an assignment shift in the Richmond office and now had suddenly taken Mrs. Finch and Davie somewhere. "He's killed his phone, so we have no tracking option. Ethel might have returned to the house in case he brings them there. That's a smart play on her part. Meanwhile, I've alerted all of our East Coast offices and the state highway patrols of Virginia and neighboring states. I don't know what O'Hara's game is, but he might be trying to negotiate an escape and has taken the Finches as hostages."

"Do you want me to approach the house?"

"No. O'Hara knows you by sight. Keep watch from a safe distance. Call me if anything changes. And if you see O'Hara, don't confront him. We'll get you backup."

"Yes, sir."

"And keep your phone charged so we can trace you."

———

"I want you to back into the driveway." Ethel gave Jesse the order as they neared the Finch house.

"Why?"

"Because you're staying in the car as lookout. There's a chance O'Hara could bring them here, and I don't want to be caught flat-footed. We can also get away quicker if you're facing out." She retrieved her lockpicks from the large handbag. "I'll be as quick as possible. Honk once if you see anything suspicious."

She got out of the car, and then leaned back in. "You brought the revolver?"

"It's packed with the computer."

"Get it out where you can reach it." With that ominous instruction, she left.

Having picked the lock once, she was able to enter the house in half the time and went straight to Davie's room. She took the model of Jonathan's SUV off the shelf and removed the LEGOs hiding the hard drive, the KryptoFold, and the strip of paper with the private key to the smaller wallet.

Her phone buzzed with an incoming text. *Right on time,* she thought.

The message read—

> We know you have the wallets and keys. Give them to us and no harm will come to the woman and boy.

The address was blocked, but a Reply icon was available. She assumed the text came from some secured device.

Ethel typed—

> Okay. In-person exchange only. You choose the place.

She pressed Send and waited.

The response came a few minutes later—

> No. Text the private key and we'll tell you where to find them.

Ethel didn't know if she could send a photo, but she used her phone to take a picture of the hard drive and KryptoFold. She linked it to a reply and wrote—

> I'm not stupid. I give you the keys and I have no leverage.
>   You'll get the drive for Davie, the KryptoFold for Susan.
>   We both walk away with what we want.

The immediate response—

> SEND THE KEY NOW!

Ethel steeled herself. What she did next would be the biggest gamble of her seventy-five-year life. Bigger than when she confronted her father's betrayer alone. This time two lives were at risk. And she chose to do nothing.

Five long minutes passed. The text arrived—

Don't think we're not serious. We've nothing to lose.

She quickly typed her response—

20 million is nothing? You see the KryptoFold we just found in Davie's LEGO model? You walk away, I keep the money. Your choice.

Maybe they'll ask Davie to confirm, she thought. That would be helpful as long as he said nothing more.

Another five minutes crept by. Ethel imagined some kind of conference must be underway.

The text came—

We're monitoring law enforcement frequencies. Any sign that they're moving toward us and everything's off. Understood?

Understood. I also have a tail I'll need to lose.

You have fifteen minutes. Then you'll get directions one leg at a time.

She replied with one word—

Understood.

Then she placed a voice call.

Curt Foster sat in the office at the rear of his house, watching the blips move across Google Maps. He answered with two words, "Things happening?"

"They've made contact," Ethel said. "You following me?"

"Yes, I've got you at the Finch home. Player number two is a few blocks away. Looks like a gas station."

"What about Pete?"

"We're on a landline. I'll put you both on speaker." He paused a few seconds. "Okay. Go ahead." His voice now had a hollow echo.

"Pete, what's your status?" Ethel asked.

"Player number one appears to have bailed and is looping back to DC."

"Or some other destination," Ethel said. "Keep monitoring. I'm about to get segmented directions to a rendezvous site. My own phone might be monitored until they text me the final leg. Then they may shut me down."

"I don't like it, Ethel," Pete complained. "You're being lured into a trap with no immediate backup."

"Let's hold that concern in reserve till I have a better idea of where this is going down."

"It's your call," Pete reluctantly agreed.

"How's your weather?" Curt asked.

"Rain and low visibility," Ethel said. "I wouldn't want to fly in it."

"We love it, don't we, Pete?" Curt said. "Makes it harder for the enemy to shoot us down."

Ethel couldn't help but laugh. "You two geezers. For this mission you're both grounded. Just be vigilant and be ready to follow my instructions."

———

Douglas Gray breathed a sigh of relief when he saw Ethel's car parked in the driveway. Then he carefully scanned the surrounding area for any sign of Ed O'Hara. The guy had been a pain in the ass to work with. On the New York counterfeiting case, O'Hara was always giving him the menial duties and calling him the "new boy," as if daring Douglas to take it as a racial slur. Ironically, Trevor Norwood had been the one to admit Douglas into the fold. Although he and O'Hara were tight, Norwood didn't hesitate to tell O'Hara to knock off the hazing. Norwood brought Douglas fully into the team and fully into the operation. Douglas had appreciated what the man had done for him, and if O'Hara had betrayed them, Douglas wanted to settle the score. That meant being ahead of Ethel Crestwater.

He was thinking about the sly old woman when he saw her return to the carport. He used his binoculars. She not only carried the same leather pouch from earlier but also a large model of an SUV. What the hell was she up to?

Standing just under the carport's roof, she shouted something, and Jesse hurried from the driver's seat, ran around the front of the car in the rain and opened the passenger door. Ethel dashed from her shelter, dumped her load on the passenger seat, and then went to the driver's side and got behind the wheel. Jesse rearranged things so he could sit down, and for the next few minutes the two of them seemed to be busying themselves with whatever Ethel had brought from the house.

When the Infiniti's headlights and wipers came on, Douglas started his Honda. The chase was on.

Chapter 33

Davie left the portable wheelchair and squeezed into a desk chair with his mother. He looked down at his hands and murmured a never-ending loop of words. It took Susan a few minutes to realize he was repeating "Miss Crestwater, come together, Miss Crestwater, come together…" It was like a mantra and seemed to calm him.

"What's he saying?" Ed O'Hara sat on the edge of the desk beside the open laptop. His arms were folded across his chest and the pistol returned to its holster.

"A name."

"Whose?"

"Ethel Crestwater. Heard of her?"

"Yeah. She's supposedly a legend around the FBI."

"She is. And she's coming after you for killing my husband."

"I never killed him. I never killed anyone."

"Then who did?"

O'Hara looked at the boy locked away with his repetitive mumbling. "He's been taken care of, if it's justice you want."

"I want you to let us go."

O'Hara nodded his agreement. "And I'd like nothing more.

Now it depends upon your Ethel Crestwater. If she does the right thing, no one gets hurt. I fly away, and you'll never see me again."

"And what's the right thing?"

"Return the money your husband stole. Ethel got a copy of his laptop somehow and knows the way in. She gives us that, and everybody wins."

"My husband's not a thief."

O'Hara shrugged. "Believe what you want. But you'd better believe Ethel Crestwater will come through for you." He looked at Davie again. "What's wrong with your boy?"

Susan bristled. "There's nothing *wrong* with him. He's sweet, gentle, and kind. That's all you need to know."

"Okay. Let's all just relax. A few more hours and this will be over."

Over. The word was anything but reassuring.

———

Jesse put the hard drive, the KryptoFold, and the strip of paper with the handwritten long sequence of numbers and characters for the smaller wallet into Ethel's bag.

"You told Tracy not to contact you?" Ethel asked.

"Yes. She should have returned the ten thousand to the wallet we control and is waiting for further instructions. It's close to seven in London, and she's staying up and logged in all night if necessary."

"Good." Ethel handed him her phone. "I'll lose our tail while you watch for directions. We'll trade places when I know the final destination."

"I'm a good driver. I could lose the surveillance."

Ethel shook her head. "It's not so much that we lose a tail as that it looks like we're trying to lose a tail. As far as we know, Douglas is following us and reporting our actions. But a person or persons unknown could be following him. We need to appear to be playing by their rules."

Jesse expected the car to rocket out of the driveway and neighborhood. Instead, Ethel let the car coast to the street and then drove at a speed that would have placed third behind the tortoise and the hare.

"Now, he'll either have to drop back and stay out of sight or pass us," Ethel explained. "But if he matches our speed, he'll draw attention to himself."

Once they left the neighborhood, Ethel moderately accelerated onto a commercial boulevard. The concentration of strip malls, gas stations, and fast-food chains also created a concentration of traffic lights. She kept stopping and starting as the lights changed until she got what she wanted, a light that turned yellow as she approached the intersection. She slowed, trying to time the change to red. A horn blared behind her as another driver urged her forward so that he could make the light. Ethel stopped on the crosswalk, saw the yellow go red, and then made an illegal left turn across three lanes of traffic. The cross street was clear for the next block, and she did fifty in a thirty-five-mile-per-hour zone. She took another left, effectively circling behind her surveillance like a fox backtracking the hound.

That hound found himself stuck in bumper-to-bumper traffic in the middle of the block. With a sickening feeling, Douglas saw the Infiniti take a sharp left against a red light and accelerate out of sight. The maneuver left no doubt that Ethel was trying to shake free of him. And she had succeeded. Now he could only report the setback to Bradshaw. The director would not be happy, but Douglas would be free of his constant oversight and could pursue his own agenda, an agenda that would bring them all to the same place.

Ethel continued breaking the speed limit as she alternated right and left turns in a diagonal route away from Douglas. She glanced at Jesse. "Check Google Maps for the fastest route to I-95."

Jesse reached out one hand to steady himself on the dashboard as she braked hard into a right turn. "North or south?"

"Doesn't matter. I just want to put some miles behind us."

Ten minutes and ten miles later, the first text came—

> Go to Montpelier. 23192. Acknowledge and power off phone till arrival.

"Vermont?" Jesse exclaimed.

"No. There's a Montpelier, Virginia. And there's also a Montpelier Station, where James Madison's house is located. That's closer to Charlottesville. People get them confused, so whoever's sending the text added the zip code. Reply 'understood,' and then enter the town and zip into the GPS."

Jesse did as she said. "We're about forty minutes away. Looks like Highway 33 is the best bet."

"All right. Kill the phone. We'll stop for gas and then hopefully make good time despite the rain."

It was nearly three o'clock when they pulled into the parking lot of a U.S. Post Office. The zip code 23192 was prominently displayed on the front of the building.

"Here's as good a place as any. Turn the phone back on and text 'Arrived.'"

A few minutes later—

> Go to Gum Spring. Same procedure.

"That's about twenty-five minutes away," Jesse said after checking GPS. "State roads all the way. Gum Spring looks to be a crossroad community."

Ethel nodded. "They're winnowing down the traffic. We'll probably wind up in an isolated spot. Let me send a quick text and then power off." She took back her phone, scrolled to another thread and typed,

What's happening?

The immediate reply—

looping back toward you

Ethel's response—

Okay. Time to move forward as planned. Give him Montpelier 23192 and keep him one location behind. I think you're safe for voice if it's easier. We're headed to Gum Spring.

Ethel looked out at the rain and dark skies. "Jesse, I think I'm at the point where I have to trust that integrity, fairness, and justice are more than words for some people. Trust my instincts as to who those people are."

"What do you mean?"

"One question for two men. Whether their answers are the same or differ will tell me a lot."

"What's the question?"

Ethel gave him an enigmatic smile. "The question is, 'What's the relationship?'" Without saying anything further, she composed her texts.

When she handed the phone back to Jesse, he was tempted

to look at her sent messages. Instead, he powered it off and gave her directions to Gum Spring from memory.

At three thirty, they pulled into the lot of another small post office.

"We should have brought some letters to mail," Jesse said.

"The post office is what these unincorporated communities have in common. Also, if we had an entourage, we'd be easily spotted. Someone's being very careful."

"Want me to send them the text?"

"The rain's eased up a bit. You drive, and I'll handle the phone."

They opened their doors, and as they passed each other in front of the car, Ethel quipped, "Well, Cousin, you could be in a nice, dry classroom."

"Yeah. A nice, dry, boring classroom."

When they were in their seats, Jesse added, "And I wouldn't be helping a mother and child."

"We wouldn't have gotten this far without your computer skills. Let's hope you're back in class tomorrow." She took her phone and texted—

Gum Spring.

The immediate response—

Last leg. Look for single lane. Wait outside structure.
37.9498446, -77.9084076

"They've given us coordinates rather than a town or road names," Ethel said. She entered them into the GPS. "Well, well, according to this we're another twenty minutes away from a location just outside of a town named Cuckoo."

"Cuckoo?"

"Yes, but rest assured they're not crazy. Give me a moment and then we'll go." She scrolled back to the other thread and texted—

Final destination. Pass along as planned. Wish us luck.

37.9498446, -77.9084076

She pressed Send.

Chapter 34

On QT, check out Gray and Draper relationships to Ed O'Hara. Interested in Philadelphia. Text info. Will explain later.

The text message arrived on the private cell phones of Rudy Hauser and Cory Bradshaw simultaneously. Each man was on a conference call in his office, but when each saw Ethel Crestwater's number, they quickly wrapped up. Neither man knew the other received the identical request. Both men had the same first reaction—*WHAT NOW?* The second reaction—*WHAT DOES ETHEL KNOW THAT I DON'T?*

FBI Director Hauser assumed Ethel knew he had Lisa Draper monitoring the situation. Had Draper's efforts created friction between her and Agent Gray? What was the point of Philadelphia?

Secret Service Director Bradshaw saw nothing new about Ethel's request to investigate Gray and O'Hara. They were his men, and both were tainted by the counterfeit scam. Now O'Hara had gone off the grid with Finch's family. Bradshaw asked himself if Gray had been misdirecting him in his reports. Both Gray and O'Hara had been in the Philadelphia office. And Lisa Draper? Had she started up a relationship with either or both in order to get information? She wouldn't be the first agent to use sex as a means to an end.

Both directors took similar actions. Bradshaw wanted a complete review of Gray's and O'Hara's interactions. Was there more than just the one investigation and an occasional pint at the Dubliner? Getting info on Draper would be trickier since she was FBI. But Bradshaw had his sources among the gossipers in both his agency and the Bureau. First, he'd put a tracker on Gray's phone, and if he could finagle Draper's number, then hers as well.

Rudy Hauser undertook the same steps. But he learned before Bradshaw did that Lisa Draper was off the grid.

Then both men discovered Ethel Crestwater's phone had gone dead.

———

The rain eased to a light drizzle. Ethel drove slowly along a deserted blacktop a few miles south of Cuckoo, looking for the lane that could take them to the designated coordinates.

"There's a break in the foliage ahead," Jesse said. "That has to be it."

The Infiniti bounced over the lip of the highway and turned onto a muddy washboard of cracked asphalt and potholes.

"Whoever it is certainly doesn't spend any money on upkeep," Jesse said. "Must be an abandoned farmhouse."

Ethel kept her eyes straight ahead. "Maybe, but there must be advantages beyond isolation. I would never set up an exchange with only one way out. Too easy to be trapped."

Jesse took the point a step further. "But isn't it also the only way for us to get out?"

"That's why you'll stay in the car and keep the motor running. And as at the Finch house, turn the car around so we're headed out."

A few minutes later, they came to the open gate. As soon as Ethel cleared it, she stopped the car and opened her door. "Let's change places before we get any closer."

She got out in the light drizzle, but instead of going to the passenger's side, she walked to the gate. Jesse followed.

Ethel lifted one end of the chain where the open padlock hung from a link. "Note these are new. The gate's bars are rusty but sturdy." She removed the padlock, snapped it shut, and threw it into the underbrush. Then she yanked the shiny chain free and tossed it under some briars on the other side. "Now if someone closes the gate at least they can't lock it."

Back in the car, Jesse used his jacket sleeve to wipe water from his eyes. "So, if I'm with the car, I won't be able to help you."

"Your job is to get away safely and be the witness if something happens to me. No heroics." She gave him a fierce stare. "Understand?"

"Yes."

"We'll make a final logistics decision when we see the layout, but, bottom line, I need you to be prepared to fly out of here. Now, let's go forward nice and slow."

Jesse set the automatic transmission in low gear and continued along the rough road.

When they broke through into the clearing, Ethel exclaimed, "So, that's their way out."

Jesse stopped at the edge of the parking lot. "What? That one car?"

"No. The airstrip behind the hut. One of my former roomers worked a case involving drugs flying into central Virginia. This must have been abandoned while the owner's getting his room and board courtesy of the Feds."

"There's a plane in that hangar?"

"I doubt it," Ethel said. "Otherwise it would be out and

prepped for a quick takeoff. No, I think someone's coming to fly our culprits out of the country. They know the game is up, and this is their last effort to take twenty million dollars with them."

"So, now what?"

"We circle around and park face-out about twenty yards from what I suspect is O'Hara's sedan. I'll get out and demand to see Susan and Davie. You keep the car running. I'll first make the trade of the hard drive for Davie. When that's done, we exchange the KryptoFold and the private key for Susan, and we leave."

"Okay." His shaky voice betrayed his lack of bravado. As he crossed the lot and swung wide to turn around, he saw the small door of the Quonset hut open. Susan and Davie were just inside the threshold, she standing and the boy in his chair. Behind them, the man Jesse recognized as Ed O'Hara held a gun aloft. What little confidence Jesse had left evaporated when he saw the fear on the faces of the mother and child and then the gun and the grim expression of the rogue agent.

"Stop here," Ethel said. She reached into her bag on the floor for Finch's drive and then grabbed an umbrella from the back seat. "Leave the KryptoFold and the private key in the bag for when I return."

As soon as she shut the car door, O'Hara bellowed, "Show me your hands!"

Ethel refused to be intimidated. "They're at the ends of my wrists, dumbass. One's holding the umbrella and the other has Finch's drive. You know, the one I accessed to get to his crypto wallets? The one you'll get when you release Davie."

"How do I know it's the real deal?"

"What do you care? It's only the backup to Finch's computer, and you already have that. But it's proof that we control the accounts. So, let the boy go, and you can inspect the drive."

"Bring it to me."

"No. I take the boy to the car, and then I bring you the drive."

"And then?"

"Then I go back for what you really want. The private key and the KryptoFold."

"And how's that exchange going to work?"

Ethel started walking closer to him. "Like this. I walk to you as Susan walks away from you. You'll have me and what you want. I figure you'll either let me go or you won't. Either way, the car leaves."

She stopped and waited.

O'Hara thought for a moment. Then in a softer voice, he said to Susan, "Tell your son to wheel himself to her."

Davie clutched his mother's arm.

"Come together, Davie," Ethel said, lifting the umbrella as if it were a tent of safety. "I brought some LEGOs for you."

Susan bent down to her son. "You know Miss Crestwater. Mommy will be right behind you. Show her how fast you can roll through the puddles."

"Puddles," he repeated. "H_2O. Miss Crest-H_2O."

"That's right," Ethel said. "I brought some Tinkertoys too. It's all in the car."

Susan gave the chair a gentle push to start its momentum. When the raindrops hit his face, Davie wheeled faster for the shelter of the umbrella. Ethel shifted it to make sure he was well covered as she rolled him to the car. Davie smiled when he saw Jesse and climbed out of the chair and into the back seat.

"LEGOs?" he asked.

"When Mommy comes," Ethel said. "I'll be right back." She gave a nod to Jesse and closed the door.

"Well, come on," O'Hara shouted. "We've haven't got all day."

"We'll see how fast you move when you're seventy-five."

O'Hara grabbed Susan by the elbow and pulled her clear of the doorway. "Just bring the drive inside."

Jesse watched Ethel disappear into the hut. He was uncertain what to do if she didn't return soon. It shouldn't take O'Hara long to verify Finch's drive mirrored his computer, and that the ten thousand dollars had been returned to the smaller wallet. He was so fixed on the doorway that he jumped when he heard a light tap on the hood.

Lisa Draper crouched down, using the car to hide all but her head and shoulders. She wore a dark green slicker with a hood. She touched a finger to her lips and then mouthed, *"Where's Ethel?"*

Jesse gestured to the hut. Then he lowered his window a crack so that his whisper could be heard. "O'Hara has Susan Finch. He's released Davie. Ethel's coming back for Parker's KryptoFold and a private key. They'll be exchanged for Susan. But O'Hara will watch from the door. You could be seen at any time."

Lisa nodded that she understood. Then she broke from her position and ran on tiptoes to O'Hara's sedan, putting the car between her and the hut. Jesse watched her creep along the side until she had an angled view over the hood through the open hut door. He wished there was something he could do to help her, but Ethel had been explicit in her instructions, so he stayed with Davie.

Inside, O'Hara kept his pistol trained on Ethel. "Set the drive on the desk by the laptop and then step away."

She did as he ordered. "Mrs. Finch can verify the handwriting on the drive. And you should have seen we used it to re-transfer Bitcoins back to the smaller wallet."

"And why haven't you touched the millions?"

"Because that's evidence. We weren't after money. We were after murderers."

"Well, that wasn't me. I only—"

"FREEZE! FBI!" Lisa bellowed the order from the doorway, where she gripped her pistol with two hands.

Ethel pushed Susan away from the line of fire. O'Hara wheeled around, surprise in his eyes, gun still raised. Without hesitation, Lisa fired. The deafening boom of her pistol rattled the metal walls.

The impact of the bullet tore through O'Hara's chest and hurled him backward against the desk. The gun flew from his hand and clattered near Ethel's feet. O'Hara's expression of surprise remained as he slid to the concrete floor.

Lisa kept her gun on him. "Ethel, you and Mrs. Finch step farther away."

Ethel nudged Susan to move but held her own ground. She shook her head and said, "Let me at least try to stem the bleeding."

She knelt beside O'Hara. His eyes blinked rapidly. His breath gurgled. "She shot me," he whispered, as much to himself as to the others. Then the blinking stopped. And the breathing stopped.

Ethel stood. "He's gone."

Lisa stepped closer, still keeping her pistol on O'Hara. "Did you give him Finch's key?"

"No. The KryptoFold's still in the car with Jesse and Davie. How did you find us?"

Lisa dropped her pistol to her side. "Hauser gave me a tracking device to put on your car. He thought you knew more than you were telling."

"And have you called for backup?"

"Yes. As soon as I saw Ed O'Hara at the door. Now I need to take custody of the KryptoFold and computer."

Ethel said nothing. She stood motionless, listening.

The distant hum of an airplane became audible above the patter of rain on the roof.

"So, your backup's a plane?" Ethel asked.

"I don't know what that is. Maybe Hauser's sending a helicopter. But the Parker case is a Bureau case, and I insist you turn everything you have over to me."

Ethel bent over and picked up O'Hara's gun by the barrel. "Or you'll do what? Shoot me? You see, Lisa, we know at least three people had to be involved in the counterfeit-currency-for-Bitcoin scam."

"Yes. Hauser and I think it's Douglas Gray. He worked with both Norwood and O'Hara. And he wasn't in his room the night Norwood was killed."

"A logical line of inquiry. But where is Douglas now?"

"What do you mean?"

"If this is the last hurrah for the rogue team, why isn't he here for the rendezvous?"

"I don't know."

Ethel shook her head. "Sure you do. Because you're the third member. That plane is coming for you. You and O'Hara. Only you shot him just like you shot Norwood."

Lisa's face hardened. She swung her pistol to Ethel. "Drop the gun, and just give me the damn KryptoFold and key."

Ethel saw a flicker of movement at the door behind Lisa. "Wait. Hear me out. For all your smarts, you made some dumb mistakes. Faking the break-in was the first. You broke the window after you knocked Jesse out. I saw the photos of what you cleaned up before I got home. Jesse might not have noticed because he was worried about the money in the basement, but he would have had to step over some of the peripheral specks of glass that landed farthest from the door. Glass particles that should have stuck to his socks. Yet his socks were clean."

Lisa forced a laugh. "That's your proof? Socks?"

"That's what made me suspicious. So, I tossed out a little lie. I told you, and only you, that Director Bradshaw was requiring all of the counterfeit team to give a DNA sample. That he was looking for an internal match to the blood in Jonathan's SUV. That wasn't true. Bradshaw hadn't said that. And the FDDU, that's the Federal DNA Database Unit," she said for Susan's benefit, "the FDDU doesn't keep agent DNA profiles. You know those are only taken if a crime scene could have been contaminated by an agent, and investigators need to rule out the errant sample.

"So, I told you the lie over our evening banana ritual, and the next morning Trevor Norwood was found dead with the missing money. How easily you could have slipped out in the middle of the night, driven the few miles to Roosevelt Island Park, and eliminated your perceived threat."

Ethel looked at the body of O'Hara. "And then there's your partner's dying whisper. 'She shot me.' He was still surprised as he died."

"You're making all this up. You're trying to keep the money, aren't you?"

"No. I'm happy to wait for Rudy Hauser. After all, you did call him, didn't you?"

The noise of the plane grew louder. It seemed to be circling before a final approach.

Lisa's eyes narrowed. "All right. No more games." She waved the gun between Ethel and Susan. "I can shoot you both and take what I want from Jesse. And there's always the boy."

"Ethel?" Susan Finch's frantic plea rose to a wail.

Ethel lowered O'Hara's pistol to the floor. "All right, Lisa, you win. But there's been enough killing, hasn't there?"

"I only did what I had to do. We had no idea Jonathan Finch was the one selling the Bitcoins." She glanced at Susan. "No one was supposed to die."

"Don't kid yourself," Ethel said. "You shot Norwood and O'Hara in cold blood. And for what?"

"What do you think? Money. I see fortunes swindled by accountants with half my brains. Even the ones we catch serve minimal time in a country club prison. I've already got a little nest egg offshore, and with Parker's millions, I'll never worry about money again."

She stopped, and all three women listened as a second plane engine became audible.

Lisa shifted her weight nervously from one foot to the other. Her grip on the pistol tightened. "What's going on?"

Ethel looked beyond her at the figure moving quietly in the outside shadows. "Frank, tell the lady what's going on."

Detective Frank Mancini stepped into the doorway, his Glock level in both his hands. "Lay the gun down, Lisa. And then turn around."

Still facing Ethel, Lisa gritted her teeth and glared at the older woman. For a few seconds, no one moved. The sound from multiple planes circling overhead rattled the metal hut.

Then Lisa shouted, "I'm lowering my gun." She bent her knees and eased down.

Ethel read the desperation on her face and saw her leg muscles tense as she prepared to spring from her crouch.

"No!" Ethel leapt forward as the agent launched herself toward Susan Finch, firing at Mancini at the same time. Ethel caught Lisa around the ankles, dragging her back before she could reach a potential hostage.

Lisa fired again, and the bullet nicked Ethel's ear. Ethel clawed for the gun, turning the barrel away, using every muscle toned by her every exercise. They were eye to eye as she bent Lisa's wrist down. Lisa pulled the trigger, and Ethel felt a punch and burn in her stomach.

The struggling ceased. Ethel rolled away. She started to stand, and then the world went dark.

Chapter 35

Ethel felt the cold concrete floor against her back. She heard ringing in her ears and garbled distant voices. Her mind cleared, and she realized she must have blacked out. Had she been shot? Did Lisa still have the gun?

She opened her eyes and saw Frank Mancini kneeling over her, his brow furrowed with concern. Susan Finch peered over his shoulder. She looked horrified.

The words became clearer. "Ethel! Ethel! Are you all right?" Mancini scanned her body head to toe.

"Lisa?" Ethel whispered.

Mancini shook his head. "She's dead."

Ethel looked down at her blouse. Powder burns had scorched the fabric. She understood what had happened. When Lisa's semiautomatic fired, not only had there been blow-back but also the recoil of the slide had punched into her abdomen. Better that than the bullet coming out the other end of the pistol.

"Just got the wind knocked out of me." She struggled to get up.

"Here. Let me help you into a chair." Mancini rolled one of the desk chairs beside her and gently lifted her into it. "Your ear's bleeding."

Ethel touched the mangled lobe. "I'm fine. Stopped wearing earrings years ago. What about those planes?"

"I think they just landed."

"Well, hadn't you better check if they're friend or foe? If you see a short guy and a tall guy who look like Mutt and Jeff, don't shoot them. They're on our side."

"You're sure you're fine?"

She waved him away. "Go make yourself useful. Arrest somebody."

Mancini gave a quick glance at the two bodies as if to make sure they were still dead and then hurried away.

Ethel turned to Susan. "Do what I say and don't ask questions. Take your husband's laptop and hard drive to my car. Stay with Davie and tell Jesse to bring his computer and backpack on the double. If you're asked questions later, say O'Hara thought your husband had something of value, but you have no idea what."

"That's the truth," Susan said.

"Of course it is. Now hurry."

Ethel stood, felt the room spin, and sat back down. Her heart was racing. Jesse bolted through the door, backpack swinging by his side. He halted, eyes wide, when he saw Ethel sitting between two bodies.

"Get over here and focus," she yelled. "Open your laptop on this desk." She pointed to the spot where O'Hara had set up Finch's laptop. "I'm hoping Frank won't notice the difference. Have you got your backup drive?"

"Yes."

"How long will it take to replace Jonathan's data with yours?"

"Maybe thirty minutes, if I don't have to offload Jonathan's data first."

"Too long. Can you just reformat your internal drive?"

"Yes. That would be quicker."

"Then do it. As soon as that happens, start restoring your system. I'll come up with some explanation."

A few minutes later, Jesse gave a final click on the touch pad. "Okay. Restoration is underway."

"Good. Go to the car and hide Jonathan's computer and external drive."

"And the KryptoFold?"

"Definitely hide that. Then bring the bag. It should contain my phone, which is still off, and the LEGOs."

"Including the SUV model?"

Ethel smiled. "That's the whole point. Frank knows I'm not stupid. He'd expect me to have some kind of plan. Again, be quick."

When Jesse returned, Ethel told him to place the bag under the desk. "Let me do the talking. The bones of the story are that when Susan didn't know what they wanted, I received a text threatening to kill Susan and Davie. That message and the subsequent messages are all on my phone. I decided not to run the risk of involving the FBI or Secret Service because I didn't know whom to trust. And we have two dead conspirators, one from each agency, to prove my instincts were correct. We'll see where things go from there. Now give me my phone. I need to see if I've had any word from Rudy and Cory."

She powered on her phone. Two text messages chimed. Both began the same way—

CALL ME!!!

FBI Director Hauser's continued—

Learned O'Hara and Draper had been living together in Philly. Will contact Cory.

Secret Service Director Bradshaw's text was essentially the same—

Gossip is O'Hara's girlfriend was FBI agent. Possibly Lisa Draper. Will alert Rudy.

Ethel showed the messages to Jesse. "That's good news," she said. "Neither of them is shielding their agents, which leads me to believe both Rudy and Cory are in the clear, as far as being involved."

"You really didn't think one of them was guilty, did you?"

Ethel took a deep breath. "I'd like to say no. I can't see it for the counterfeit currency scam, but twenty million dollars? My father was betrayed for a lot less."

Rapid footsteps clicked on the concrete floor. Detective Mancini came through the door followed by Curt Foster and Pete Varner. The two octogenarian pilots wore identical leather flight jackets. They broke into a run when they saw Ethel in the chair surrounded by guns and bodies.

"Jesus, woman," Pete exclaimed. "Is there no end to your stupidity? Detective Mancini said you tackled an armed FBI agent half your age."

"My stupidity? You two flyboys were hotdogging in a cloud cover. What the hell did you think you were doing?"

Rather than tower over Ethel, Curt knelt beside her chair. "When you sent us the coordinates to text to the detective, I thought they sounded familiar. I make it a point to know every potential landing site in the region in case I've got to make an emergency landing. Those coordinates meant someone was either coming in or leaving by air. Turned out to be an old Beechcraft B55 Baron. Pretty good range on that puppy. Headed out of the country, they might have made Bermuda. Might have. Let's just say Pete and I got here in time to play hell with his landing approach."

Pete laughed. "Shaved him so close he'll have to change his underwear. And we found Lisa's car parked behind this hangar. She got here before you. My phone was under the seat."

"That's how you tracked her?" Mancini asked Ethel.

"Yes. And Jesse's phone was in Douglas Gray's. For all I knew both Lisa and Douglas could have been bad. Last night, while Lisa and Douglas were having wine with me, Jesse raided their car keys and planted the phones."

"We tracked Gray back to Fredericksburg," Curt said. "I believe he's watching the house of Mrs. Finch's sister."

"His only play is to wait for Susan and Davie to return." Ethel turned to Pete. "Any ID on the pilot?"

"I got two digits of the tail number as he flew off with his own tail tucked between his legs."

"I've given the numbers to Rudy Hauser," Mancini said. "It's a long shot, but it might be enough to ID the plane's owner."

"You've talked to Rudy?" Ethel asked.

"He and Cory both. Each has a corrupt dead agent so they're inbound."

"Helicopter?"

"Yes."

Ethel tried to get up, but Mancini motioned for her to stay seated. "And they'll probably insist on using the chopper to transport you to the nearest medical facility."

Ethel waved her hand dismissively. "Don't be silly. I'm a little winded, that's all."

Mancini shrugged. "Then you can begin explaining what happened here."

"A bluff is what happened here. This confederacy of thieves, Draper, Norwood, and O'Hara had planned the counterfeit-money-for-Bitcoin scam. Maybe they'd done it before. Lisa admitted she had money offshore. I think Jonathan Finch got suspicious and set a trap to flush them out."

Mancini looked skeptical and glanced at Jesse.

"Her room was next to Jonathan's," Jesse chimed in. "He could have overheard her talking."

"Okay," Mancini said. "I get that, and Draper knocking you out to retrieve the counterfeit money, but why didn't it end there?"

"Because of the Parker embezzlement," Ethel said. "Twenty million dollars had been hidden somewhere. Lisa knew about it because she worked the investigation. She also knew Jonathan had been first on the scene when Parker committed suicide. When Jonathan made an offer of Bitcoin for cash, she became convinced that he had Parker's money."

"And went after the family?" Mancini asked.

Ethel pointed to the door. "You were just outside, weren't you? Didn't you hear her admit that?"

"Yes, I'd parked far enough away to not be heard on the approach. Lisa shot O'Hara before I could get here. When you told Lisa, 'Wait, hear me out,' I interpreted that as a signal to me as I'd seen you glance my way."

"I wanted you to hear the confession. You know what happened after that."

Mancini walked over to Jesse and the laptop. Data was still being loaded from the external drive.

"So, this is your bluff?"

"I told O'Hara I had the wallets and keys on an external drive. They would release the boy first, and Jesse would stay with him, ready to speed away if things went south. Then Susan and I were to be let go when they got the hard drive and laptop. In truth, the only data was a clone of Jesse's computer, but it bought us time."

"But they must have searched you. And when they found they'd been duped..."

"They didn't search the right place." Ethel nodded to Jesse.

He lifted the bag from the floor and set it on an adjacent desk. Mancini was surprised but decided he must have overlooked it during the initial chaos. Jesse pulled out the large LEGO SUV model.

Ethel enjoyed seeing the three men's puzzled expressions. "Jesse was to come to the door and ask for this to keep Davie amused. I would carry it to him." She nodded to Jesse. "Demonstrate."

Jesse picked up the model and walked to the door. With his body shielding his hands, he broke the model apart, wheeled around, and leveled Ethel's revolver at Mancini. Instinctively, Curt and Pete moved away.

"Jesse," Ethel scolded. "Point that at the floor. We don't need to add an Arlington detective to our collection of dead law enforcement officers."

Mancini laughed. "Ethel, you expect us to buy that story?"

"I expect the public to buy the story. And I don't think either Rudy or Cory will see any benefit in contradicting it. Not unless they want to needlessly besmirch Jonathan Finch, his wife, and their son with unproven and unprovable allegations. His three killers have been brought to justice. You three brought them to justice. That's the story I plan on telling."

Mancini said nothing. He looked at the LEGO pieces, the gun, the running computer, and hard drive.

Pete Varner and Curt Foster stepped closer to the detective.

"That dog will hunt," Pete said.

"Yeah," Curt added. "Why would anyone want to hear anything more?"

Mancini chuckled. "Why indeed?"

The *whop, whop* sound of a chopper filled the air.

"Here come the big boys." Ethel pushed off the chair, took one step, and collapsed.

Chapter 36

Courtesy of FBI Director Rudy Hauser, Jesse sat in a secluded waiting room at the Inova Trauma Center—Fairfax, in Falls Church, Virginia. Hauser had sent Ethel and him to the Level 1 facility via the chopper with a promise to handle the logistics of transporting Susan Finch and Davie home. Jesse knew both Hauser and Bradshaw were torn between being with Ethel and personally attending to the crime scene. Neither wanted the other to take charge, and each wanted to control the narrative of corruption in their respective agency. So staying at the scene won out.

The fact that the shootings occurred at an abandoned airfield meant no involvement of the public or the news media. With luck, a lid could be kept on the whole debacle as all of the culprits were dead. The story would be what they agreed it would be. And since Mancini, Hauser, and Bradshaw didn't know the whole story, it also could be the story Ethel wanted.

During the flight, Ethel had been conscious. It had been hard to talk above the roar of the engine and rotors, but talking too loudly risked the chance of being overheard. She had managed to make one thing clear—none of Jesse's answers could reveal the existence of the virtual wallets, private keys, and the KryptoFold device.

After two hours elapsed, the door opened and Mancini, Hauser, and Bradshaw entered. For the first time, Bradshaw's dark suit looked wrinkled and his white shirt was stained with perspiration.

Jesse stood from his chair. "Are Susan and Davie okay?"

"Yes," Bradshaw said. "I had an agent drive them to her sister's. Since Agent Gray was there, I instructed him to stay in case they need anything. What's the word on Ethel?"

"Not much. A doc was in about an hour ago. His diagnosis is heart block."

"Clogged arteries?" Mancini asked.

"No. Something to do with electric signals to the heart. He said she should have a pacemaker. They'd like to do that as soon as they can determine she's stable."

"Oh, God, can we bribe them to give her one that will slow her down?" Bradshaw asked.

"Believe it or not, the doc says her heart rate is too slow. Overall, she's healthy and has the slow rate of a conditioned athlete. But she can't fight Father Time, and her electrical nerve impulses aren't what they once were, especially if she undergoes sudden activity."

Hauser shook his head. "I would say attacking an armed foe qualifies." He gestured for Jesse to sit. Then he, Mancini, and Bradshaw pulled up chairs and boxed him in.

"Detective Mancini shared what Ethel told him," Hauser continued. "That she'd suspected Lisa Draper after the attack on you. And that Draper had convinced herself that Jonathan Finch had access to the Parker money."

"Yes. But we didn't believe that to be the case. Ethel used it as a lure to bring them out in the open. Even I didn't know all that she was doing."

The three interrogators nodded in unison.

"Welcome to the club, son," Mancini said.

"So, you never had any information on the Parker case?" Hauser pressed.

"Just what Lisa told me."

"Lisa?"

"Yes. I understand now that she was pumping me for information. I think she was trying to get me to confirm her suspicions that we'd gotten information from Jonathan. We didn't know anything about the Parker case until Lisa brought it up. Ethel was just playing along." Jesse looked first at Hauser and then Bradshaw. "She wanted to trust both of you, but with twenty million dollars hanging over an interagency conspiracy? Well, you know her history with betrayal."

The two directors were silent.

Mancini took advantage of the pause. "That's why she brought me in first. And why she used those two vet pilots to pass along information to me. And why she tracked Lisa and Douglas with planted cell phones. She wanted to stay out of possibly compromised internal communications in both your agencies. Given the circumstances, you have to admit she acted with good reasons."

Jesse leaned forward. "She was really happy when both of you texted the same answer to her question about Lisa and O'Hara. That you didn't try to cover up that relationship."

"You mean that we weren't part of the conspiracy," Hauser said. "I guess I was pushing too hard to recover that money. It gave Lisa Draper cover for pursuing her own agenda."

"And I think that agenda started months ago," Bradshaw said. "She never broke up with O'Hara. She moved into Ethel's because Jonathan was there. She'd already developed her theory that he had the Parker money, and she wanted to get close to him."

Hauser frowned. "But if Finch didn't have the Parker money, where was he getting the funds to buy the counterfeit stash, assuming he was setting a trap?"

No one spoke. It was the one question that defied an exonerating answer.

"Did you ever find his computer or phone?" Jesse asked.

"No," Bradshaw said. "If it had links to Draper or the others, then both phone and computer could be at the bottom of the Potomac."

Mancini cleared his throat. "So, as a lowly Arlington detective, I see your federal agencies responding one of two ways. First option—you close the case and give Finch's family the honor of a fallen hero's funeral with the appropriate financial consideration for being killed in the line of duty. Second option, you keep the case open, creating a cloud of suspicion over Finch, who can't defend himself, waste money dredging the Potomac or some equally hopeless search for what is probably the only potential evidence of any guilt on Finch's part, and your efforts only encourage media exposure that will upset a widow and her special-needs child. To what end? Return money to some hedge fund managers who deal in millions like we deal in twenties? Well, it's your call, gentlemen. I'll let you answer to Ethel."

"Low blow," Hauser grumbled.

Bradshaw had to smile. "Yeah, kick us when we're down."

The door opened and a nurse entered. "Mr. Cooper?"

Jesse stood. "Yes?"

"You are next of kin, correct?"

"Yes."

"Would you follow me, please?"

The others rose from their chairs, and Mancini stepped forward. "Is something wrong?"

"No, sir. The patient would like to consult with her next of kin regarding treatment options. You're welcome to wait until he returns."

Jesse and the nurse walked through two sets of secured doors to a section of patient rooms visible from a monitoring station.

"I'll be at a desk right outside." She stepped back and let Jesse enter.

Ethel lay in a slightly reclined bed, a sheet tucked up under her arms but not so high as to conceal that she wore a hospital gown. Wires disappeared to electrodes that lay hidden underneath. The monotone beep from some kind of high-tech equipment and the subtle whisper of air-conditioning were the only sounds.

Jesse hesitated. Ethel looked so frail. Her eyes were closed and her breaths shallow. He realized how near he'd come to losing her, the only family he had left. And he was the only family she had left. Two double-first-cousins-twice-removed.

Her eyes opened. "Well, stop gawking and get over here. I'm not dead yet."

He hurried to the bedside.

She tried to prop herself up. "Raise this thing so I don't have to look at you sideways."

Jesse found the control and adjusted the bed's upper half to a vertical position.

"That's better." She looked beyond him. "Are you by yourself?"

"No. Hauser, Bradshaw, and Mancini are in a waiting room."

"Are Hauser and Bradshaw grilling you?"

"Not too hard. I think they're working out a consistent story. Mancini is our ally. He's basically told them they can have a tidy closed case or a messy open case."

Ethel laughed. "That's Frank. I love him. Rudy and Cory were all about climbing the power ladder in their careers. All

Frank wants to do is solve cases. If I were twenty years younger, I'd jump his bones."

Jesse blushed.

"Well, I'm not a nun. I've had my flings in my time."

"Um, that's, um, good," he stammered. "I mean Frank's a good man."

She winked at him. "And a widower. But back to Rudy and Cory. What have they told you?"

"They think Jonathan's computer and phone have been destroyed."

"They're probably right about the phone, but unless they're playing games, they haven't searched my car. Do you have the keys?"

"I gave them to Curt Foster before we boarded the helicopter."

Ethel reached out and patted the back of his hand. "Perfect. He and Pete can get my car to the house. I guess Rudy and Cory still have your computer and drive."

"Yes, but there's nothing of Jonathan's clone left on either. As far as I'm aware, no one can prove Jonathan Finch was ever tied to the Parker money. Things lead no further than the counterfeit scam, and, as Mancini said, it's a tidy case better closed than left open."

"Good. Then get Jonathan's stuff out of my car as soon as Pete and Curt bring it. But hold on to it, don't destroy it."

Jesse edged closer to the bed. "Ethel, between us, what do you think happened?"

She rolled on her side to get closer to him. "I think Parker knew the jig was up and killed himself. Jonathan found his computer, his KryptoFold device, and either a written private key or used Parker's finger to access his crypto wallet. You know better than I do what he could have done, but I think he moved that money to a wallet of his own and then destroyed Parker's drive, claiming Parker had done so before his suicide."

"So, the KryptoFold hidden in the LEGO model was Jonathan's?"

"We'll never know for sure since both he and Parker are dead, but once Jonathan had transferred the money to his own wallet, he could have purchased and programmed his own device."

"Why did he create two wallets?" Jesse asked.

"In setting up the cash-for-Bitcoin exchange, isn't it likely Jonathan would have had to show them he had the necessary Bitcoin balance?"

Jesse nodded. "You're right. And he would have only wanted to reveal the half a million dollars, not the twenty million. But when they stole his computer, they discovered the real fortune. Do you think Jonathan was trying to sell all the coins?"

"Jonathan knew he was dying. I think he was selling a small part to leave for his family. Twenty million was just too much to deal with and would have put his wife in the terrible position of knowing his crime. He could have arranged for some trust to be activated after his death without involving Susan in the details. I doubt if she'd turn down the income."

"And the rest of the money?"

Ethel shrugged. "With no private key, it would sit there for eternity, wouldn't it?"

"Yeah, like millions of dollars' worth of other lost coins."

"But his illicit attempt to provide for his family intersected with our unholy trio who were selling and then recapturing counterfeit currency. One person motivated by need, the others by greed. Then they got hold of Jonathan's computer, discovered the source of his funds, and the search for the twenty million began. I suspect Lisa Draper was the driving force. Men might be cunning, but women are ruthless. She probably would have shot her pilot once he delivered her to her final destination. An offshore account and access to her globally available cryptocurrency would have enabled her to disappear completely. Am I right?"

"Yes," Jesse agreed. "She would have gotten away with murder and the funds to keep her in luxury for the rest of her life."

"And we stopped her."

"So, what do we do now?"

"We let Jonathan Finch be remembered as the fine agent and loving husband and father that he was."

"And the pacemaker?"

Ethel grimaced. "If I must. It's not that I'm afraid of dying."

"Why then?"

"Because they might revoke my damn pilot's license, that's why. Now go tell the nurse to let Rudy, Cory, and Frank back here. Maybe they'll go easy on me if I look like I'm on death's doorstep."

Jesse bent over and kissed her on the forehead. "They won't. But you can handle them, Cousin."

"You'd better believe it. Then we go for the secret Jonathan really wanted to tell me."

Chapter 37

Four weeks later, Ethel and Jesse made a return trip to Richmond and treated Davie and Susan Finch to lunch at IHOP, Davie's favorite restaurant. They hadn't seen one another since Jonathan's memorial service where both Rudy Hauser and Cory Bradshaw spoke glowingly of Jonathan's career. The two directors especially emphasized his bravery in taking on corruption and his invaluable contributions to the internal investigation conducted jointly by the Secret Service and FBI that led to the final confrontation with his killers.

After lunch, Susan invited them to stay at the house for coffee.

As she and Ethel headed for the front door, Jesse asked, "Is it okay if Davie helps me get something from the trunk?"

Susan looked puzzled. "Yes."

"Jesse wanted to get a present for Davie," Ethel whispered. "Can they open it in his room?"

Susan smiled. "Of course. How sweet. Davie," she called to her son trailing behind on his walker, "help Jesse. He has something he wants to show you."

Davie watched with excitement as Jesse lifted a large package wrapped in brown paper from the trunk.

"For me?" the boy exclaimed.

"We'll have to see. Lead the way to your room."

Jesse set the box on the solar system bedspread. Everything was neatly in place. The SUV LEGO replica was back on the shelf along with the model of the house. A few Tinkertoy water molecules lay on his desk.

"Can I open it now?" Davie asked.

"You can, and then I have some questions for you."

The boy meticulously searched for a taped seam in the wrapping and then worked it loose without tearing the paper. When he'd finished, he clapped his hands and beamed at the *LEGO City Space Port—Deep Space Rocket and Launch Control with over 837 pieces.*

"Build it now?" Davie asked.

"First my questions."

Davie sat on the bed, never taking his eyes off the prized gift. "Okay."

Jesse went to the shelf and got the model of the house. He sat on the bed beside the boy. "Can I see inside?"

Davie looked uncomfortable, but nodded.

Jesse removed a section of the roof. "This is your room. Your daddy told me about your room. Like he kept a secret in the model of his SUV, he gave you a secret to keep with you. Something he made for you and you made your own slip of paper like it to put in your LEGO room." Jesse lifted the loop of paper and handed it to Davie.

"A Möbius strip," the boy said. "Only one side. Daddy said it goes round and round forever."

"But it's something else, isn't it? You wrote Davie's secret."

Davie nodded. "That's what Daddy called it." He slipped it over his hand so that it shared his wrist with the Medic Alert bracelet.

"Can I see the real one?"

Davie hesitated, then slid the narrow part of his small wrist through the gap in the silver bracelet. He handed it to Jesse.

"Osteogenesis Imperfecta—Fragile Bones" had been engraved in block letters across the faceplate. Simple, clean, and legible.

Jesse turned the bracelet over and examined the inside surface. Jonathan Finch's steady hand had etched the string of letters, characters, and numbers onto the interior length. Ethel had been right. She'd seen more than a Möbius strip, she'd seen a twenty-million-dollar bracelet.

Jesse pulled out a pen and paper from his pants pocket and started writing.

——

Jesse and Ethel returned from Richmond around four. They were the only ones in the house since Douglas was traveling with the vice president, and Ethel hadn't yet taken in new roomers to replace Jonathan and Lisa. Still, they decided to wait until after dark to proceed. Detective Mancini had been occasionally dropping by in the late afternoons, claiming he was checking on Ethel's recovery. Jesse thought he was suspicious. Ethel said he was looking for a home-cooked meal, and she had invited him for dinner a few times.

At eight, Ethel pulled Jonathan Finch's laptop from the back of her closet and took it down to her RBG workout room. Jesse was already sitting on the weight bench with his computer.

"Have you set up your accounts?" she asked.

"Yes. Two new wallet addresses and two private keys." He set his laptop to one side and took Jonathan's from her. He patted the bench beside him. "Sit. This will take a few minutes."

"Wait. I want to get something. But go ahead and set things up." She hurried up the stairs.

A few minutes later, she returned carrying her scrapbook.

"What's that for?" Jessie asked.

"We need a place to hide those keys. I mean we'll also keep them in a safe deposit box, or even two, but this will be handier."

"If it works." He took the strip of paper from his pocket. "You think that's what he was trying to say, 'Tell Ethel the secret is with Davie?'"

"Maybe. Or 'Tell Ethel the secret's on Davie's bracelet.' Something like that. Jonathan was clever, putting the medical information and financial information together."

"Not as clever as the woman who solved his murder and saved his family." He handed the paper to Ethel. "So, do the honor of reading and I'll enter."

She began. "Lowercase q, five, uppercase U..."

When she'd finished, Jesse said, "Here goes nothing," and pressed Enter.

The screen went blank for a few seconds, and Jesse feared Davie's Secret had been a fail-safe defense Jonathan had designed to destroy the link to the wallet, not to bridge it.

Then the beautiful words, "ACCESS GRANTED."

"Yes!" Jesse pumped his fist in the air.

"Make the first transfer," Ethel instructed.

"The five hundred thousand?"

"Yes. Jonathan's original intention. And give me the private key." She opened the scrapbook to the photo of her and her father standing in front of the plane after her first solo flight. She slid it out from beneath its protective plastic, turned it over, and wrote on the back as Jesse read the new sequence.

When the allotted coins had been transferred, Jesse said, "And now the balance into the second wallet."

Ethel wrote that private key on the photo's back and returned it to its proper spot in the scrapbook. Jesse stared at the screen of his own computer as the wallet grew in value with each coin transferred into it.

"Did you tell Tracy you're sending her back that ten thousand dollars?" Ethel asked.

"Yes. She didn't want it, but I made up a story that we'd received a reward for helping with the case and this was her share of the money."

"Good. Then we can destroy Jonathan's wallets and computer and terminate any trail to him."

"And the trust fund for Davie?"

"I've got an appointment with an attorney friend who can set it up. Of course, an anonymous donor will fund the half million."

Jesse looked at the larger transfer still in progress. "And the twenty million?"

"Well, we could just destroy the private key and let those coins be lost forever. I think that's what Jonathan was planning."

"But what is Ethel planning?"

She gave him a sly smile. "I've always believed in recycling. Why throw away a resource that could do so much good?" She held out her small hand. "Do you agree we could use it with integrity and fairness to see justice done?"

Jesse clasped the offered hand. "Your father's words."

"Yes, but I realize we're a little short in the integrity category if we're keeping the money."

"Keeping the money for the greater good. My conscience is clear."

They shook and sealed the deal.

Then Jesse held on to her hand a little longer. "There is one thing I'd like to use some of the money for."

"If you say a Ferrari, I'll kill you myself."

"Flying lessons. That is, if you expect me to go up in a plane with a pilot whose pacemaker could conk out at any moment."

Ethel shook his hand again. "Done. And I'll even throw in a set of lockpicks." Then she hugged him. "Welcome to the family."

AUTHOR'S NOTE

Although this story is fiction, it contains factual elements. Millions of dollars in Bitcoin and other cryptocurrencies are now inaccessible to their owners because private keys have been lost. Cryptocurrencies also appeal to criminal enterprises that value the anonymity and impenetrable security of the virtual wallets. Such criminal activity is clearly demonstrated by ransomware attacks that demand cryptocurrency as the medium of payment. What the future holds for Bitcoin and other cryptocurrencies remains to be seen, but it appears they are here to stay.

UFOs do exist. United Flying Octogenarians, that is. Although Ethel is too young to be a member, her friends Pete and Curt are worthy examples of this elite group.

Osteogenesis imperfecta is a serious genetic bone condition that ranges from lethal at birth to milder manifestations that allow for a relatively normal life. Davie is midway on that spectrum and could face life-threatening vulnerabilities as he ages.

ACKNOWLEDGMENTS

This novel certainly benefited from the help of others. Special thanks to my editor Diane DiBiase for championing Ethel's story. Thanks to Beth Deveny for eagle-eyed copyediting and to the Poisoned Pen Press team that connects books with readers.

I'm indebted to former U.S. Associate Attorney General Webb Hubble, who provided guidance in jurisdictional matters of the FBI and Secret Service. Thanks to Mark Thornberry for navigating me through planes and flight procedures to get Ethel up in the air and down again, and to Bill Hamby for his knowledge of Richmond.

Grandson Charles Thomson showed me how to construct a hollow LEGO box that made for an excellent hiding place. Thanks, Charlie!

Finally, thanks to family and friends for the support and love that I wish could be a part of everyone's story. And to you, dear reader, for giving Ethel Fiona Crestwater the chance to tell hers.

ABOUT THE AUTHOR

Mark de Castrique was born in Hendersonville, North Carolina, near Asheville. He went straight from the hospital to the funeral home, where his father was the funeral director and the family lived upstairs. The unusual setting sparked his popular Buryin' Barry series and launched his mystery-writing career.

Mark is the author of twenty-one novels—seven set in the fictional North Carolina mountain town of Gainesboro, eight set in Asheville, three in Washington DC, one science thriller set in the year 2030, and two mysteries written for middle-graders and set in the Charlotte region.

His novels have received Starred Reviews from *Publishers Weekly, Library Journal,* and *Booklist.* The *Chicago Tribune* wrote, "As important and as impressive as the author's narrative skills are the subtle ways he captures the geography—both physical and human—of a unique part of the American South."

Mark is a veteran of the broadcast and film production business. In Washington DC, he directed numerous news and public affairs programs and received an Emmy Award for his documentary film work. Through his company, MARK et al., he writes and produces videos for corporate and broadcast clients.

His years in Washington inspired his DC thrillers, *The 13th Target*, involving a terrorist plot against the Federal Reserve, and *The Singularity Race*, a winner-take-all quest for artificial intelligence.

Mark lives in Charlotte, but he and his wife, Linda, can often be found in the North Carolina mountains or the nation's capital.